MW00957703

AUGUST FORTRESS

KILENYA CHRONICLES BOOK THREE

ANDREA PEARSON

August Fortress

Printed in the United States of America

This is a work of fiction, and the views expressed herein are the sole responsibility of the author. Likewise, characters, places, and incidents are either the product of the author's imagination or are represented fictitiously, and any resemblance to actual persons, living or dead, or actual events or locales, is entirely coincidental.

ISBN-13: 978-1981488995

ISBN-10: 1981488995

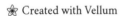 Created with Vellum

DEDICATION

To my husband
As always
For his love and support

1

J acob rolled out of bed. It was well past midnight, and he was thirsty. He slowly pulled his door open, hoping the squeak wouldn't wake anyone, then crept downstairs to the kitchen. He filled a glass with water and leaned against the bay window near the table, looking outside as he drank.

The moon was bright enough to see nearly anything, and Jacob studied the trees, thinking over the past two days since he'd returned from getting Aloren out of Maivoryl City. It was so awesome to have her back. She was smiling a lot more now, and even laughed at Matt's jokes.

Speaking of Matt—he'd been careful not to tread on Jacob's toes where Aloren was concerned, assuring Jacob that Sammy, his girlfriend, was the only girl for him. Jacob really appreciated that. He frowned—he still hadn't had the opportunity to ask his parents how Matt had come to be in the family.

He brought the cup to his lips one last time, staring out the window, then nearly dropped it when several shadows passed near the brush about twenty feet away.

He set the glass on the counter and peered out the

window. Was it Kevin and his friends? Probably not—they hadn't played pranks on the Clarks for a while now.

Was it the Lorkon? Jacob felt his pulse quicken.

Only one way to find out.

He got on his knees and crawled past the window to the mud room. Grabbing his darkest hoodie, he put it on as he scrambled to the back door, then slipped outside.

Jacob squinted through the darkness, trying to see where the shadows had gone. There! Men—not boys. It wasn't Kevin after all. The last of them looked back in his direction, then entered the forest. Jacob crept forward, following. He had to know who they were, and if they were from Eklaron.

He straightened behind a tree when he entered the woods, looking around. He'd lost the group. Where did they go?

Jacob shaded his eyes from the bright moon, trying to see through the branches. A *ping* sounded in the air, and wind brushed his cheek. He put his hand there and looked to the side to see what had passed him. He saw nothing.

Another *ping*, and this time he instinctively dropped to the ground. There was a loud *thwack* right next to his head and he shied away, then stared.

An arrow was embedded in the tree right where his head had just been.

A third *ping*, then the loudest human howl Jacob had ever heard sounded through the air—made even louder by the cool of the night.

Jacob's heart nearly leaped from his chest, and he scrambled away from the arrow and the source of the scream, burrowing deep into a large bush.

Everything went still.

Then the forest erupted into a frenzy—several pings from either side of Jacob—and arrows flew everywhere. A set of legs appeared near him, and he looked up in shock at a man dressed like a Native American. Dark-colored war paint was smeared across his face, and he held a dagger in one hand and a bow in the other. Bright red colors swirled in the air around him—anger. He put the dagger into a strap on his leather leggings, then pulled an arrow from his quiver, peering through the night.

What was going on? As far as Jacob knew, there weren't any Indians on Eklaron, and this definitely was still earth. He held his breath, trying to be as quiet as he could.

The man got on one knee near the bush, but somehow didn't see Jacob. He raised his bow, the arrow already nocked in place. He glared through the trees, ignoring the arrows flying around him.

He let his arrow go, and raised his chin when someone nearby screamed, then fell to the ground with a thud. Jacob gasped—that person hadn't been far away at all. Had Jacob somehow jumped into the middle of a war reenactment? And what would the Indian do if he saw Jacob? What was going on? And if it was a reenactment, why did he see anger earlier?

Another Native American strode up to the one near Jacob and spoke a language that seemed to be only garbled words, helping the first to his feet. They laughed like the funniest thing ever had just happened, then the first turned and called in the strange language, and there were hoots and hollers. The forest around Jacob was swarming with more Natives.

Jacob had to get away. But how? They'd most definitely see him. He leaned forward, keeping his eyes on the Native American who'd been closest to him. The man strode to a crumpled form, grabbed the figure by the hair, pulled his knife out, and before Jacob could look away, scalped him.

Jacob nearly retched into the bush, fighting to keep the bile down. He'd seen a lot of things, but none of them were as sickening as what he just witnessed. Barbaric!

Soon, the group of men, still hollering and shouting

happily, moved far enough away to give Jacob an opening to escape through.

He scrambled to his knees and slipped out of his bush, then, without looking backward, crawled as fast as he could through the forest toward his house. He held his breath, waiting for the Native Americans to see him.

They didn't.

Jacob blew out a small breath in relief that no one seemed to be paying any attention to him. But he couldn't figure out what was going on. They'd spoken a different language—were there enough people nearby to put together a reenactment that thorough? Or was there an Indian reservation close to Mendon that Jacob didn't know about?

His pulse sped when he heard feet rushing toward him. He was being chased—they must've seen him after all. Would they kill him? Kidnap him? What about his family?

He curled up in a ball, protecting his head, when the runners reached him.

And passed by.

Peeking through his arms, he watched as several pairs of brown legs zoomed through the trees on either side of him. They were racing toward his house—his family was in danger!

Jacob lurched to his feet, tuning out the tingling sensation in his legs as blood rushed back into them. He stumbled forward and pushed himself into a fast jog, then a run. He rounded the last tree in the forest, then stumbled again, falling to the ground.

His home was gone. Completely. Nothing was there except . . . except for an Indian camp. Devastation and panic flowed through him—he was too late. The Native Americans had already destroyed his home!

But . . . logically, they couldn't have done so in such a short amount of time. And he would've heard it. This had to be a nightmare. There was no way any of this could be happening.

He squeezed his eyes shut as tight as possible and pinched himself. The house was going to be there when he opened his eyes. This was all just a dream! It wasn't real.

Except, he couldn't shake the feeling that said it *was* real.

Jacob jumped when feet rushed toward him, then jerked away when a strong hand grabbed his arm, trying to pull him to his feet.

"Son!"

Jacob squinted, opening his eyes. Dad! How did he get here?

"Did you see the Indians?"

"Jacob. Jacob!" Dad said, fear in his voice. "Come on, you've got to shake yourself out of this."

Jacob tried to get out of his dad's grip. "No, Dad, no! We're not safe. Indians are attacking—they scalped a man, Dad. We've got to go!"

Matt stepped into view, rubbing his eyes. "What are you talking about?"

Mom joined them and Jacob's body tensed up. Then he looked at the house behind her. It was there! But where did the Indian camp go?

"Jacob honey, what's wrong?"

"He's hallucinating again," Dad said.

"Not a hallucination. There's no way—they were real, Mom!" What he'd witnessed couldn't possibly be fake. Not at all.

She put her arms around him. "Who was real?"

He didn't realize tears were streaming down his face until just then, and he quickly wiped them away. "The Indians—attacking. Their camp is right here—was—where the house is now!"

"That's not possible, son," Dad said. "Let's get back inside. We'll figure this out together."

Jacob ignored the expressions of concern his parents

shared. He couldn't shake the fear from his system—the sense of danger and urgency. What had happened? If none of it was real, was it a sign? A warning that something was coming? Or was he going completely crazy?

His legs shook really badly, and his mom helped him sit on the couch when they got in the living room. "Start at the top. What did you see?"

Jacob swallowed a few times, trying to collect his thoughts. "I couldn't sleep. Got a drink. A bunch of people were outside, and I went out to see who—in case they were the Lorkon or something."

"You should've woken me up," Matt said. "I'd have gone with you."

"I followed them into the forest. They were crouching—trying to be quiet. Then arrows started flying through the air, and I saw Indians! All over the place—and—and they scalped someone! Then they raced toward the house and I thought they were going to attack all of you."

Jacob's parents exchanged a glance. Mom looked panicked.

"It couldn't have been real, Janna," Dad said. He turned to Jacob. "You're sure it wasn't a dream?"

"I'm positive it wasn't." Then he hesitated. "But . . . something weird—they didn't see or hear me or anything."

Dad frowned. "It had to have been a night terror."

"Isn't sixteen a bit old for night terrors?" Mom asked.

Dad paced the carpet in front of Jacob. "Don't know."

"But it felt so real," Jacob said. "Not like a dream at all. And I actually felt wind from one of the arrows passing by."

"Night terrors can be like that."

Matt grunted, leaning up against the doorway to the kitchen. "I still think you should've come and got me."

Mom glanced at him, tucking a strand of loose hair behind her ear. "Get in bed, Matt. You have school in the morning."

"So does he."

"He's not going."

Matt grumbled, practically dragging his feet on the way out of the room.

Jacob accepted a blanket from his mom, putting it around his shoulders. He sank back into the couch, still trying to calm down. What was he going to do? He couldn't keep doing these sorts of things.

2

Dad sat on the couch opposite him and leaned forward, resting his elbows on his knees. "What can we do to help?"

Jacob shook his head. "I don't know, Dad. I don't understand most of what's going on around me anymore." He looked up. "I wish *you* did, though. I wish you could figure all this out."

Dad nodded. "I know. We could take you to a doctor again, but I really don't think that'll help."

Mom sat next to Dad, a blanket for the two of them to share in her hands. "No, it didn't last time. These must be night terrors. But why? He's never had this problem before."

No one responded. Jacob snuggled further into his blanket, feeling the panic finally leave him. His parents were smart and had access to smart people—they were royalty, after all. They'd figure things out.

His mom left to make three cups of hot chocolate. He and Dad didn't speak, and he was fine with that. He wanted to relax and stop thinking about his hallucination. Or night terror. Whatever it was.

A few minutes later, Mom returned, handing out mugs. Jacob sipped his hot chocolate, enjoying the warmth as it flowed down his throat and into his stomach. After a moment, he put the cup down, ready to ask something he'd wanted to know for a while.

"Where did Matt come from?"

Mom looked up, surprised. "You don't know already?" She turned to Dad. "You didn't tell him?"

"No—haven't had the chance." Dad's eyes glowed and he rubbed his hands together. "You already know that when I came to Arien's kingdom, I brought my best friend, Kelson, with me."

Jacob nodded. "And he helped distract the Lorkon when you got Mom and me."

"Yes. He fought alongside me—faithful as always. He wanted to rescue his queen, even though he didn't have to. His wife, your mother's best friend, had been badly abused and left to die. We found her and made sure she was comfortable. I gave Kelson the choice to remain with her or to continue with me, and he chose to continue."

"And was killed trying to get the Shiengols." Jacob thought he could see where this was going. "He left a son behind, didn't he?"

Mom nodded, rubbing her eyes. "Yes. There was no way we were going to leave a one-year-old boy in Maivoryl City with the Lorkon coming to power—especially the child of parents who were so important to us, and loyal." She looked at Jacob. "His mom had been my biggest help in the castle—my best friend. She and I were inseparable. And when your father and Kelson came from Troosinal, Midian fell in love with Kelson while I fell more in love with your father."

His parents beamed at each other, Mom's cheeks glowing. Green swirled in the air around them and Jacob looked away, embarrassed by their obvious affection. They'd always been so . . . so *mushy*.

"When we found out Midian had passed away, we brought the boy with us, intending to raise him as our own."

"Does he know he'd been adopted?"

"Of course. But we've never treated him like he wasn't one of ours."

Jacob thought over this new information. Matt wasn't from earth either! Did he remember living in Eklaron? How would he have forgotten it? "How'd you explain to him the whole being-from-another-world thing?"

"Didn't have to. He'd been very traumatized when the Lorkon attacked the castle, and his memories of that time have always been vague. He didn't know the difference between the two worlds."

"But now he knows the truth, right?"

Mom folded up the blanket she and Dad had been using. "Yes. I told him the night your father and Amberly were kidnapped. He wasn't as shocked as we'd expected."

Dad laughed. "Quite the opposite. He thought being from another planet was great." He leaned forward, a serious expression on his face. "Kenji told me Gallus wants to get a group together to find the Shiengols."

"Yeah. And they'll need my help." Jacob hesitated. "That's okay, right?"

"Of course. And I've been thinking a lot . . . I've decided I'm coming too."

Jacob sat up. "Really? Awesome!"

A half smile crossed Dad's face. "And it's about time we taught you how to fight with a sword."

"Great."

Dad nodded. "The Makalos want to go during Thanksgiving break."

"That's this month—good."

"All right," Mom said. "I'm tired. It's time to get back in bed." She brushed Jacob's hair off his forehead, feeling his temperature, then took his mug. "Will you be okay now?"

"Yeah, I think so." Jacob didn't mind his mom fawning over him—it would probably never stop, regardless of how old he got.

Jacob climbed the stairs to his room, excited at the thought of learning how to fight from his dad.

He pulled the blankets up and sighed contentedly. This would be the best month ever. As long as he didn't hallucinate —or have a night terror—again.

JACOB DIDN'T WAKE up until nearly noon—he was surprised Mom let him sleep that long. After showering, he went downstairs to the kitchen, where Mom was eating a tomato sandwich.

"The Makalos have been asking about you all morning—everyone over there is worried, especially Aloren."

Aloren? Jacob's mouth went dry. "What did you tell them?"

"That I'd send you as soon as you got up."

Jacob hesitated. "I can go visit them?"

Mom laughed. "Of course—you're not a prisoner, and you're not sick. Just overly exhausted. I excused you from classes all day."

"Thank you." Jacob hugged her.

She patted his arm, then pulled away, looking him over. "You've been really stressed. I don't want it to ruin your feelings toward Eklaron."

Jacob rolled his eyes. It didn't surprise him that she'd want him to fall in love with her—their—world. "It won't, Mom. I promise."

"Okay. Get going—they're anxious to see you."

Jacob grabbed an apple and dashed upstairs to get the key and his shoes. After he'd swallowed the last bite of apple, nearly choking on it in his hurry, he keyed himself to Taga Village. He couldn't wait to see Aloren.

The dark interior of Kenji's place let him know no one was home. Rather than key over to the tree, he decided to walk there.

Jacob started down the path that wound between the Makalo dwellings. He put his hands in his jacket pockets and nodded at people as he passed, picking up speed. It was cold.

When he got to the ledge, he saw that Kenji and Ebony were down by the tree, talking to Aloren.

"Hey," he called, waving, then quickly descended the wall, using the holes etched into the stone.

He turned as Aloren threw her arms around him. "You're here. And you're alive!"

He laughed. "'Course I am."

She flushed and stepped away, tucking her hair behind her ear. Jacob's heart thudded in his chest—she liked him! Right?

Ebony and Kenji caught up. "Your mom told us what happened last night," Ebony said, "and we've been very worried about your hallucination. Especially after what took place when you were in the tunnel with the Ember Gods."

Jacob nodded. "Yeah, it's pretty frustrating, not knowing what's going on."

"We'll figure it out soon," Kenji said, clapping his hand on Jacob's shoulder. "Or, you will. We really won't be much help here."

Jacob chuckled. "Good to know."

Ebony grabbed Kenji's arm, pulling him away. "We were on our way to visit some friends when we saw Aloren. Dear, let's keep going. We can leave these two to catch up."

Aloren's face split in a grin as she turned to Jacob, and he marveled at the change in her from the first time they'd met. Where had this enthusiastic, happy person been back then?

"You've got to see what I've done with the tree!" she said.

Jacob followed her, wondering if she'd added a secret room or something. The idea of being alone with her was definitely appealing.

She opened the door and waved for Jacob to go in first.

He stepped into the slightly darker interior and raised an eyebrow.

3

Aloren had hung blue polka-dot curtains, used a matching tablecloth and a huge, brightly-colored rug, and put random things on the bookshelves. Vases or statues or something—Jacob didn't go close enough to see what they were.

"Isn't it awesome?" she said, spreading her arms wide. "I love it. And what's even better—there aren't holes in the ground like at the tower."

"It's, uh . . . it's great." Jacob grinned, putting his hands in his pockets. They'd started sweating the moment he and Aloren had walked into the tree. They were alone. Alone. He crossed his fingers that things would go well—that he wouldn't embarrass himself by saying something stupid.

How would she feel if he tried to hold her hand again? Would it be better to wait? Or should he just reach out and grab it? He chewed the inside of his cheek. No, he'd wait—he needed to figure out how not to be nervous around her first. The last time he'd tried, it had taken him several minutes to get up the courage, and just as he had, she pulled away.

"Do you want something to drink?" she asked, walking to

the refrigerator. "This thing keeps food cold. It's pretty awesome."

"Yeah, I love them too."

Jacob shook his head at himself. He loved fridges? He hadn't ever even thought about them before—aside from being something that was in the kitchen. "And yes—I'd like a drink. What've you got?"

"Water. And soda. Do you like soda?"

"Definitely."

She pulled out a two-liter bottle of root beer and poured him a glass. After putting the soda away, she sat across from him at the table, tracing patterns on the tablecloth. The colors in the air around her changed from bright green to a light orange—nervousness.

She took a deep breath. "I've been thinking . . ."

He put his cup down. "About what?"

"And I've talked to the Makalos and they think it's okay if . . . I . . . I'd like to attend your school, so I can meet humans my age and learn more about your world."

She'd told Jacob a couple days before that there weren't a lot of teenagers in Macaria. He was constantly amazed at how many people were killed by the Lorkon. After Jacob and his parents had escaped, the Lorkon went around killing infants and children, trying to find him. Guilt flooded over him. He'd caused so much destruction to Eklaron, simply by existing.

Then what she'd said hit him. "Wait. You want to come to school? That's a great idea!" It made him excited to think he'd see her on earth too. He paused. "We'd have to ask my parents, though. Make sure it would be okay."

She nodded. "Can we do that right now?"

"Why not? Mom's home, and she'll call my dad at work."

"Great. Let's go." Aloren got up from the table, stepped to the door, and turned, smiling at Jacob.

His heart skipped around inside his chest—her smile was

so pretty—and he felt his ears redden. He looked down, fumbling with the key in his hands. Finally, he got it in the lock the right way and took them to his house.

"Mom?" he called out. "You here?"

"In the office, honey."

Jacob started across the living room, heading to the doorway of his parents' study, but paused when he noticed that Aloren wasn't following. She stood at the front door, staring as if she'd never seen it before. He looked around, seeing things through her eyes. The piano, fireplace, couches, pictures on tables and walls would all be foreign to her. He couldn't wait to show her the TV and sound system in the family room!

"Wow," she said, running a hand across the worn couch, fingering an old blanket, then crossing to the fireplace. "I love it—it's so . . ." She turned to him, and he was surprised to see tears in her eyes. "So much like a real home. Where people who care for each other live."

He raised an eyebrow, then quickly hid his surprise. That wasn't what he'd expected—she didn't even comment on the things that wouldn't be in her own world. He cleared his throat, determined to ignore her emotions. "Yup." He motioned her to follow him to the study.

"Um . . . Mom, you remember Aloren, right?"

"Your Majesty," Aloren said, sinking to one knee.

Jacob's mouth popped open, and his mom blushed.

"Oh. Oh, dear," Mom said, walking around the desk. "Thank you—very much." She pulled Aloren up.

"It's such an honor to finally meet you—Gallus spoke of you and King Dmitri all the time."

Mom's cheeks flushed even redder. "It's been many years since I was anywhere other than Taga Village."

Aloren nodded. Then she looked at Jacob, her expression reminding him why they were there.

"Oh," Jacob said. She wanted *him* to ask. He quickly explained Aloren's idea to Mom.

"Well, I think it'll work—it's an excellent opportunity for you to increase your experience." She walked around the desk. "But I need to talk it over with Dmitri first. Step out for a moment, please, and shut the door. I'll call him."

They left the room and Jacob sat next to Aloren on the couch—his mom had just called Dad Dmitri! Weird.

Neither said anything. Jacob folded his arms and looked at the wall in front of him, careful not to inadvertently touch Aloren. She leaned back and gazed at the ceiling, staring at the light fixture, twirling a strand of hair in her fingers. Mom's muffled voice came through the door, but Jacob couldn't understand what she was saying. Finally, she put the phone down and came out.

"King Dmitri and I would like to talk it over with both of you before giving our go-ahead. Come on in." She held the door for Jacob and Aloren.

"Aloren?" Dad's voice came out of the speakerphone.

Aloren jumped, then leaned forward, looking at the device on the desk. "It's really a phone. Wow."

"Yes. We want to make sure you're absolutely clear on something before we allow you to attend school here."

Aloren nodded. "Whatever you think is necessary."

"No one—not one person—knows anything about another world and the link to it near our house. You must be extremely careful in your communications with others—both students and teachers."

"I will. I promise."

"And we'd rather you not get involved in any after-school activities. Once the final class lets out, you'll return to Eklaron right away."

Aloren folded her hands in her lap. "That won't be a problem."

"Last, have you spoken with Gallus about this? He's the one who needs to give permission."

Aloren blushed. "I haven't—it didn't occur to me."

"Do you have your Minya with you?"

Aloren lifted the knapsack she always carried. "Yes—Hazel is here. I'm getting her out now."

"Good."

No one said anything while Aloren opened Hazel's container. Hazel's eyes sparkled as she looked up at Aloren, then she waved to Jacob, who grinned back at the little creature.

"Okay, she's ready."

"Hazel, can you hear me?"

Hazel nodded. "Yes."

Dad asked the Minya to deliver a message to Gallus, telling the man about Aloren's desire to attend school on earth with Jacob.

Jacob leaned forward in his chair, paying close attention to the conversation between Gallus, his parents, and Aloren as Hazel flitted back and forth, delivering messages. He crossed his fingers, hoping everyone would agree that having Aloren attend school would be a good idea.

Hazel flashed back with Gallus's final message, giving his permission just so long as Aloren made sure to follow the king and queen's instructions closely.

"All right, Aloren," Dad said from the phone. "It looks like you're going to be Mountain Crest High School's newest student."

Aloren grinned broadly, getting to her feet. "Wonderful!"

Mom smiled. "I'll take you to the school in a minute to meet with a counselor and set up classes—we'll say you're an exchange student." She looked over Aloren's clothes. "Those should work for now—the leather pants aren't too different, and people here occasionally wear cotton tops like that. You won't stand out too much, and I'll take you shopping later." She paused, thinking. "But we want to make sure your first day isn't awkward. Jacob, how about you take her over to Tani's after school lets out?"

Jacob knit his eyebrows. "Why?"

"It would be nice if she already knew someone outside of our family."

"Oh, yeah. Tani's great."

Mom and Aloren left right away. Jacob shot hoops in the driveway until it started snowing, then he stood looking up at the sky, enjoying the feel of the falling snowflakes. They didn't stick to the ground, and nothing would for probably another month.

He waited outside for a long time, then finally gave up when it got too cold and went to read in his bedroom.

4

An hour later, he heard the front door open and went to investigate. Dad was carrying several pizza boxes. He handed them to Jacob. "Matt'll be home soon, and your mother took Aloren shopping. We'll eat when they're all back." He went into his study and sat at the desk, opening up the laptop.

Jacob put the pizza on the counter, then sat in the living room, occasionally looking out the window. He jumped to his feet when a car pulled up, then sank back down with disappointment. It was just Matt.

"What'cha doin'?" Matt asked, plopping on the couch next to Jacob.

"Mom took Aloren to the school and signed her up for classes, and they've—"

"Wait, what? Really? That's freakin' awesome!"

Jacob bounced his feet up and down rapidly. "Yeah, I know. Anyway, they're out shopping now or something. I'm waiting for them to come back so I can take her over to meet Tani."

Matt raised his eyebrows. "Why? You think they'll fight over you and you want to be there to break it up?"

Jacob snorted. "Right. Tani has a boyfriend."

Matt snickered, punching Jacob's shoulder. "Two girls who'll follow you everywhere."

"Whatever." Jacob shoved his brother, and Matt chuckled again.

"So . . . does she like you?"

"Who, Tani?"

"No, doofus. Aloren. Obviously."

Jacob felt his cheeks flush. "Don't know—and I'm not going to ask her."

"I can, if you'd like. Give her a nudge in the right direction."

Jacob's jaw dropped. "Don't, Matt. Please, please don't."

Matt rolled his eyes. "Dude, you've got to get over this phase you're in. Be the man—ask her out."

Dad entered the living room. He sat on the couch opposite the brothers. "What's this I hear? Jacob, you're looking for advice on girls? I've got plenty of experience—you know, wealthy, handsome prince. I courted a lot."

"'Court?' Are you serious, Dad? We're not in Eklaron, and I'm not *courting* anyone." Jacob shook his head, and his dad and brother laughed.

The garage door opened, signaling Mom's return, and Dad jumped up to meet her by the car.

Matt turned to Jacob. "Your car is still in the shop, right? I assume you want me to drive you and Aloren to Tani's house."

Jacob nodded. "If you could."

Matt shrugged. "Shouldn't be a problem. Let me put my stuff away." He went up the stairs, lugging his backpack and gym bag with him, then returned just as Aloren and Mom came in, followed by Dad.

Aloren stepped to Jacob, carrying all sorts of bags. "Check

this out." She glanced at Mom, an admiring expression on her face, and whispered, "You're so lucky. The queen understands fashion."

Jacob didn't know how to answer that. He was still adjusting to the fact that his parents were—*he* was—royalty. And he'd never noticed his mom's fashion sense.

"How'd it go? With the school?"

Aloren held up a sheet of paper. "My classes."

Mom turned, smiling. "She'll be with you for most of the day, minus your third and fourth periods."

Jacob nodded. "What classes is she taking during those times?"

Aloren read from her schedule. "Art while you're in history, and science while you're in the woodworking class."

"Art, huh? That's cool."

Aloren nodded. "I love drawing and painting." She sat on the couch, going through her bags.

Mom looked Jacob right in the eye, lowering her voice. "Honey, the counselors wanted to put her in remedial courses. I wouldn't have any of that—she's here to experience things as an ordinary teenager. You're really going to have to help her catch up. Her grades might not matter so much, but I don't want her to be completely miserable when she doesn't do well. Plus, if she decides to attend college here, it would be good if she figured things out in high school."

Jacob nodded. "Shouldn't be too difficult. It's not like my classes are super hard." And it was true. Math had been his most difficult subject, but Mr. Coolidge no longer required him to attend early, and had stopped giving him a ton of extra work to do.

She laughed. "Don't get complacent."

"I won't," Jacob said. Helping Aloren catch up meant more time with her. This semester was going to be amazing—they'd be spending a lot of time together.

Mom looked at her watch. "Let's eat dinner, then you can head to Tani's."

THE RIDE to Tani's house after dinner went quickly—Jacob was very aware of Aloren sitting next to him, between the brothers. Aloren's colors were so bright, it was difficult to see past them. She was seriously excited about meeting Tani and going to Mountain Crest High School. He smirked to himself —she'd probably get over her excitement once she saw how much homework she'd need to do to catch up.

"What's this vehicle called?" she asked.

"It's a Toyota—a truck," Matt said. "Isn't it amazing?"

"Yes! I love these things." She hesitated. "They're . . . so fast, though."

Jacob sighed in disappointment. He'd missed Aloren's first car ride when she went to the school with Mom—it would've been really great to see how she reacted.

Tani opened the door when they rang the bell. "Jake!" she squealed. Her smile grew when she saw Aloren and Matt. "Hey!" She turned, yelling to the back of the house. "Mom, the Clarks are here. Can we hang out for a while?"

Kim, Tani's mom, stepped into the front room, drying her hands on a towel. "Only for a few minutes—you've got too much homework." Her eyes sparkled when she looked at the brothers. "Jacob and Matt. We haven't had you around for some time. And who's your friend?"

Jacob introduced Aloren as their exchange student, and Aloren shook hands with Tani and Kim.

He turned to Tani. "We're hoping you could help her in school when she's not with me. Mom thought you two would get along well."

Tani nodded. "Yeah! It'll totally be awesomesauce. I'll introduce her to Sheena and Jen and everyone."

"So, Aloren, where are you from?" Kim asked. She must have noticed Aloren's leather pants. Definitely not American.

"Eklaron," Aloren said. "More specifically, the land of Gevkan." She gasped, realizing what she'd just said. Her face turned white and she turned to Jacob and Matt.

"Huh?" Tani said. "Where's that?"

Jacob mentally kicked himself. They hadn't decided which country she'd be from!

Kim looked just as confused, and Jacob's mind raced. Aloren wouldn't know enough about earth to come up with an appropriate answer. "It's, uh . . . near Hungary. It's a really small English-speaking province-region-place."

Kim looked confused, but Tani accepted the explanation immediately. "That's why you don't have an accent. Cool!"

Aloren nodded, clearly still panicked.

"Exactly." Jacob rushed to change the subject. He already felt bad enough for leading them on. "So, Tani, if you could help her feel welcome in school, that would be cool."

"Sure." She grabbed Aloren's arm. "Just hang with me and Jacob and you'll be fine!"

Jacob blew out a breath in relief. "Thank you, Tani."

"You're welcome."

Everyone said goodbye, and Jacob, Matt, and Aloren returned to the truck.

"That was close," Aloren said, doing up her seatbelt. "We've got to find a better story than that."

Jacob nodded. "Yeah, especially since Kim is probably going to Google Eklaron now. Hopefully she'll get distracted on her way to the computer."

5

Jacob looked forward to taking Aloren to school with him. He keyed to the tree to get her, but she wasn't ready yet, so he waited by the door. When she came downstairs a couple of moments later, he sucked in a breath of air. Something was different about her face—her eyes were even prettier than usual. It took him a second to figure out why. She was wearing makeup. Wow. She looked so . . . so . . . *hot*.

"Is this going to be okay?" She waved at what she was wearing. "Queen Arien picked it out."

Jacob nodded. She was wearing jeans and a bright pink T-shirt. He'd seen clothes like that at school before. "I think so. Girls wear jeans all the time."

She laughed. "You probably don't know much about fashion."

He shook his head.

"I kept up with it very well in Macaria. I was sad when your mom told me that Macarian fashion wouldn't be helpful while attending school at Mountain Crest."

"She's right. 'Course, there are dances throughout the year

where you'd probably be fine wearing one of the more fancy dresses."

Her face lit up. "Really? Great!" She motioned to the door. "Let's get going."

Aloren peppered Jacob and Matt with questions the entire ride into town. Math was interesting. Shirley nearly freaked out when Mr. Coolidge made her move to an empty chair two seats behind Jacob and Aloren took Shirley's spot.

"This is stupid!" Shirley said, throwing her bag on her new chair. "I've sat there the entire semester! Why do *I* have to move? Why can't *she* sit *here*?"

"I'm truly sorry," Aloren said. "I'm fine with going back there."

Mr. Coolidge shook his head. "No. The note from the front office is very specific. She's to stay near Jacob."

Shirley pouted, pushed her bag off the chair, and plopped down. "Ridiculous."

Instead of continuing to make Jacob come early, Mr. Coolidge simply gave him other material to study during the period. Jacob had given up trying to convince Mr. Coolidge to let him just transfer to a different class.

Luckily, things weren't frustrating anymore—his relationship with Mr. Coolidge had changed. They had an understanding that worked for both of them. Jacob helped out in the class whenever needed, and Mr. Coolidge didn't ask him about anything odd he'd noticed—including Jacob molding wood and metal with his bare hands.

Math ended and Jacob walked Aloren to English, and the teacher rearranged the seating so Aloren could sit next to him. Being an attractive "exchange student" who wasn't shy and spoke perfect English really helped her fit in with the others.

Jacob reluctantly left her as he headed to history and she to art. When the period finally ended, he ran to the locker room to get his gym clothes, excited for Aloren to see him play basketball.

Kevin was in there too. "Hey, no more ball during lunch."

"What? Are you sure?"

"Yeah. Dad told me this morning—the principal decided it was time to end the tradition. He thinks more work will get done if the admins aren't reffing games."

"That's ridiculous."

"Totally."

Jacob's stomach churned at the thought of no longer being able to play basketball, but he set the feeling aside, determined to find out for himself if what Kevin had said was true. He wouldn't put it past the guy to lie just to prevent Jacob from playing.

Jacob grabbed his clothes anyway and jogged to the orange gym. Tani, Josh, and Aloren waited near the doors. Jacob stopped when he saw their expressions.

"Is it true? No more ball?"

Tani nodded. "Stupid principal."

Jacob dropped his stuff. "Why, though?"

"Oh, the usual. They want to be 'more efficient.'" She flipped her hair back. "It's dumb, I know."

"Now what?" He wasn't sure where to eat lunch if it wasn't in the gym. He'd only eaten in the cafeteria once since starting his junior year. It felt weird, thinking about eating there again.

"We could try the commons area," Josh said.

"Yeah—that's where Matt and his girlfriend usually eat, right?" Tani asked.

"And the rest of the football team." Jacob wasn't sure he wanted to eat with all the football players, but he and his friends turned and walked there anyway. Matt scooted over when Jacob, Aloren, and the others sat near him and Sammy.

"Heard about basketball," Matt said. "Sorry 'bout that, dude."

Jacob rubbed the back of his neck and didn't respond. He didn't feel like talking about it anymore.

While they ate, Aloren and Tani got on the topic of guys. Jacob rolled his eyes, but his heart froze when Aloren mentioned seeing a cute one.

"What did he look like?" Tani asked.

"Tall. Very pretty eyes. We don't have a lot of blue-eyed people where I'm from."

Was she talking about him? But then she continued, and his heart fell.

"And his hair was blond."

Jacob's hair was dark brown. Really dark brown.

Tani nodded. "I'd have to see him to know who he was. Did he talk to you?"

"Oh, yes. Quite a lot. We sit next to each other. He's an athlete—he spoke of some sort of sport. I think Jacob plays it as well." She turned to Jacob. "What's the name of the sport you play?"

"Basketball," Tani said before he could answer.

"Yes! That's it."

Jacob tried to control the feelings of jealousy that hit him in the pit of the stomach. He'd never once considered that Aloren would crush on someone else. He felt like kicking himself. What had he been expecting? That he'd save her life and she'd melt all over him? He sighed in frustration. None of that gave him a claim on her.

No one seemed to notice him withdraw from the conversation. That irked him, which, in turn, bothered him even more. He'd never been the type to get worked up like that.

Everyone cleaned up and Jacob walked Aloren to class, neither saying anything.

THE RIDE back to Mendon went quickly—Aloren babbled about her first day of school, Jacob stared out the window, and Matt sang along with the radio.

Dad was home when they got there, waiting on the front porch. "Jacob, take Aloren to the tree, then come back."

He looked upset. Had something happened? Jacob did as he was asked, then found his dad. He was already speaking with Matt, but filled Jacob in on what they'd discussed.

"Someone left the chicken run and coop open last night, and the chickens wandered away this morning. Since they usually come back on their own, and haven't, I was just telling Matt they're either dead or stolen by now." He glared at Matt and Jacob, daring one of them to deny what he'd just said.

The brothers exchanged glances. Matt looked extra guilty. "Sorry, Dad, it was probably me—I put them away last night."

Dad nodded. "Thank you for your honesty." He sighed and didn't say anything for a moment. Then, "You won't do anything else until every chicken is found—alive or dead."

Matt looked at his feet, but didn't say anything.

Dad turned to Jacob. "I'm home early because we were planning to have a meeting in Eklaron today. That's still going to happen. I need you to round everyone up and take them to Kenji's place. When you're done, return here to help your brother."

Jacob's mouth popped open. He'd never been left out of a meeting before! "But—"

Dad put a hand on his shoulder, addressing both him and Matt. "Come as soon as you've found all the chickens."

Jacob nodded, and took Mom, Dad, and Amberly to Taga Village. Amberly surprised him by rushing up to Kaiya, Akeno's little sister, as soon as she stepped through the door. They giggled, jumping up and down, then ran off to play. Jacob looked at his parents.

"She knows Kaiya really well."

His mom laughed. "Yes. We figured it would only be a matter of time before we were able to come here as a family, and I started taking Amberly for walks a couple of months ago while you were at school and Dad at work. We wanted her to get used to the Makalos, and have a good experience on Eklaron."

"Good idea."

Jacob keyed to Macaria and the Fat Lady's cabin. After he'd dropped her and Gallus off at Kenji's place, he returned home and found Matt.

It took the brothers an hour to locate the chickens and get them back to the coop. Luckily, none were injured, but it was dirty, frustrating, and annoying work. Matt apologized several times.

When they were done, they cleaned up and keyed to Kenji's.

"We're nearly finished here," Dad said. "But come—have a seat."

"Where's Aloren?" Jacob asked, looking around. He ignored the slight pang that hit him when he remembered what had happened in school that day.

Kenji motioned out the window. "In the tree."

Jacob frowned. "Why isn't she here?"

"Are we positive she should be a part of these meetings?" Brojan asked.

"Of *course*," Jacob said. He couldn't believe the patriarch would even ask something so . . . *stupid*. "She already knows everything that's going on—plus she'd be able to help a lot."

"All right. Go get her."

Jacob got to his feet and opened a link to the tree, inviting Aloren to join them.

6

Kenji had to bring another table and more chairs from a back room so there would be space for all in attendance. The two tables together nearly filled the entire place.

Jacob was glad everyone had been able to come. He looked around, smiling at the people he'd grown to love so much. Sweet Pea was by Aloren, and Jacob hid a grin when he watched the Makalo fail to get Aloren's attention. He was obviously enthralled that such a cute girl was near him. He clenched his jaw when he remembered she had a crush on someone else.

Ebony gave cups of water to Matt, Aloren, and Jacob, and put the pitcher on the table.

Dad turned to Jacob, his voice taking on a tone of authority Jacob had never heard before.

"We've gone over many things—we'll review in a moment —but so you know, our main focus, of course, is to get the Shiengols out of August Fortress."

"August?" Matt asked. "Is it some sort of summer retreat?"

Jacob's parents laughed. "No, son," Dad said. "August is an

adjective—it means majestic, supreme, grand. Don't they teach you anything in school?"

Matt snorted. "Yeah. That August is a month."

He had a point. Jacob chuckled. He'd never heard the word used in any way except when speaking of the calendar.

"All right," Dad said. He stood and paced. "Kenji and Ebony are building as many doors as possible. We'll place them everywhere we feel we'll need quick access. The first we're installing will be at Aldo's cabin to replace the one that was destroyed. Jacob, you'll key Sweet Pea, Jaegar, and Akeno to Macaria today so they can head there."

Matt's face clouded. "Jaegar's really young, isn't he? Only eleven or something? Wouldn't it be better if someone else went?"

Kenji chuckled. "I'm sure you've heard by now that Makalos age differently than humans. Jaegar isn't a child, even though by your standards, he would be. In earth terms, he's around fourteen. And since Sweet Pea and Akeno are basically adults, he'll have plenty of supervision."

Matt slowly shook his head. "Akeno is an adult?"

"Yes. We reach adulthood at fifteen, so Jaegar isn't far from that."

"Weird."

Dad raised his hand and everyone went quiet. "Jacob, tomorrow after Aldo's new door is in place, you and the Fat Lady will go through Aldo's things there. She's looking for a remedy for what he's done—"

"Yes, yes! I'm positive it's reversible," the Fat Lady said excitedly. "Only a matter of finding out what he did—he had to have left a clue in his cabin. And Jacob, this isn't going to be easy work—the place is in ruins, from what I've heard." She looked at Jacob's dad. "Oh. Sorry, Your Majesty. Continue."

"Friday after school, a scouting group will head to the fortress, camp there overnight, and put up doors in a few locations around the area so we'll have easy access through Jacob and the key, should anything go wrong. They'll get a feel for the valley, then come back Saturday morning."

Dad grabbed his glass and took a drink, then resumed pacing. "We'll need time to prepare before we attempt to free the Shiengols—find out everything we can about what we're facing. For all we know, the Lorkon traps are still active. We should expect it to still be exceptionally difficult to break in. You all know that every member of the group who tried it before died."

Dad sat again, then drummed his fingers on the table. "Ebony, Gallus, Akeno, and Jacob, of course, with the key, will make up that scouting group."

Matt started. "What about me?"

"And me?" Sweet Pea asked.

"Excuse me, Your Majesty," Gallus said, "but I won't be able to spend this much time away from the shop. I need to focus on providing a living for my family."

Dad nodded. "That's fine, Gallus. Take care of your store and family. We appreciate everything you already do."

"I'll help wherever," Aloren said. "Gallus has trained me in many areas—including scouting and tracking."

"I'm like Aloren," Sweet Pea said. "Well, not like her, obviously, 'cause she's taller, but—"

"*That's* the only difference you can think of?" Matt asked.

"Well, no—"

"'Cause I haven't seen a beard on her yet." Matt looked at Aloren. "Maybe she shaves her face."

Aloren looked confused. "Shave my face? Why would I do that?"

Sweet Pea growled, then mock-glared at Matt. "The point is, I can help wherever I'm needed."

Akeno nodded. "Same."

"Send Aloren," Gallus said. "She's got a brain on her. She'll find anything I would."

"Then it's settled," Dad said, ignoring Matt's "No fair!" and Sweet Pea's "Whatever!" "You'll leave as soon as Jacob returns from school." He waved his hand toward Jacob and Matt. "That concludes what we'd gone over before you came. Now we'll discuss the people in the scented air. We need to pull them out. All of them." He looked over the group. "How many of you have taken the Malono potion?"

Matt, Sweet Pea, Gallus, Ebony, Aloren, the Fat Lady, and Akeno raised their hands. Jacob hadn't taken it—as far as anyone knew, he was immune to the traps of the Lorkon.

"Good. That's enough. This Saturday after the August Fortress scouting group returns, we're going to do a mass rescue. Those of us who haven't taken the potion will wake the people outside the scented air. The rest of you will pull them."

Jacob lifted his hand. "If the people stuck there aren't marking where the scented air begins, how will everyone know it's there? Won't more people get stuck?"

"Good point," Dad said. "Kenji, will you and Ebony put warning signs together before Saturday?"

Kenji nodded.

Dad took a deep breath. "There's one other thing we need to discuss, and that's recruiting Wurbies."

"That's going to be very difficult," Gallus said. "They live in Ashay Hills—the most impassible mountains in this part of the land. We don't even know if the tunnels are still open. Especially . . . especially after what happened to Jacob's group."

Jacob's throat tightened just thinking about what had happened to Seden, and how powerless he'd felt.

"True, but it's necessary. They're the only ones who can actually help fight against the Dusts."

Aloren raised her eyebrows. "You've been having problems with Dusts? They're really easy to deal with."

"In small groups, yes," Brojan said, "but the Lorkon have gathered a huge army of them. In the war nearly fifteen years ago, they'd been trained quite efficiently and caused a lot of destruction."

"Why are the ones I've come across so stupid, then?" Jacob asked.

"The Lorkon haven't spent as much time on tactical things lately," Brojan said. "And Dusts have really short memories. They forget nearly everything they've been taught after five or six months and have to be re-trained. Plus, they only live around five years."

Dad nodded. "My guess is that the Lorkon will work directly with them again." He paused. "The point is, we must have the Wurbies. It's time to recruit." He looked at his watch. "We'll end now. Jacob needs to take Akeno, Jaegar, and Sweet Pea to Macaria, and he and I must begin his sword-fighting lessons."

Jacob felt his chest expanding. His dad was going to teach him how to fight! He got up and stretched, enjoying the pops in his back. Most of the others didn't stand right away—they looked somewhat overwhelmed, the colors swirling in the air around them switching between excitement, nervousness, and a little fear. He certainly felt the same. It was going to be a busy week.

7

Jacob keyed the three Makalos to Macaria after returning everyone else to their proper homes, then he met Dad in their back yard in Mendon.

"We'll use wooden swords while we catch up to what you remember," Dad said. He tossed one to Jacob. "After you're comfortable with a few of the moves, we'll switch to metal. I'll teach you as many of the basics as possible, but you must recognize something—good sword fighters practice hours every day for years. The chances you'll pick any of this up within the next month—year, even—are pretty slim."

"Why are we doing this at all, then?"

"Because you're a prince. And princes become kings. And people don't respect a king who can't defend himself, even if he never has to."

With that, Dad jumped forward, swinging his weapon at Jacob's head. Jacob barely blocked the blow in time and fell to his knees under the force.

"Hold on! You didn't tell me we were starting."

"Rule number one," Dad said. "Real fighting isn't like the movies. Your opponent won't wait for anything. If they're going for the kill, they'll take the first opening they see, regardless of how ready you are."

He attacked again, this time swinging at Jacob's midsection. Jacob was only partially able to block the attack and he was knocked to the ground again, gasping for air.

Dad circled around him. "All right, get up. Let me teach you a few defensive moves."

"Shouldn't that have been the first thing we went over?"

"I wanted to see if you remembered anything."

"*Right.*"

Jacob took his time getting up—his side really hurt. When he finally got to his feet, his dad showed him several defensive tactics, each more painful on the hands, wrists, and arms than the one before. Then, as if that wasn't enough, Dad wanted to teach him offensive moves.

"I thought this was going to be fun," Jacob choked out. He grimaced when he saw the grin on his dad's face.

"It *is* fun!"

Jacob snorted. "Whatever."

"Trust me—when you've been doing it for a long time and are evenly matched with your opponent, it can be quite enjoyable."

Jacob rolled his eyes. "I'm sure."

Dad told Jacob to attack, and attack he did. He'd show his father a thing or two! But Dad stopped him only a couple of moments later.

"You're breaking two more rules. First, go for the opponent's *body*, not their *weapon*. Striking their sword will alert anyone watching to the fact that you're . . . what do you kids call it? A noob?"

Jacob laughed. "Okay, Dad."

"Next, you've got a lot of energy, but if you stream it the wrong direction—flailing around like you just were—you'll burn out really quickly, giving your opponent the perfect opportunity to strike you down. We'll focus a lot of time on ensuring you're channeling your energy into the correct movements. I want to make sure you're learning this completely."

They practiced for an hour more—Jacob was positive he'd never regain feeling in his hands and arms again. This was worse than fighting with Sweet Pea! Though, maybe enough time had passed to where Jacob didn't remember the pain from that anymore.

Finally, Dad called it quits. "We'll go at it again tomorrow after you finish working with the Fat Lady."

Jacob groaned, pulling himself inside and up the stairs to his room. He collapsed on his bed and fell asleep before remembering to change his clothes.

AFTER SCHOOL THE NEXT DAY, Jacob keyed himself, Aloren, and the Fat Lady to Aldo's cabin, using the door Jaegar, Akeno, and Sweet Pea put in place. Jacob had keyed them to Macaria the day before, and they'd made the trek to Aldo's cabin overnight. The group was there waiting when they arrived.

"'Bout time," Sweet Pea said lightly, hands on his hips. "Can we go home now?"

Jacob keyed the three Makalos back to Taga Village. He was glad Aloren had volunteered earlier to help. The Fat Lady put them to task immediately, and it was hard, messy work. Most everything was covered with debris left over from the Bald Henry's attack—bits of brick and mortar, wood shavings, glass, etc. Jacob looked around the place, then made a quick decision and keyed home to get a broom and dustpan, along with several garbage bags.

The Fat Lady insisted on cleaning up the entire cabin.

Jacob held in a chuckle—why she wanted Aldo's place clean when hers was always a wreck, he didn't understand. She collected everything that looked remotely important—papers, books, pictures, random objects Jacob didn't recognize, and even plants and leaves.

Finally, after Jacob didn't think he could get sweatier or dirtier, she said they were done. She seemed very excited about a book she'd found. Jacob looked at it curiously—it had plant pictures on the front and was full of illustrations.

Jacob keyed them to her house, and she had the two teenagers go through the salvaged stuff while she went through the papers.

Aldo perked up when they entered the cabin, sitting cross-legged in his usual corner of the room. He grinned at Aloren and held up something he'd made—from where Jacob stood, it looked like several handfuls of grass tied around a bunch of paper.

"I'm free dogs!" Aldo said. He jumped up, knocking over a stack of papers in his excitement to get to the group.

When he reached Aloren, he shoved the thing into her hands. She looked at him skeptically, obviously trying to figure out what he wanted her to do.

He clapped. "This is what happens to shoes in springtime! Sometimes they dance and sing!"

Aloren looked to Jacob for help. "What's he talking about?"

Jacob sat on the couch, thoroughly enjoying Aloren's discomfort. "Who knows. Just talk to him."

"Okay. Uh, Aldo, tell me about this." She motioned to the paper and grass mess.

"I asked to her dad about it."

"You asked to her . . . her dad?"

"Sure did not. Winter is true. It's true!"

"Yes, winter is very t—true." She turned the thing over. "What is it called?"

"It's my frustrating break!"

Jacob chuckled. "That's a great name. 'Frustrating Break.'"

The Fat Lady took Aldo's toy from Aloren, shoved it in Aldo's hands, and motioned for Aloren to sit next to Jacob. "Okay, we've got work to do."

Aldo returned to his corner, sitting cross-legged again, and the others started sorting books and papers.

Some of the books Jacob looked through were written in a form of English not hard to understand. Many of them, however, were in a different language. Aloren was able to read it, so Jacob gave those to her, and he read over the English books.

"I don't even know what I'm looking for," Aloren whispered.

"Anything that might make someone go crazy on purpose." He wasn't entirely sure either.

After nearly an hour of searching, the Fat Lady squealed. "I think I've found it!" She held out a book Jacob had already discarded as useless. "The mushrooms that grow near Kaith trees are poisonous!"

"Yeah, I saw that." Jacob remembered learning about Kaith trees a couple months earlier. They were magical and let people leave messages for other people in their trunks.

"Taken in very small amounts, the poison doesn't kill the person, but renders their brains nearly useless! And where there's a poison, there's a cure!"

"Um . . . I'm not sure how that works," Jacob said, "and it doesn't prove that's what happened to Aldo."

"No, not the book alone, but when you see what I've found here, it does!" She showed them a piece of paper. She'd circled something on it, and Jacob had to hold it up close to his eyes to decipher the scraggly writing.

FAT LADY – REMEMBER to stir twice before administering.

JACOB RAISED AN EYEBROW. "What does this have to do with anything?"

"First, it was written by Aldo—I know his handwriting. Next, it's for me, obviously. Third, it's a remedy. He and I used to discuss the differences in potions and cures. Cures nearly always require an exact number of stirrings. Even numbers, usually."

"But—"

"Look what it's written on."

Jacob inspected the paper, knitting his eyebrows. At first he didn't notice anything, but then he held the paper up and realized it had a very large, elementary depiction of a mushroom on it—faint enough not to be noticed with a cursory glance. Almost like a watermark. "So . . . this means he poisoned himself with a mushroom?" He still didn't see how she'd made the connection.

"Yup!" she said. "We can get to work on the cure immediately." She bent over her papers again. "Keep looking —books that deal with remedies are what we want now."

"Oh, I've got several here," Aloren said. She handed over a stack.

The Fat Lady fluttered through pages quickly—Jacob wasn't sure how she was taking anything in at all. She squealed again, much louder this time. "This is it! Lots easier to find than I'd expected. And look! I own this one! I wonder why it never occurred to me to go through my own collection."

She frowned, staring at the shelf opposite her, then glanced at the first page of the book in her hands. "This *is* my book. How'd he get it? And why didn't I notice it was gone?" She scowled at Aldo. "That wasn't very smart of you. You know better than to borrow something from me and not return it."

Jacob laughed. "You didn't even notice it was gone."

"Don't matter."

Aldo snickered, watching the Fat Lady. Jacob couldn't tell if the old man laughed at what she'd said, or how she'd done her hair that day. Thin locks were wrapped around her head, not in a braid this time. They looked plastered to her scalp. Not attractive at all.

"Time for you to go home—" She stopped. "I need some of the mushrooms first, though. Take me to Taga Village."

"Didn't you say the mushrooms grow around Kaith trees?"

The Fat Lady looked at Jacob like he'd just said the stupidest thing ever. "What do you think that tree in the village *is*?"

He looked down. "Oh." How was *he* supposed to know what kind it was?

He keyed there, and he and Aloren followed the Fat Lady around as she inspected the bark.

"Ah-hah!" she said. "Here they are."

"Those aren't mushrooms," Jacob said, recoiling from the huge beetles the Fat Lady stood near.

"Of course they are!"

Jacob bent as close to them as he could without getting within bug-jumping distance. "Are you sure? Looks like a beetle to me."

"It's not. See how it attaches itself to the tree?" She pointed.

"Oh, yeah. I see." It looked like one half—in this case, the left half—of the beetle had been stuck into the wood. The creature-plant-thing didn't appear to be a living insect. That brought a little relief to him.

"They grow that way. See, over here." She motioned to a much smaller one.

"Why's it always growing with the left side of the beetle sucked into the tree?"

"Mushroom, not beetle. And don't ask dumb questions—"

"That's not a dumb quest—"

"I need two—no, three of them." She plucked the ugly mushrooms from the bark, putting them in a cloth bag she'd brought.

Jacob cringed when the "mushrooms" moved inside the bag.

"That's so *disgusting*," Aloren said. "I can't believe he'd willingly eat one."

Jacob agreed.

The Fat Lady circled to the door. "He just ate the legs, I think."

Jacob grimaced, not wanting to imagine eating a mushroom with legs. Sick.

SWORD-FIGHTING LESSONS WENT BETTER that evening than they had the day before. Jacob wasn't sure why, but he felt like he was better able to concentrate, even though his entire body still ached.

Dad congratulated him, then helped him gain perspective by saying he only had a few more years to go before he'd successfully be able to fight someone who really wanted to kill him.

"I'm sure that when we finally win this war, there won't be anyone like that left."

Dad chuckled, gathering the swords, and the two walked to the garage. "We had enemies before the Lorkon came, you know."

"I haven't heard about anyone else."

"That's because the worst was my father. And other people feel awkward reminding me of that."

"What happened to him?"

"Last I heard, he killed himself."

Wow. "Really? That's awful."

Dad nodded, pausing by the kitchen door. A dark expression crossed his face. "Yes, well, at least he's no longer a threat to my people."

Jacob pondered over this for a while. How would it be to have a father like that? One so evil, you're relieved he's not alive anymore? He shook his head, not wanting to follow that train of thought.

8

During lunch on Friday, Jacob groaned inwardly when Tani and Aloren started another conversation about the blond guy from her math class.

"Oh!" Aloren exclaimed. "He's coming! What do I do?"

Jacob turned to see who Aloren had been crushing on for the past few days. He nearly spit out the food in his mouth. *Kevin* was walking toward them.

Apparently it shocked Tani too. "Kevin?" she hissed. "Kevin's the guy?" She looked at Jacob, possibly trying to gauge his reaction. He put on his best poker face.

"Hey, Aloren," Kevin said. He paused when he saw she was with Jacob. "So . . . are Jacob and Matt your host family?"

Aloren blushed, looking down. She actually blushed! "Sort of. Jacob and I are in many classes together. He's helping me with my homework."

"Hmm." The two guys eyed each other. Jacob tried to mask his frustration and jealousy. He could tell by the swirling colors that Kevin felt the same way, but it didn't show on his face—apparently he was good at hiding his emotions.

"Mind if I join you?"

Aloren scooted closer to Jacob, patting the spot on the other side of her, before Jacob could tell him to get lost. "Sure. There's plenty of room."

Jacob's mouth popped open and he felt red creep across his face. How could she do that?

Kevin sat on the other side of Aloren, and she turned toward him. They flirted and talked. Josh was busy chatting with one of the football players, and Tani looked like a third wheel, though she tried to join the conversations around her wherever possible.

Matt elbowed Jacob. "Competition, huh?" he whispered. "What are you going to do about this?"

Jacob shook his head. "Nothing I can do," he whispered back, making sure Aloren and Kevin couldn't hear. They were obviously in their own world. "She's been talking about him non-stop."

"Oh, don't I know it."

Sammy leaned forward and whispered, "You like Aloren, Jacob?"

Jacob flushed again and was about to answer when Matt cut him off. "Isn't it obvious?"

"Actually, no, it isn't," Sammy said. "I wouldn't have guessed if you hadn't said something."

"Great, Matt. Thanks." Jacob glared at his brother. "Don't say anything to anyone else, okay? It's no one's business."

Matt put his hands up. "No worries. I won't."

Jacob relaxed—Matt could be trusted, as long as he knew the boundaries.

"So, what are you going to do?" Sammy asked. "You can't just let Kevin have her."

"There's nothing I *can* do," Jacob said. "She makes her own choices."

No one said anything, and Jacob tried to focus on finishing his lunch.

EBONY AND AKENO were ready and waiting when Jacob, Aloren, and Dad arrived at the tree.

"I'm on a late lunch," Dad said, "so I'm only here for a moment." He motioned for everyone to sit. "How many doors did Kenji make?"

"Twenty. They're all here." Ebony lifted a knapsack. "Shrunk and ready to go."

"Okay. I've got a map of August Township." Dad pulled it out and indicated things as he spoke. "First, place doors here, here, and here. Make sure they're well hidden. After that, place one every half mile or so. We'll want to have as many escape routes as possible."

Ebony nodded. "We numbered them so Jacob won't have a problem figuring out which door to use."

"Good," Dad said. "Next, you have to go through the forest before you can get into the city itself. Be extremely careful— the Lorkon don't use ordinary traps, as we know. I hoped Aldo could give you more instructions. He's very familiar with the area. Unfortunately, the remedy won't be ready until tomorrow, so in the meantime, we're going to learn as much about the place as we can." He folded the map. "We'll need one of you to keep a detailed journal of what you find." Dad held up a small leather book.

"I'll do that," Aloren said. "Gallus has me make notes of my trips all the time."

"Excellent." Dad handed her the book and the map. "Mark the placement of the doors on the map, and keep it with the journal." He sighed, running his hand through his hair—what remained of it. "You'll leave now, or as soon as possible. Check back with us frequently. Oh, and also, which Minya are you taking?"

"Mine," Aloren said. "And Kenji will use Early, should he need to get in touch with us."

Dad nodded. "Be safe." He looked out the window of the tree. "I wish I could go."

Kenji and Brojan had insisted Dad stay behind—he was too important to Gevkan to put himself in potentially dangerous situations. "Maybe when we get the Shiengols." He put his hand on Jacob's shoulder. "Be careful, son. Take care of the group. And the rest of you," he motioned to the others, "watch over my son."

9

J acob couldn't believe they were out on another trek. He, Akeno, and Aloren—the only difference this time was the presence of Ebony.

It only took a couple of seconds to key to Aldo's ruined cabin. It looked a bit silly, having a fully intact door when the walls were broken down. At least Kenji had tried to make the door look old, so no one would suspect the cabin was still being used.

Ebony and Aloren chattered a great deal about parties and clothes as the group left the cabin. It didn't bother Jacob—he was still so relieved to have Aloren out of Maivoryl City, safe and sound, that even this kind of conversation was refreshing.

Right then, the women were discussing clothing fashion in Macaria versus Taga. Jacob hadn't even been aware there *was* a fashion in the village.

Akeno playfully nudged Jacob. "Let's hope this trip through the infected forest won't be as . . . *fun* as the last."

Jacob stared at Akeno, then laughed. Makalos so seldom used sarcasm in their speech that it always caught him off guard when they did. "Yeah, seriously. I'd rather not deal with that *and* the two of them." He jerked his thumb over his shoulder toward Aloren and Ebony.

Akeno chuckled.

The trail led them to the outskirts of the woods, and Jacob looked at Ebony. "Which way to August Township?"

"Just follow the trail," Ebony said. "Luckily, the forest doesn't remove this part of it. When we get to the intersection, we'll go straight."

"How close will it lead us to the female Lorkon's manor?"

"Not very. You'll see—we should be okay."

Jacob couldn't help the shudder that hit him when he saw the trees shift slightly away from the intruders. He knew it would happen, but it still unnerved him.

The group rounded a corner and came to the intersection. A weathered sign, partially covered with vines, pointed straight ahead for August Township. Jacob hadn't noticed it last time he was in that forest, and probably because he'd been so distracted by the swarm of bugs chasing him.

He couldn't help the excitement that crossed over him, mingled with nervousness. He could very well meet his first Shiengol that night! These were creatures he'd heard a ton about—they had to be amazing!

"Let's put a door here," Ebony said, pulling one out of her knapsack. Jacob noticed that the Makalos had put legs on the back of it—probably to support it without a wall. She handed it to Akeno.

Akeno held his arm out straight, squinted, and dropped the door. It appeared about twenty feet away, and Jacob and Aloren rushed forward to drag it into the undergrowth. The trees freaked out, but the two of them were quick at getting it into place, so no real harm was done. Aloren marked the location and number of the door on her map.

They continued on. Ebony was right—the trail didn't lead

them anywhere near the manor, and Jacob was relieved that they didn't see any snakes.

Two hours later, they stopped for a break at the end of the forest, sitting on top of a big hill which overlooked a small valley. A thin forest blanketed a large part of it, and on the other side, the walls of what must have been August Fortress rose between the trees.

Jacob couldn't stop gawking at the fortress. It was magnificent—tall, without adornments, and very demanding. Imposing, actually, compared to the land. If he'd been involved in its design, he would have chosen something that graced the countryside, rather than dominated it.

"So, that's August Fortress?" He looked at Ebony for confirmation.

"Sure is."

How were they going to break in? Winding walls of brick and stone merged with rock outcroppings all over the other end of the valley. It looked like a maze, and Jacob couldn't tell if the outcroppings were put there by the Shiengols or by nature. Ebony answered his unasked question.

"Most of the walls are natural. A few hundred years ago, that mountain behind the fortress," she pointed to a large, craggy hill with a dip in the top, "was a volcano. The top of the mountain burst off when the volcano erupted, and rocks landed everywhere. The Shiengols incorporated them into their defense." She folded her arms. "'Course, they didn't really need defense. Nothing could beat a Shiengol."

Jacob had to say it. "Until the Lorkon."

No one responded.

He sighed. "Where should we begin?"

"We'll put another door here," Ebony said, handing one to Akeno.

After it was set into the forest, out of sight, Ebony started down the hill, followed by the others.

The group waded through nearly waist-high grass. Jacob held his hands out, feeling the tops of the grass hit his palms as he passed. He jumped when something large at his feet moved, but relaxed when he saw bright blue petals. It was a flower Akeno had introduced him to when they'd gone to get the Key of Kilenya. According to Akeno, the petals—which the Makalos used to season foods—continued to wiggle in your mouth when you ate them. So disgusting.

Akeno laughed. "It's just a reca flower."

"What did you call it?"

"Reca. That's their name."

"This one is huge." Jacob knelt beside it, examining the vivid petals. It was shaped somewhat like a pansy from earth.

Ebony got down by him. "I've never seen a reca get this big. And yes—they're really quite tasty." She motioned for Jacob to go ahead and try one.

He hesitated, then decided it probably wouldn't kill him. He reached for the plant and tore off a corner of one of the petals—smaller than bite-size. He let it fall into his palm and watched it wiggle. "That's so gross."

"Creepy, as Matt would say," Aloren said, watching over Jacob's shoulder.

Jacob laughed. "Yes, creepy." He inspected the petal, then popped it in his mouth, chewing. Nothing happened. "I can't taste it."

"Are you positive?" Ebony bent to examine the plant. "That's interesting."

"Maybe I should try a bigger piece?"

She didn't answer his question. "It's possible this plant is too old—maybe the flavor has left."

Aloren shook her head. "They don't lose flavor as they get older."

"I didn't think so." Ebony crossed her arms, contemplating the plant. "Have they been changed somehow?"

A sensation of vertigo hit Jacob so strongly it made him fall, knocking the wind out of him, the world spinning.

"I think I'm going to be sick." The cold sweat that hit him confirmed this. He rolled away from the others just before his stomach emptied itself. He was vaguely aware of Ebony patting him on the back and Akeno and Aloren standing together, watching. Awkward.

He coughed a few times, clearing his throat. Akeno gave him water, and he rinsed his mouth and sat up. The dizziness slowly dissipated. "Wow. Sorry 'bout that."

Ebony was inspecting the reca flower. "Why would it make you become ill? And why couldn't you taste it?"

"Maybe it's not really a reca," Akeno suggested.

Aloren shook her head again. "It is. I see them this big near Macaria all the time. And they've never made me sick before."

Jacob took a few deep breaths, waiting for his heart to slow and his stomach to calm down. After a moment, he realized with surprise that he felt completely fine.

"Weird." He slowly got to his feet. "I feel great now." As if nothing had happened. He took a few more swallows of water, then held his hand out to Akeno. "And I'm starving. Can I have some jerky?"

Akeno gazed at Jacob like he was crazy, then handed over the knapsack. Jacob rummaged through it, insisting he was fine and they needed to keep going. He found the bag with beef in it and popped a good-sized chunk in his mouth, then knit his eyebrows.

"I can't taste this, either."

Aloren knit her eyebrows. "Is something wrong with you?"

Jacob sighed with exaggeration. "Of course there isn't. Here, you try." He handed the bag to Aloren.

She fished out a piece and ate it. "It doesn't have any flavor."

Ebony glowered. "It does *too* have flavor—I made it." She

snatched the knapsack from Aloren and sniffed. "Smells fine." She sampled a chunk, then frowned. "Odd."

She lowered the bag, her expression changing from irritation to frustration, then shock. "The Lorkon. I wonder if they're behind this. They must be!"

"But how?" Akeno asked.

"It's the area. Maybe it's one of the traps? If so . . ." She gasped. "Those reca plants are probably poisoned!" She turned to Jacob, grabbing his arm. "What was your first instinct when you couldn't taste the petal?"

"To eat a bigger piece."

She nodded. "What you *did* have was very small, and you got sick—imagine what would've happened with a much larger section."

"It would've killed him, probably," Aloren said.

"That is so brilliant," Akeno said. Ebony scowled at him, and he ducked his head. "Sorry."

Jacob motioned to Aloren. "Maybe we should put it in the journal."

She nodded, pulling the book out of her bag, then hesitated. "How do we know where the trap starts?"

"Just mark the general area," Ebony said.

Jacob looked over the meadow around them. "Include a note not to eat anything from the land here. We need to assume that everything edible is poisoned."

Ebony tucked a strand of blonde hair behind her ear as she gazed at Jacob. "If this really is a Lorkon trap . . ." She paused. "Jacob, you aren't immune to it. And you probably won't be safe from the rest around the fortress either."

Jacob raised his eyebrows. He hadn't thought of that. He'd relied heavily on his resistance to Lorkon traps in the past, but if Ebony was right, he'd struggle just as much as the others in their group.

After a few more minutes of walking, they came across

many, many more recas. Jacob shook his head, wondering how many people had died here, eating these things. He couldn't help but wonder how the Lorkon had poisoned them. Was it genetic modification? Or could it have been like the scented air and more of a blanket potion that covered the area?

Soon, the meadow of flowing grasses ended and the group entered the thin forest, placing doors every hundred feet around the edge of the forest—making sure there were plenty of ways to escape. Jacob kept his eyes open for potential problems—Lorkon, Molgs, Dusts, and other dangerous creatures—occasionally looking at the fortress through breaks in the trees to judge how far they'd come in relation to it.

As he stared at it, he noticed something odd and paused, the rest stopping as well.

10

"Can you see the glow around the fortress?"

Ebony squinted, shading her eyes. "No." The color swirling in the air around her changed to a light yellow-green —interest. "Describe it."

Jacob frowned in concentration. "It's not really a glow. There are a ton of different colors, swirling together. Very bright colors. It's like . . . emotions! I can see emotions coming through the walls! I've never had that happen before." How cool! He beamed, meeting eyes with Ebony.

"The Shiengols!" Ebony said. "It has to be them."

Jacob nodded. "Awesome! I can't believe I can see them this far away!" The group was at least two miles from the fortress.

Ebony snorted. "Doesn't surprise me. They're rather . . . exuberant in the way they feel about things." She looked at the fortress. "What are the colors you see?"

"Red—angry."

"Makes sense."

"Green—excited. That's odd. Why would they be excited?

They've been in the same place for a long time—I hardly think that's worth getting excited about."

Ebony shrugged and Akeno and Aloren exchanged glances, looking as intrigued as Jacob felt.

"Also, they're sad. And disgusted. There's some fear, too— that's the bright yellow." He rubbed his chin as he tried to make out the rest of the colors. "There are some very deep colors, too. Harder to make out. Depressed, bitter, and a little thrilled."

Aloren chuckled. "You're like a palm reader." She grabbed his arm, getting his full attention. "What emotions am I feeling right now?"

Jacob flushed at her touch, but recognized she wasn't flirting with him. He wished she were. "You're a little nervous and slightly bored."

"No, I'm not!" She swatted at him and he jumped away, laughing.

"All right," Ebony said. "Let's keep going. I think we've set up enough doors around the perimeter. We'll see if we can get in closer."

After a few minutes of walking, Jacob started feeling restless. Jumpy, even. It took him a moment to figure out why. It was like they were being watched, and not just by one person or creature, but by hundreds. He couldn't help the shudder that came over him.

A few times, he swore he saw eyes on either side of them, marking their progress, but when he looked, all he saw were thorny bushes.

Even the bushes were somewhat different. Not their height, which was knee to thigh high, but their branches, circling in on themselves, surrounding a center mass. Nearly perfect spheres. And the strangest thing—all of them had a slight green glow. Was it because of the leaves? Jacob didn't think so. It reminded him too much of the emotions he saw coming from people and intelligent creatures. But undergrowth didn't have emotions, right?

"I think I've seen this kind of bush before," Aloren said.

Ebony nodded. "Yes, I've been thinking the same."

Jacob paused, peering at one. He decided to voice what he'd discovered. "They're glowing." The others looked at him. "They are. A green color—excited, or happy."

"Emotions?"

"I don't know. Why would plants have emotions?"

"I can't see anything but their natural colors," Aloren said.

Akeno stopped walking. "That's it. I can't stand it anymore. I have to know what's around us." He stepped to a tree, putting his left ring finger on it. A shocked expression crossed his face.

"What is it, son?"

"We're surrounded. Completely surrounded!"

Jacob started, his heart pounding, and looked into the bushes. "By what?"

"Tarri!" Aloren yelled, jumping to Ebony's side. Akeno did the same and Jacob followed suit, not sure what was going on, but wanting to stick to the others.

Ebony drew her sword. "Get your weapons out."

Aloren pulled two long knives from sheaths on her thighs, and Jacob found himself wishing he was wearing his father's armor. At least he had his sword. Though, with only two lessons, he wasn't sure how effective it would be. "What are tarri?"

"There's one." Aloren pointed.

Jacob turned. The thigh-high bush moved, and he gasped.

It rolled, unfolding tons of branches that surrounded a dense circle in the center. A face with two sets of eyes and sharp teeth appeared in the middle of it. A moment later, the branches finished unfolding, and Jacob's mouth popped open.

Arms! They were arms! How many did it have? At least fifteen, maybe more, coming out on all sides.

The creature paused and glared at Jacob and his friends. It spoke something unintelligible and the entire forest around them shivered, then stirred. Jacob squeezed in closer to the others as hundreds, if not thousands, of bushes moved.

He *knew* he'd felt eyes watching!

The first tarri spoke a few more garbled words, and Jacob shifted his grasp on the hilt of his sword.

"Everyone, backs to each other!" Ebony yelled. "They're extremely dangerous and fast. Make sure to use your water!" She pulled out her canteen with the hand not holding her sword.

Water?

All at once the tarri attacked, rushing forward and surrounding the group. Jacob yelped when a branch—an arm —whipped him across the knees, and he knocked the creature away. It was surprisingly light, even with all the branches. As soon as it was gone, two more jumped at him. He tried kicking them too, but one of the little beasts grabbed his ankle, making hime stumble into Aloren. He struggled, finally getting out of the thing's grasp.

Jacob swung his sword back and forth, swiping at the tarri. He found himself wishing he had daggers like Aloren's—his sword was too long, and he almost hit his friends several times.

"Your water—use it!" Ebony called.

He heard splashes and Ebony yelled in rage, her sword making swishing sounds through the air. Tarri all around them hollered in pain, more garbled screams issuing from their mouths.

Jacob pulled out his water bottle, then knocked a tarri away from Aloren, who was busy with her daggers. "How?"

"Pour it on them," Ebony said.

Akeno growled, scrambling to get away from one of the tarri. "I thought plants like water!"

"Not these!" Ebony shrieked.

Jacob undid the top of his bottle, then shook water on the nearest tarri. It hissed, two of its brown eyes turning black, and backed off. Several more took its place, and Jacob sprinkled them as well. They dashed off.

The rest of the group did the same, Jacob noticed, with similar results. But it didn't seem to matter how many creatures got wet—there were hundreds more streaming in.

"I'm out of water!" Aloren called.

Jacob used the rest of his on some of the beasts near her, then yelled that his was gone too.

Aloren stabbed at one of the tarri, then swung around, attacking several near Jacob. "We can't hold them off any longer!"

Jacob yelled when one of the creatures bit him on the arm. He shook it off, then drop-kicked it away. "This isn't possible! There are too many of them!"

"To the fortress!" Ebony shouted. "Fast!"

The group rushed forward, kicking tarri out of the way, prying the things off each other's backs. Akeno tripped and fell and Jacob turned back to grab him, throwing the Makalo over his shoulder. Several tarri clung to the boys, whipping both of them with their long, branch-like arms, getting in bites wherever possible.

Akeno called out in pain and swung his legs and arms wildly, beating the creatures off as best he could.

Jacob caught up to Aloren and Ebony and helped them force a path through the beasts. He swung Akeno from his shoulder, using the leverage to fling off the rest of the tarri.

Then, just as quickly as the attack started, it stopped.

The group fell to the ground panting, watching. The

creatures were behind them, speaking angrily, trying to rush forward. But something was stopping them.

"Why aren't they coming?" Jacob asked.

Ebony got to her feet, pulling out a cloth. "Looks like that's the end of the trap—that's as far as the Lorkon want them to go." She wiped her face with the rag and cleaned her blade. Then she got out a Kaede sap package and treated everyone's wounds.

After she finished, she put her blade and the leftover sap away. "Why didn't we smell them? I would've known they were near if I'd smelled them."

Aloren nodded, glancing up from the journal where she'd been taking notes. "Good point."

"They stink?" Jacob asked.

"You wouldn't miss their stench. It's incredibly overpowering. Like sewage mixed with the smell of old socks and rotten eggs."

Jacob stopped watching the tarri and wiped off his sword, then re-sheathed it. "I'm betting it's another trap of the Lorkon."

"It would seem so," Ebony said. "In fact, I still can't smell anything." She rolled back on her heels, an intense expression on her face when the rest mentioned they couldn't, either. "Jacob, the fact that you can't smell them shows for certain you aren't immune to these Lorkon traps."

Jacob thought over that, then considered what else the traps meant. He got to his feet and paced. "I'm not sure if you guys realize it, but this is important. Five senses. Two gone: taste and scent. Three remain." He counted them off on his fingers. "Sight, sound, touch." He looked at Ebony. "Should we continue? We have to recognize that losing one of the other senses would be extremely dangerous."

Ebony's face clouded up as she apparently thought

through the matter. "We would probably be fine without touch, assuming it's next."

Jacob shook his head. "No. Imagine if we got attacked by something. You wouldn't feel the pain. You wouldn't even know that something had touched you—you'd just keep going until you bled to death. And if you can't feel your sword, or pain, or anything else, you're as good as dead."

"Good point," Ebony said. "Taste and smell aren't as strong as the others, yet the Lorkon exploited them well. We can expect the rest of the traps to be just as dangerous—if not more so."

As if in reply, Jacob heard a roar, loud and ferocious enough to challenge any living creature.

Akeno looked at him, and Jacob saw fear in the Makalo's eyes. "That sounded like a T. rex," he said.

Jacob couldn't help the smile that crossed his face. "How would you know what a Tyrannosaurus rex sounds like?"

"I've watched the movie *Jurassic Park* too, you know."

Jacob laughed. "That's fiction. People were guessing how they'd sound." A chill went up his spine, even as he chuckled at Akeno's reaction. A dinosaur? Here? Was it possible? And would they have to face it to get the Shiengols?

Ebony took a deep breath. "We've gone far enough. Let's put a door here. Akeno, set up a couple of huts for us to sleep in. Make sure nothing can get through them, even yoons. In the morning, we'll do as much scouting as we can to the left and right—without advancing—then go back home."

Akeno nodded, pulled a door out of his bag, and enlarged it. Jacob and Aloren went to work disguising it with branches and vines in a section of underbrush. Jacob could tell Aloren was watching the foliage closely—he didn't blame her. As long as eyes didn't appear, though, they'd be fine, right?

As soon as the huts were complete, the group entered them, saying goodnight to each other.

The sun hadn't even set yet, but Jacob didn't want to be out in the open anymore. He thought over a conversation he'd had with his dad the night before regarding Kelson's death. Aldo had witnessed it. He'd been overcome with despair sixteen years when he told Dmitri what had happened.

What were Jacob and the rest up against?

11

After breakfast the next morning, the group returned to Taga Village, somewhat somber. Matt, Amberly, and Jacob's parents were just arriving, entering the meadow when Jacob and his group stepped through the door of the tree.

"How did it go?" Jacob's dad asked.

Ebony's lips tightened. "Not good," she said. "The Lorkon traps are just as strong. We think there are five, possibly more. We came across two: poisoned reca flowers exploiting our loss of taste, and tarri you can't smell. Dmitri, we need people who are experienced with the area."

He sighed. "That would be Aldo."

"What about Mom?" Jacob asked. "She was there too."

Mom shook her head. "They kept me blindfolded and tied the entire time."

Kenji joined the group, carrying a bunch of knapsacks. "Is everyone ready? I just sent Early to the Fat Lady, letting her know we'll be coming soon." He observed the group. "Doesn't look like things went very well. Is everyone okay?"

Ebony put her arms around her husband, looking like she

needed a hug. "No, we're fine. It's just going to be very difficult to get to the fortress."

Early appeared next to Kenji. "The Fat Lady needs assistance at once. Aldo is going crazy."

"'Craz*ier*,' she means," Matt whispered.

Kenji slung his bags over his shoulder. "We're on our way."

Jacob keyed the group to the Fat Lady's place. As soon as he opened the door, he could tell things were out of control. He could hear Aldo and the Fat Lady down the hall, screaming at each other.

Dad dashed forward, his sons on his heels. They entered the living area, and Jacob nearly bust up laughing. The Fat Lady had Aldo in a headlock, and the old man was trying to run away—his legs were moving while his upper body stayed put. Dad grabbed Aldo by the wrists, pulling him away from the Fat Lady.

The Fat Lady rubbed her arms. "He just freaked out."

As soon as Aldo saw the group, he relaxed. He grabbed Jacob's cheeks, his eyes glowing.

Jacob chuckled, trying to get the man's hands off him. "Hi to you too, Aldo."

The old man let go, then pushed past Matt to fling his arms around Dad. "Damitini!"

Jacob and Matt met eyes. Damitini? Must be trying to say Dmitri.

Aldo rushed to Jacob's mom, nearly knocking her over in his excitement to hug her. "Arla!"

Jacob was surprised to see tears in her eyes.

"He remembers me!" she said. "He has to."

Aldo sighed happily. "Time taking time!"

The old man hugged Ebony as well, then sat on the couch, crossing his legs and arms, smiling up at the group. He patted the seat next to him and then pointed at Jacob's parents. They joined him, Mom still wiping away tears. Aldo then pointed at

Jacob, motioning to his other side. Jacob sat reluctantly. He didn't have the relationship with the man that his parents had.

"I can't believe it," the Fat Lady said. "He was all over the place just a moment ago, nearly trying to kill me to get out."

"When did you administer the remedy?" Dad asked.

"About half an hour ago." She picked up an empty vial. "He was calm for at least twenty minutes afterwards. Hadn't really said anything. I tried to get him to open up—telling him what we were doing and how a group went to scout out August Fortress. That's when he started freaking out."

Aldo growled when she said August Fortress. "No good. No good."

Dad appraised his friend. "It seems he was trying to warn the group not to go there."

Aldo jumped to his feet. "Yes! No good!"

Matt frowned. "Does he mean, it's no good to try to rescue the Shiengols, or the fortress itself is no good?"

Aldo made some motions with his hands and arms, but they didn't make sense. He slumped to the couch, exhausted.

"He needs to sleep," the Fat Lady said. "We don't want to kill him while trying to get him better."

She helped Aldo to his feet. He resisted at first, then calmed when Mom promised they'd still be there when he woke up.

When the Fat Lady returned, Dad indicated it was time to pull people out of the scented air.

He divided everyone into teams of two. Jacob ended up with Akeno, and Aloren and Matt were paired with each other. Jacob sighed in resignation. He was glad to spend time with Akeno, but he . . . Aloren . . . He stopped that train of thought. No sense pining for someone who wasn't interested in him.

They walked to the scented air and got to work. It was long and hard, and the group pulled out person after person.

Jacob and Akeno went through their section quickly, pulling out the younger, lighter people first. Then they teamed up with Aloren and Matt to get the heavier individuals in the two sections combined.

Jacob knew Jaegar was standing guard, watching the forest and the sky, but he decided this area would always make him jumpy—he still thought about Lirone almost the whole time. The sunlight only partially comforted him, especially since the sun was about to set.

The sun set, and it gradually got darker and darker. Still, they continued. Hazel and Early flitted around, delivering messages.

After a while, Akeno volunteered to stand and hold his finger up, lighting the area considerably. Jacob hadn't realized it, but the previous times he'd seen Akeno use his finger as a light, the Makalo hadn't put all of his energy into it. The light he cast now was so bright, it hurt Jacob's eyes.

Jacob and Matt paused to take a break, Matt wiping sweat off his face. He motioned to Akeno. "He's freakin' awesome."

Jacob nodded. Akeno and Aloren were talking—they were just far enough away to where Jacob couldn't understand what they were saying. "Yeah. He's got some really neat abilities."

"But why?"

Jacob looked at his brother, squinting to see his expression. It didn't show anything, but the colors around him—which Jacob could see, even though the sun had long since set—showed curiosity. "What do you mean?"

"Hasn't it ever occurred to you to ask why he can do so much more than the other Makalos?"

Jacob shook his head. "No—not really. I just assumed he . . . he had more magic in him than the rest of them."

Matt nodded, as if Jacob had just hit on something very important. "Exactly. And how did he get that extra magic?"

Jacob didn't answer. He pushed his hair from his forehead, trying to let the breeze cool his sweat away. He considered taking off his coat, but decided not to—he didn't want to get too cold. Matt made a good point—why *did* Akeno have more magic than the rest? It didn't make sense—not when his parents could hardly do anything, and the Makalo magic was inherited.

He decided to ask Akeno about it later. But no matter how Akeno got his magic, Jacob was glad he had it.

The adults worked close to Akeno to take advantage of the extra light. Jacob couldn't help but notice the Fat Lady. She picked up adult men, slung them over her shoulder, and carried them through the door, then on to Taga Village. Obviously, she had no difficulty doing so, regardless of their size. Jacob and Matt watched her, their mouths open, until Aloren laughed.

"She's going to think you're romantically interested in her if you keep acting like that."

"Okay, Aloren," Matt said, turning to her. "We've got to work on your vocab. Especially if you plan to hang out with us on earth."

She nodded. "I'll accept any help you can give." She motioned to a nearby man. "Help me get him out, and we can work on how I say things."

Matt and Jacob jumped to the guy, each grabbing one of his arms.

"Good," Matt said. "'Cause you've got to speak American." He pointed at Akeno. "Listen to how he talks. And Sweet Pea, too. They both sound like they're from my country." He sighed in exaggeration, readjusting the man's arm over his shoulder. "But first things first. 'Romantically interested' just *doesn't* work. You gotta say 'likes.'"

"Oh, I say that all the time."

"Yes, I know, but you have to get the context right. Instead of saying 'The Fat Lady might think you're romantically interested in her,' you say, 'The Fat Lady might think you *like* her.'"

Aloren paused, still holding the man's elbow. "I don't understand the difference."

Matt chuckled. "You will. Just pay close attention, okay? And we'll let you know when you could say something better."

12
___

It took a couple more hours to get everyone out. Jacob's arms felt like they'd been ripped from their sockets over and over again. But they did it! He folded his arms, leaning against the tree in Taga Village, looking at the people. They were lying all over the meadow, with the Makalos bustling around them, taking care of their needs.

A brisk wind came, chilling to the bone. Jacob was about to shut the door, cutting off the link to the Fat Lady's cabin, when she squealed from inside.

"It worked! It worked! Come! Now!"

Jacob's family jumped to their feet, and they all rushed through the door and into the Fat Lady's front room. Aldo was lying on the couch, eyes shut.

"He's out of it still," Matt said. "Just like when we left."

Aldo raised a hand. "I'm awake."

Matt jumped back. "Whoa! That made sense!"

"Well, of course it did!" the Fat Lady said, laughing.

Mom clapped, an expression of glee on her face. "Wonderful!"

"Arien?" Aldo's eyes opened. "Oh, Arien, my dear."

She rushed forward, kneeling, wrapping her arms around his frail body. "I'm right here, Aldo." A sob choked in her throat, and Aldo tried to get up, probably to comfort her. "No, no," she said. "Stay down."

Dad sat on the short table in the middle of the room, facing Aldo. "How do you feel?"

"A little discombobulated, but otherwise fine." He grinned at the others in the room. "Birds were flying down, but the rain . . . came . . ." An expression of horror crossed his face. "Oops. Sorry about that."

The Fat Lady waggled her eyebrows at him. "I think it'll take some time before everything wears off completely."

Dad pulled Jacob forward. "This is our son, Danilo. He goes by Jacob now. He's the child Arien was carrying while at August Township."

Jacob blinked. *He* was Danilo? That was the name the female Lorkon had used in the forest. How hadn't he known before that his name was Danilo?

Aldo nodded. "Yes, yes. I remember him well." Jacob thought he saw a twinkle in the man's eye, then it disappeared, replaced by an "I'm about to lecture you" face. "Do you like nuts, Jacob?"

Jacob's mouth popped open. "Uh . . . I'm . . . I . . . No?"

A smile broke through Aldo's stern expression, and he chuckled weakly.

Jacob tilted his head, unsure how to respond. "You remember all that?"

"Oh, yes." He took a breath. "I was quite aware of what was going on around me." Another pause as he struggled to concentrate. "The fly—mushroom caused minor problems for me—it messed up my speech . . ." He wiped sweat off his face. "Made it impossible to communicate, but I almost always knew what was happening."

Matt looked confused. "But . . . but you seemed so . . . *loony.*"

Aldo laughed again, more strength behind it this time. "What's the fun of being a crazy . . . crazy old man without getting to act like it, too?"

"Oh, Aldo, I'm just so excited you're feeling better now!" Mom's eyes were still shining with happy tears. "And when you're completely well, I'm going to throw a party to celebrate! Maybe next Saturday!"

Aldo lay back down on the couch, closing his eyes. "I would love that. Your parties were excellent."

Jacob's parents stood. "We'll leave now so you can rest more," Dad said. "We're having a meeting tomorrow to catch you—and everyone else—up on what's going on."

Aldo said good-bye, and Jacob keyed everyone home.

SUNDAY AFTER CHURCH, Jacob went to Eklaron to get Gallus, Aldo, the Fat Lady, Aloren, and the Makalos. They were having the meeting in his living room on earth. He was so excited to have everyone in *his* territory!

When he returned, Mom had set up extra chairs and pushed the couches against the walls to make room. It wasn't as tight a squeeze as the table in Kenji's place, but still, pretty cozy.

Like the previous meeting, Dad was in charge. It was much less formal than last time, and Jacob sighed, leaning back against the couch. It was so nice to have everyone here.

The first part of the meeting was spent discussing those pulled from the scented air. Ebony reported that it would take time for them to come to themselves—the first group had taken a couple of months, at least.

Next, they discussed how school was going for Aloren.

"Wait—she's going to school? No fair!" Sweet Pea glared at the adults. "Why does she get to go, and I don't?"

"Well, she *is* human," Mom said. "Sorry, Sweet Pea, but you'd stand out way too much."

"No, I wouldn't!" He paused when everyone stared at him skeptically. "Okay, so maybe my exceptionally . . . exceptionally good *looks* would get attention," Matt snickered at this, "but I'm close enough to a human!"

Mom nodded. "Yes . . . but your eyes—"

"And your skin," Jacob said.

"What's wrong with them?"

Mom's tone of voice was sympathetic. "Humans have eyelashes."

Jacob nodded. "And human skin isn't blue."

Sweet Pea snorted. "It took *you* several months to see it."

Jacob laughed. It was true—he hadn't noticed that Makalos had a slightly blue tint to them until Matt pointed it out. "Yeah, well, most humans notice more things than I do."

Aloren rolled her eyes. "It's true." She glanced at Jacob, then smiled at Sweet Pea. "Sorry, Sweet Pea. I'll take notes for you."

He grunted, folding his arms.

The conversation then drifted to something else, but Jacob had a hard time following. What had Aloren meant? Was she trying to hint at something? Or was he imagining things?

"Jacob," Dad said. "Are you there?"

"Oh, yeah. Sorry. What?"

"Please give a report on what happened on the scouting trip to August Fortress."

"Ebony was pretty much in charge—"

"You're the reigning prince," Dad said.

Ebony nodded. "Go ahead."

Jacob put his frustrated thoughts of Aloren away. "Well, you already know about the poisoned reca plants. We got past those and put up a ton of doors throughout the forest. Then we headed toward August Fortress and ran into a gazillion tarri—"

Just then, Aldo jumped from his chair, flapping his hands. "No good! Butterflies briskly run!" He paused, arms held out from him. A sheepish grin crossed his face. "Oh, oops." He sat down. "I, uh . . . . My brain works faster than my mouth. I have to speak slower, otherwise random things pop out." He grimaced at everyone. "Stop being so serious. It's okay to get a good laugh in every now and then. Go ahead—it won't offend me."

A few chuckles broke the silence, and Aldo grinned before continuing. "What I was trying to say is: August Fortress is surrounded by horrible traps. I watched the whole thing with Kelson's group and was powerless to do anything." He motioned to Jacob. "I assume you suspect this already, but the Lorkon traps eliminate your senses one at a time. How did you get past the tarri?"

"It was hard—we gave up on fighting and rushed toward the fortress instead."

Aldo leaned back, putting his hands behind his head and rubbed his sparse hair. "Yes. If you'd stayed behind, as part of Kelson's group did, you would have been slaughtered. There's no stopping them."

Jacob frowned. "Not even with water?"

"You couldn't possibly carry all the water you'd need." Aldo paused. "No, the only way to get through that trap is to push forward, getting away from them as quickly as possible."

Ebony nodded. "And they didn't follow."

"No. They won't." A grave expression crossed his face. "Judging by how Kelson's group acted, the next trap would have been the loss of sight."

"Whoa, really?" Matt asked. "You guys would've been dead."

Jacob nodded. He could imagine them stumbling around, blindly feeling their way. "No wonder they didn't make it out alive."

Aldo shook his head. "That's not how they died. Yes, a few did, but not the entire group. No, they made it much farther than that, even with Argots."

Ebony gasped. "Argots?"

"Yes."

"What are those?" Aloren asked.

"They live in the dirt," Ebony explained. "Actually, they technically *are* the dirt. They make up the ground. And when you've gone far enough across them—when they sense the right amount of weight—they open up all around—"

Aloren put up her hand, her face white. "Please, no more— I can't handle it right now."

Ebony smiled sympathetically at the girl, but Jacob was surprised to find he agreed with Aloren. He didn't care about the creatures either—a first for him.

Dad looked at Aldo. "How does one get through this trap?"

"They don't have ears or eyes, so they have no idea you're there except by the weight change above them. So, you have to find a way to get across without touching the ground."

Dad looked gloomy and blew out a long breath of air. "Okay, that's going to be difficult."

Matt rubbed his eyes. "Why can't Jacob just key us into the city? Or even the fortress?"

Aldo, Ebony, and Dad shook their heads.

"The Lorkon destroyed all the doors in the entire city," Aldo said. "In the fortress, they filled the holes with concrete."

"But didn't you use the key to get in and out before?"

He nodded. "Yes, but they didn't know we had the key. They destroyed the doors of the fortress to prevent the Shiengols from coming and going, but at that point, they had left the doors in the city intact."

Jacob leaned back against the couch again. He couldn't imagine what it would be like to be stuck for so long—he'd have felt incredibly claustrophobic if it were him. "How did you know they destroyed them all?"

"I tried one last trip to the city to see if I could find Kelson's remains. I couldn't get in. Everything had been shut off."

Dad turned to Ebony. "Now we have a way past the first two traps, correct?"

"Yes."

"Are you coming when we get the Shiengols?" Jacob asked Dad.

"Yes—"

"*No*, he's *not*," Gallus said. Everyone turned to him. "Your Majesty, I know how much you want to be involved, but having Jacob go is bad enough. We still have you if he doesn't make it. But if you both go, and both of you are destroyed? We need a leader here to take us through the revolution."

Dad rubbed his forehead, looking disappointed. "Yes, I know. I . . . never mind." He put on a mask of determination, then closed the meeting shortly thereafter. The only assignments he'd given were for the Makalos to work with the people now pulled from the scented air, and for Jacob and Matt to focus on their sports. Everyone else was to continue what they'd been doing already.

13

The day and time for basketball tryouts were finally posted the next morning—Wednesday, right after school. During lunch, Jacob called up Scott—the older teen he used to practice with—and arranged to get together with the guys both Monday and Tuesday as soon as class got out.

The Makalos were busy with the people pulled from the scented air, and since Dad had told Jacob to focus on basketball, he didn't feel guilty practicing.

They played for three hours on Monday—Scott making sure Jacob knew the ins and outs of tryouts, what would happen and how things would go—then finally called it quits.

That evening, Mom helped him ice his shoulders and upper arms so they wouldn't get sore. Tuesday wasn't nearly as grueling, though, and Jacob had time leftover to do homework with Aloren.

"Uh, Jacob . . ." Aloren tucked a strand of hair behind her ear. Mom was curled up on the couch, reading a book, and Jacob and Aloren had just finished working on assignments for history and science.

"Yeah?" He grabbed her math book, glad she was a level or two below him—made it easier to check her work.

"Kevin's going to help me with my math homework. Also, he wants to come pick me up for school. And take me home. You don't need to key me from the tree anymore."

Jacob dropped the book, gawking at her. "That's . . . that's *ridiculous*."

"Why?" She paused. "You don't like him very much, do you?"

"No, and for good reason. He's a bully and a complete jerk." Jacob had been about to say something about Kevin smashing him against the drinking fountain a couple of months ago, but decided against it.

"But he lets you play *now*, so what's the problem?" She took a deep breath. "Never mind. It's just that I'm . . . roma—I really like him, Jacob."

What? What was she talking about? There was no way! "It's only been a week! How's that possible?"

She didn't answer for a moment, instead opening her backpack and pulling out her art stuff. "I don't know. He's kind to me, and I find him very attractive."

Jacob blew out his breath in exasperation. "Well, that's just *great*. Most girls *do*." Most girls thought Jacob was good looking, too. Why didn't Aloren? And wasn't *he* nice to her? He'd rescued her, after all. Didn't that count for anything?

No one spoke for a while. Jacob leaned against the couch, staring at the ceiling. He didn't feel like doing homework anymore. Aloren shuffled through her art papers, but he could tell she wasn't concentrating on them.

Mom must have sensed the tension. She set her book aside. "Aloren, why don't you tell us about your family? I haven't heard a lot about your mom."

Aloren fiddled with her backpack. "I . . ."

"That is, if you're comfortable with it. I've been meaning to ask, but didn't want to upset you."

"Oh, Your Majesty, you could *never* upset me. And you're free to ask anything you wish to know."

"Come on, Aloren," Jacob said, trying to keep the irritation from his voice. "Just treat her like she's a normal person. Mom's not a queen here."

Aloren looked at Jacob, horrified. "I couldn't possibly! She's . . . she's . . ."

"You don't treat *me* like royalty."

"That's different."

"How? Technically—"

"That's enough," Mom said. "Aloren, he's right. Here, I'm his mother, and that's perfectly fine. In Eklaron, it's different. I would expect you to wash my feet, mend my clothes, watch over my horses, and serve me food."

Aloren's mouth popped open, then she must have seen the twinkle in Mom's eyes because they both laughed. Jacob jerked the zipper down on his hoodie and yanked his arms out of the sleeves. Aloren took things way too seriously sometimes.

"I'm okay talking about my mother. It doesn't bother me. What would you like to know?"

"How did she die?"

"She slipped away quietly. Gallus thinks she went into a coma."

"What caused it? Do you know?"

Aloren rested against the arm chair behind her. "She'd sustained many injuries before I was born—possibly while she was pregnant with me—and her mind was never quite right after that. Her health was pretty bad, too."

"That's too bad." Mom leaned forward. "Did she ever talk to you about your family? Where you came from?"

"Yes, but by the time I was old enough to understand, she'd already forgotten my father's name and who her parents were. I'll probably never know if half of the stories she told were even true. Her energy to talk left soon after she got really sick, and by the time she passed, she hadn't spoken or moved for several months."

Aloren looked at the art papers in her hands. Jacob peered at her from the corner of his eye—no tears. Oh, good.

"What did she look like?" Mom asked.

"She was very lovely. Brown hair—a little darker than mine. And the prettiest, brightest smile you'd ever see. She was quiet—always said my father was the outgoing one. She missed him a great deal and spoke of him all the time."

The front door opened, and Dad stepped through, coming home from work. He put his briefcase down, hung up his coat, then kissed Mom and said hello to Jacob and Aloren.

"Dinner's in the Crock-Pot," Mom said. "We'll be eating in an hour."

He nodded, loosening his tie, and went to the family room, probably to unwind from work.

Mom turned back to Aloren. "Did your mother always live in Macaria?"

Jacob frowned. "So many questions. Aloren, you don't have to answer if you don't want."

Aloren shook her head. "Honestly, Jacob, I don't mind. It helps to talk about her." She turned back to Mom. "She was from Maivoryl City—lived there her whole life."

"Hmmm." Mom picked up her book again and fingered the pages, a contemplative expression crossing her face. "What did she do there? Was she employed?"

"Yes. As a lady-in-waiting, I think, for someone fairly high up—a noble woman, perhaps. She didn't quite remember everything."

Mom nodded slowly. "I should remember her, then.

Brown hair. Most everyone had brown hair." She looked blankly at the wall opposite her, concentrating. Finally, she shook her head and looked back at Aloren. "I'm assuming your father also worked in Maivoryl. What did he do?"

"If what she said was true, he worked in stables somewhere."

"Really? That's . . . that's very interesting." She put the book down, scooting to the edge of the couch. "What did he look like?" she asked, urgency in her voice.

Jacob perked up—the expression on his mom's face told him this wasn't a random question.

"I don't know. She never told me."

"What are you getting at, Mom?" Jacob asked.

"Nothing, dear. Only . . ." She paused. The colors for nervousness and excitement flowed in the air around her. "Aloren, what was your mother's name?"

"She called herself Mide. Gallus said her name was technically Midian of the North, but she never used—"

Mom gasped, surprise and excitement flooding her features. "Oh, my . . ." She sprang to her feet, dropping the book on the couch. "Dmitri! Dmitri, come here!"

Jacob jumped up too, eager to find out why his mom was so excited.

Dad rushed into the room, panic on his face. "What's going on?"

Mom grabbed his hand, her face shining. Jacob was astonished to see tears in her eyes.

"Dear, guess who Aloren's mother was? Guess?" She practically bounced up and down.

"I don't know . . ."

"Midian!"

"Of the North? Are you sure?" Excitement crossed his features. "That would mean . . . Her dad was Kelson!"

14

M om squealed and Dad laughed, throwing his arms around her, holding her tight. The brightest shade of green Jacob had yet seen flowed through the air around them. They were *really* excited about this.

Then what they'd said hit Jacob, and he stumbled closer to them. "Kelson? As in—you mean—*Dad's best friend?*" And then Jacob realized something else. Was it possible? Were Aloren and Matt siblings?

"Wait," Aloren said, obviously very confused. "I don't understand. You know my parents?"

Mom and Dad nodded. Both were crying now. Mom helped Aloren to her feet, and she and Dad hugged her tightly.

"They were very close to us," Dad said.

Mom laughed. "I would never have dreamed Aloren was their daughter! Not in a million years!"

"Kelson's girl!" Dad shook his head in amazement. "Midian must've been pregnant when we gave her to Gallus for care—"

"Had to have been—"

"It's the only explanation."

Aloren still looked shell-shocked. "Kelson—you mean the man who died when he tried to release the Shiengols?"

Mom nodded. She looked at Dad. "But why didn't Gallus tell us?"

"He wouldn't have known. When Kenji and I went back to Macaria, Midian had run off. Gallus assumed she'd died, since it had been a week." Dad shook his head. "Obviously, she returned after we left, and we'd have sealed off the entrance to Taga Village by then. And Gallus didn't know that we were still alive."

Aloren nodded. "She ran away several times when I was little. Gallus always found her again, though, and after a while, she got too sick to do that anymore."

Jacob held up his hands. "Okay, so let me get this straight. Kelson and his wife were Aloren's parents? And Gallus was Kenji's friend who took her in?"

"That's right, son," Dad said. "And think it through a little harder. When Kenji and I went to Maivoryl City after getting you and your mother, what were we doing there?"

Jacob scratched his cheek. "Cleaning up after the Lorkon? Taking care of people? Fixing broken buildings?"

"Yes, and we helped the orphans. Made sure there was someone to take care of as many of them as possible. And we took one of the orphans to raise as our own—Kelson's son."

Jacob nodded, a huge smile crossing his face. He'd been right! "Yeah, I remember now. That *would* mean Matt—"

Aloren gasped. "Matt . . . Matt is . . ." She put her hand over her mouth. "He's my brother?"

Mom nodded. "His name used to be Devlin. We changed it to Matt when we moved here."

Aloren laughed. "He's my brother! I've found my brother!" She grabbed Jacob and flung him around her, dancing with him, squealing. Jacob chuckled, trying to keep up with her.

Then abruptly she let go and fell to the ground, bursting

into tears. Mom dropped next to her, throwing her arms around the girl's shaking shoulders.

Wow. Jacob hadn't been expecting that. Dad didn't look shocked, though, and Jacob folded his arms, making sure his stance was casual. "This is so crazy," he said. "And it means that when Aloren went to Maivoryl City, all that time her brother was here, safe and sound."

Aloren sobbed louder.

Jacob couldn't believe it. Matt was Aloren's brother! He never would have guessed it.

Just then, Matt walked through the front door.

Dad chuckled. "Speak of the devil . . ."

Matt dropped his backpack and gym bag. "Whoa. What's going on here?"

"Would you like to tell him?" Mom asked.

Aloren shook her head.

Matt focused on Aloren, orange-yellow—the color for concern—flowing around him. "What did you guys do to her?" He grabbed a box of tissues from an end table, holding them out to Aloren.

"Oh, nothing," Dad said, a huge grin on his face. "Just told her the most important information she's ever heard. And it involves you."

Matt's face went white. "What's going on? Who died? Am I being sent to prison?"

"No, of co—" Dad paused, the expression on his face and colors swirling around him showing his suspicion. "Why would you be sent to prison?"

Matt laughed. "No reason. It was the first thing that popped out of my mouth."

"I'll tell him—if you'd like," Mom said.

Aloren nodded, keeping her face in Mom's shoulder.

Mom took a deep breath. "Son, you know you're adopted from Eklaron, correct?"

"Of course."

"Well, when we brought you back, we had no idea your mother was still alive. Alive and pregnant."

Matt's face blanched even more. "She was? Where is she now?"

"I'm sorry, honey, but she passed away several months ago."

Matt looked confused, as if this was too much to digest. "She's de—dead?"

"Yes. A lot to hear right now, I know. But, the point is, she wasn't having just any old baby."

"She was pregnant with me." Aloren finally pulled her face away from Mom's shoulder and took a deep breath. "Matt, you're my older brother."

Matt fell onto the couch. "No way! Are you serious?"

Everyone nodded.

"Oh." He expelled a big breath of air, the colors around him showing he was shocked. Very shocked. "Wow."

Mom put a hand over her heart, her eyes bright. "We just now figured it out."

Matt bounced to his feet. "It's freakin' awesome! So cool! I've got *another* sister! Does Amberly know?"

"She's playing with Ida Mae's grandkids." Mom picked up her book and closed it.

Matt rubbed the side of his face. "Wow. It's a good thing I was dating Sammy. 'Cause things might've turned into a Luke-and-Leia relationship. You know, before they knew they were siblings and Leia was trying to make Han Solo mad—"

Dad laughed. "That's enough, son. We get the picture."

Matt sat back down on the couch, staring at Aloren. "We look nothing alike! I mean, I've got blond hair and blue eyes, and hers are all brown."

"There's always the smile," Mom said. "You both have Kelson's smile."

JACOB HAD GROWN up with Aloren's brother! It just wouldn't compute.

Wednesday, he'd gone to math and history, completely in a daze, and was now walking to woods class, still trying to digest this new piece of information. It was weird—really weird. And almost made her his sister. That thought made him stop completely, several students calling out to him in impatience when they ran into him.

Did she think of him as a brother? He definitely didn't think of *her* that way. She'd fallen for Kevin, so it didn't matter either way.

Finally, as school neared an end, Jacob's thoughts turned to tryouts that afternoon. He was nervous, but surprised at how calm he felt, too. He'd practiced his hardest. He'd been working toward this for years. He was as good as any of the seniors on varsity, and definitely as good, if not better, than Kevin, Coach's son.

Right when the bell rang after choir, Jacob sprang from his seat and rushed to the locker room. He changed into his basketball clothes as quickly as possible, then raced to the gym where tryouts were taking place.

Fear hit him when he saw how many people were there. Where had they all come from? He only recognized a handful of them—a couple of which he knew for a fact had *never* played a game in their lives. He jogged onto the court with his ball and shot baskets, warming up.

After a couple of minutes, the assistant coach blew his whistle, and Coach Birmingham stepped away from the bleachers, calling everyone over.

"Many of you have tried out for varsity before and so you know what we'll be doing. For the rest of you, we start by shooting drills, and then we'll practice lay-ups. Next, we'll test your endurance and strength. We finish off with a few timed games."

The students lined up in front of the different hoops, and Coach and his assistant meandered through the players, watching closely and taking notes. Jacob kept his eyes on the others too, making sure to play harder and faster than they did. He mostly paid attention to how Kevin was doing. Excellently, of course. Kevin waved at him before slam-dunking the ball. Jacob rolled his eyes, but smiled just the same. He'd spent more time with Kevin in the past week—through Aloren—than he had since third grade. And . . . he hated to admit it, but Kevin wasn't all that bad.

Jacob growled at himself when that thought crossed his mind. Kevin and Aloren . . . Okay, that was it. He had to focus on basketball, not the problems in his social life. He put everything else behind him, and pressed forward as hard as he could.

Sweat poured down his face, and his limbs burned from exertion. Coach was having them run across court in a complicated way, dodging cones borrowed from the driving range. The guys had to step over and around the cones, going both forward and backward.

Gratitude for Scott and their team rushed over Jacob—they'd practiced something similar to this during the past two days, and he knew he was doing well. He felt the assistant coach's eyes on him several times and made sure to be at the front of the line every time. If he wanted to make the team, especially as a point guard, showing leadership was essential.

Finally, everything was over. Coach congratulated the players on how well they'd all done. Jacob looked around—a few of the applicants had fallen out, but he wasn't sure when. Maybe twenty had made it all the way through, and out of those, only three were point guards. Jacob was much better than the others.

"First cuts will go up tomorrow morning. After school, we'll have the next—also last—round of tryouts. Final cuts will be posted Friday morning."

The students filed toward the locker room to shower and change. Jacob's heart swelled inside him—he'd done exceptionally well. Possibly the best he'd ever done.

As soon as Jacob got home, Mom had him run an errand to Taga Village—taking a huge box of Walmart stuff to Ebony. It looked like Mom was planning her party with a lot of energy and excitement, and Ebony would be helping. He sighed in relief about the errand—he'd wanted an excuse not to be around when Kevin brought Aloren back from school, and using the key to get to Taga Village meant not running into her as she walked past his house. She'd attended tryouts, and Jacob was grateful he hadn't seen her there until it was all over. She would have made him too nervous.

After he dropped off the box to Ebony, he spent some time with Akeno until dinner was ready back on earth. He'd missed hanging out with the Makalo.

The next morning, Jacob, Matt, and Tani rushed to see the list of who'd made first cuts. Jacob's name was second from the top. He nearly dropped his bag in excitement. He'd made it! His first response was to look for Aloren, but she wasn't anywhere to be seen. Tani threw her arms around him, saying over and over again that she knew he'd do well.

Jacob laughed. "I'm not on the team yet."

"Yeah," Matt said. "For all you know, he's going to fail miserably this afternoon."

"Oh, be quiet," Tani said, elbowing Matt in the side.

WHEN THE ASSISTANT coach blew his whistle during tryouts that afternoon, Jacob knew things would go well. He was alert and energetic—definitely in the mood to play. He was ready for this. Nothing could stop him.

An hour and a half later, he dropped his ball near Tani and Josh, completely satisfied with how he'd done. If that performance didn't get him in, he didn't know what would.

"Congrats on making varsity," Tani said.

Jacob waved her off, looking around to see if anyone had heard her. "We won't find out until tomorrow morning."

"Oh, I know. But you're definitely on the team. They'd be complete idiots if they didn't let you."

Jacob hoped she wouldn't jinx him by saying that.

15

When Jacob and Matt got home, Jacob was surprised to see Brojan there. Had he walked the entire way? He was sitting on the couch, looking very uncomfortable. He got to his feet after Jacob burst through the door.

"How are you?"

"Good. You?" Jacob dropped his backpack and took off his coat.

"I'm well."

"Are you waiting for my mom or dad? Are they around?"

Brojan shook his head. "No, I'm here to see you."

Jacob pushed his bag into the closet by the front door, then joined Brojan near the couch. "Okay. Did you want to talk about something?" The colors swirling around the Makalo said he was nervous.

"Yes. Would you mind taking us somewhere private—not Taga Village? I don't want to run into anyone."

Jacob nodded, his thoughts racing. What could the Makalo patriarch have to say that he didn't want others to hear? And where was Jacob going to take them that would be guaranteed private? "How about Aldo's cabin?"

Brojan shook his head. "No—there aren't any walls."

Jacob looked at his watch. Six o'clock. Tryouts had gone longer than he'd thought they had. "Well, we could always go back to my school and find an empty classroom. The cleaners were just finishing up when Matt and I left. As long as no teachers are hanging around, we should be fine there."

"Yes, that would be excellent."

Jacob keyed them to the school, but went through the door near the pool, just in case someone was in the offices near the main entrance. The hallway was dark, and Jacob found himself wishing Akeno was there to light it up. He'd asked Brojan once to do it, but the Makalo had said no. Jacob didn't want to ask again. He quickly walked them to the math section of the school and breathed a sigh of relief when he found it empty.

"We should be fine here," he said, opening Mr. Coolidge's classroom with the key.

Brojan motioned for Jacob to sit, and the Makalo chose a student desk. Jacob stared. It was so weird to see a Makalo—especially this one—sitting at a desk. In his school.

After a moment, Brojan got to his feet and paced. Then he turned and faced Jacob, bright orange swirling around him, showing he was even more nervous now.

"I've been meaning to talk to you for a while. Tell you something—confess—what I did years ago."

Jacob frowned. "Confess?"

Brojan sat again. "Do you remember the story of Onyev? How he and his people left the trees to live together as families?"

"Yes . . ."

"Do you remember why they did this?"

"They'd been focusing too much on power and their own abilities, and had forgotten the important things in life."

Brojan nodded. "Yes, exactly. I'm not sure if Akeno told

you, but they entered into an agreement that Makalos would never again introduce Kaede sap into the finger of an infant."

Jacob realized he'd been absentmindedly molding his desk. Mr. Coolidge would kill him if he saw that, so Jacob worked to fix it while it was still warm, concentrating on what Brojan was saying.

"And that agreement wasn't broken," the patriarch continued, "until fourteen years ago."

"By who? You?"

Brojan folded his hands, looking at them. He flushed, his colors changing to show embarrassment. "Yes—I did it. To one of the Makalo children." He looked up. "Jacob, you must understand my reasons for doing so before you judge me."

Judge him?

"I couldn't stand how helpless we were against the Lorkon. So many Makalos were slaughtered—it was horrendous. Absolutely terrifying and heart-wrenching. And, what's worse —my beloved Sabelle . . ." His voice faltered, and the pain written on his face shocked Jacob.

"What happened?"

He sniffed. "She . . . and our children decided . . . They turned themselves over to the Lorkon."

Jacob gasped. "Why? That's insane!"

Brojan shook his head. "She hadn't seen everything I had. They thought they could help the Lorkon get better. Our children were adults—they made their own decisions, and wouldn't listen to me."

"It doesn't make any sense. Why would they even try, after what the Lorkon had done to the kingdom?"

Brojan buried his face in his hands. "I might have led her to . . . believe that things would work out . . . that they would end up helping us in the end." He rubbed his eyes. "I was what your country might call an opportunist. I saw the Lorkon as powerful beings who desired control. I felt if we talked to them, channeled that desire, they'd come to see our side of things and we could help each other."

Jacob nearly scoffed, then remembered his manners, softening his voice. "I'll bet I can figure out what happened."

"The Lorkon refused to acknowledge us, and I realized I'd been foolish. Sabelle wasn't sure. She thought that if they were exposed to even more Makalos, they'd see our potential to create a more dynamic world."

Jacob bit his lip. Why would anyone think that? "And the Lorkon killed her?"

Brojan nodded. "Didn't even let her speak. Slaughtered my entire family." He closed his eyes, turning his face from Jacob.

Goodness. No wonder Brojan acted the way he did—gruff, never personal with people. He'd been hurt really badly by what happened.

Finally, he spoke again. "After we moved into Taga Village and sealed the entrance, I had plenty of time to think about how things had gone. I recognized how weak the Makalos had become. We all did. But *I* decided to do something about it."

He stood again. "What I'm going to tell you, you cannot repeat to anyone." He turned and looked Jacob in the eye. "No one! Not even your brother."

"I promise I won't." Jacob was nearly positive he could see where this was leading.

"Akeno . . . Akeno was the firstborn Makalo in Taga. During the Welcome Ceremony, it is customary for the Makalo patriarch to place a shield on the left ring finger of the baby—symbolic of the early Makalos' decision to protect that finger from Kaede sap. While I was doing it, I pretended to put it on wrong, injuring him in the process. He cried, as was to be expected, but quickly calmed when Ebony held him. The shield covered the wound he'd received when I put a little sap in his finger."

Brojan looked up quickly, probably to analyze Jacob's reaction.

Jacob realized too late that his **mouth** was hanging open. And even though he'd heard **nearly** exactly what he'd expected, it was still kind of brutal. Brojan had actually stabbed Akeno's finger. "Okay, well . . . **wow.**"

"I understand your shock. I also understand what you quite possibly do not: I have broken a very serious Makalo law. And it's incredibly wrong that Akeno and his parents don't know about it."

"What would happen to you if they found out?"

Brojan shook his head. "I don't **know**—we don't have a consequence in place for this **sort** of action. It was unthinkable that anyone would ever **do** it."

Jacob scratched at some pen **markings** on the desk, trying to figure out what to say. "Why are **you** telling me all this?"

"So that someone knows the **real** reason behind Akeno's abilities. Why he's more powerful **than** the others. So that person can help him progress more quickly than he would otherwise."

That made sense. "My brother already asked me why—he'll figure it out."

Brojan shrugged, looking worried even though his body language said otherwise. "Just . . . just do your best."

"Okay."

"Akeno shouldn't know for several more years what's happened to him. At least, not until after I've gone."

Jacob scowled. "Why, so you don't have to face all of this yourself?" He immediately felt bad for his disrespect, and quickly said, "I'm sorry. It's just . . . I'm just trying to understand."

Brojan held his hands palms up. "It's been difficult living with this lie for the past thirteen, nearly fourteen years."

"Wouldn't telling them help get rid of the guilt?"

"I've told *you*. Why would I need to tell anyone else?"

Jacob blinked in surprise. He decided to keep his thoughts to himself, but it was very much unlike a Makalo to act so selfishly. "How am I supposed to keep this a secret? What if you live another twenty years?"

"You've become very adept at hiding things. How many of your schoolmates know what's going on in your life?"

Jacob didn't answer. He didn't have to—Brojan was right. Some of the biggest things he'd ever experienced couldn't be shared with anyone aside from his family and the Makalos.

"It's time for me to return. If you wouldn't mind taking me home, I'd appreciate it."

Jacob did so, his thoughts jumbled.

16

J acob rushed to the locker room Friday morning, so
excited and nervous, he felt like his insides were about
to jump into his throat. A group of people already
clustered around the list, and Jacob had to push his way
through.

"Sorry, man," a guy said, putting his hand on Jacob's
shoulder.

Jacob ignored him, determined to see where he'd ended
up. He quickly scanned the sheet for varsity, a sick feeling
dropping his insides back into place when he didn't find
his name.

What? No way. He scanned again, making sure he hadn't
missed anything. How did he *not* make it? Wait—Kevin's name
was on the list. Kevin? He got in and Jacob didn't? Jacob was
much better!

He looked at the paper for JV and found his name there.
What a . . . a . . . He couldn't find an appropriate word to fit his
thoughts. It had to have been rigged. Or—and Jacob's heart
nearly stopped when this new thought hit him—Kevin's dad

was still favoring his son. Of *course* he was. Hadn't they gotten past that?

He backed away from the list, oblivious to the people around him, and left the locker room in a daze. He barely acknowledged a couple of girls saying hi to him as he wandered the halls. What a piece of junk tryouts had turned out to be. He'd played so well! So much better than anyone else. Why hadn't he made it? He and Kevin played different positions—there was room enough for both of them!

Jacob didn't notice Tani and Aloren until Aloren touched his arm, making him jump.

"You didn't make it, did you?"

He shook his head.

Tani's mouth popped open. "Not any team? Not even sophomore again?"

"I made JV."

"What's that?" Aloren asked.

"Junior varsity," Tani said. "It's a step below varsity. Jacob, you were robbed!"

"Where did they put Kevin?" Aloren asked, her voice too nonchalant.

Jacob fisted his hands, too frustrated to answer at first. Why was she even asking? She probably knew already. "Varsity, of course. His dad wouldn't have him anywhere else."

Not wanting their words of sympathy, he left, heading to math early. Aloren and Kevin. Kevin on varsity. This was the worst day—no, the worst *week*—of his life.

Math, woods, and lunch crawled by—Jacob ate in his car, wanting to distance himself from Aloren and Kevin—but history and science were especially painful. Not only did Aloren keep trying to comfort him, but Shirley tried, too. He could barely handle Aloren's awkward attempts—knowing that she was keeping her excitement for Kevin well hidden—but Shirley put him over the edge. She did everything she could to get the attention of the entire class, and by the end of the period, Jacob had heard "Dude, I'm sorry" so many times, he couldn't stand it.

Anytime he saw Kevin in the hall, he turned and walked the other way. Even when Kevin called to him to stop.

There wasn't a thing he could possibly have to say to Jacob.

THAT NIGHT WAS the last game of the football season. Jacob sat with his family, Tani, and Josh to watch Matt in all his glory. Jacob glowered nearly the entire game, barely able to keep up with what was happening on the field.

His parents had been disappointed that Jacob didn't make varsity, but said maybe Coach thought he'd still been too young. Until he told them Kevin was on the team. Neither said anything, but Mom's lips tightened, and she and Dad shared an annoyed expression.

During half-time, Jacob was listening to Tani and didn't notice Kevin and Aloren coming until they sat right in front of him. He didn't have the opportunity to escape.

"I don't want to talk about it," he said before either could say anything.

"Dude, knock it off," Kevin said. "Stop being petty. I'm not trying to gloat—I want to tell you how mad I am that you didn't make it too."

"Yeah, well, that's good and all, but . . ." Jacob paused. "What?"

"You heard me. Dad knows varsity needs you, but he says you don't have enough experience."

"That's the stupidest thing I've ever heard. I'm just as experienced as you are, and you know it!"

"That's what I told him. He's being an idiot."

Aloren nodded, the expression on her face showing how badly she wanted Jacob to understand.

Jacob sighed in frustration. He believed them. Kevin had been a lot nicer since he and Aloren had hit it off. It didn't make Jacob any happier. At that moment, he'd rather be talking to the Lorkon.

"Okay, well, thanks for saying something. The game's about to start again." He turned back to Tani and Josh. He knew it was rude, but he didn't care anymore. From the corner of his eye, he saw Kevin and Aloren leave.

Tani acted like she wanted to say something. Finally she blurted, "How do you feel about those two going out?"

"It doesn't matter—they can do what they want," Jacob mumbled under his breath.

Tani blushed. "Oh, sorry—bad timing." She turned back to watch the game.

Jacob had a hard time paying attention to the last quarter. He was glad it was the weekend—he didn't think he could handle going to school in the morning and facing more disappointment and "I'm sorry"s.

Matt led Mountain Crest to victory. Jacob didn't realize it until Tani pulled him to his feet, jumping up and down, screaming, "We won! We won!"

17

Saturday morning, Jacob's mom burst through his door, making him jump up in bed. "Whoa, Mom. Everything okay?"

She nodded excitedly. "We're having a ball!"

"The ball?" The first thing that popped into Jacob's mind was that she was really enjoying herself. "Did you want me to join you? Oh, wait. You mean one of those big dances."

"Yes!" She hesitated. "Well, no. Much smaller. No carriages or big dresses. More like a party. Remember? We're celebrating Aldo's recovery!" She pulled his hand. "Get up! I need your help—we're going to make this place shine."

"It's going to be here?"

She scowled at him. "Of course. Where else would it be?"

"Somewhere bigger? Maybe in Eklaron?"

She folded her arms. "And where in Eklaron would be big enough? Everything in Maivoryl City is off limits."

She had a point. He knitted his brows, thinking. "The castle in Macaria?"

"Oh, Sondalane? That's a great idea. It's completely falling apart, and we couldn't get it ready in time for tonight."

Jacob jumped out of bed, glad he always slept in a T-shirt and pajama pants. "It's tonight? Why didn't you say so? The yard's a mess!"

"I know! I'll get Matt up. Could you guys rake the leaves? The weather is going to be nice enough for us to BBQ and to have a couple games of football or basketball or whatever you want—so the yard needs to look good."

He agreed to help, and she bounced out of the room. Jacob hadn't seen her so hyper since she'd found out she was pregnant with Amberly, and that had been a really long time ago. Nine and a half years, at least.

He changed quickly, putting on warm clothes before going outside with Matt.

The brothers took turns raking the leaves into a pile, then jumping into it, scattering the leaves everywhere. Amberly joined them, and they tossed her into the pile a few times before getting serious and cleaning everything up.

After a couple of hours, the place was perfect. Mom came out and looked the yard over—made sure the BBQ grill was ready and the yard presentable. She reported that Gallus was bringing his wife and kids.

Dad came back from running errands. He and Mom had decided to have a full-out feast, including steak, ribs, hamburgers, chicken, and hot dogs.

Jacob picked up Aloren, who'd volunteered to help Mom make sure things were ready.

Matt watched her enter the house with Mom. He shook his head. "I can't believe she's my sister."

Jacob chuckled. "Yeah, I've been having a hard time adjusting to it too."

"I'll bet!" Matt elbowed him in the side. "You having a crush on your brother's sister is definitely weird."

Jacob pushed Matt away, laughing. "Stop it. I don't want to think about that."

The brothers pulled stuff up from the crawlspace under the house—old Thanksgiving decorations that Mom hadn't used in years, folding tables and chairs, and boxes of cloth napkins and tablecloths.

Eventually, everything was ready. Jacob, Aloren, and Matt followed Mom around the house and yard as she inspected things. Tables were set up in the back yard so they could take advantage of the unusually warm weather. The grill was heating up, with Dad watching over it. The house was absolutely perfect. Mom approved.

She had Jacob, Matt, and Aloren change into clean clothes, then she sent Jacob off to pick up everyone. Even Early was coming.

Meeting Gallus's family for the first time was entertaining. His wife was very attractive—taller than Matt and Jacob, with dark skin and hair. Not as dark as Gallus's, though. Her eyes were a brilliant honey color—Jacob couldn't stop staring at them, and Gallus laughed when he noticed.

"She's from the same country as Aloren's mom. They have darker hair and skin, but very light eyes."

Gallus's children were fun—they were really excited to meet Jacob, but didn't jump all over him like little kids usually did. Instead, they followed him around the yard until Gallus called them back.

Finally, everyone was at Jacob's house and in their places.

Jacob ended up next to Matt. He wondered briefly where Aloren had gone, but decided to try to get over it and move on. Maybe she'd gone to the bathroom or something.

Dad welcomed them all and explained how the evening would go. They'd start out by eating a small snack, just to make sure no one was absolutely starving, then they'd break for various things—games and activities, etc.,—and would end with dinner, dessert, and a movie. Matt and Jacob were really excited about this since most of the people from Eklaron hadn't ever seen movies. Aldo and the Makalos were the exceptions.

The snack was a sort of food Jacob had never seen his mom prepare before. She said it was a delicacy from Gevkan. It was made with creamed chicken and cheese sauces, and was sucked out of small bowls with straws that were actually a vegetable growing in Eklaron. You would then eat the straw. Disgusting.

"What *is* this stuff?" Matt asked.

Jacob shook his head. "No idea. It looks gross."

Matt leaned over his bowl and sniffed. "Smells okay. Should we try it?"

"You first."

"No—let's go at the same time."

Jacob agreed and pulled the green straw toward him and sucked on it. The stuff came faster than he expected, and he nearly breathed it in. He coughed, trying to clear his airways. Matt had the same reaction. "Is Mom trying to kill us?" Jacob asked.

Matt didn't answer. He was staring wide-eyed across the table toward the path between the forest and the garage. He nodded his head in that direction, and Jacob looked.

Kevin and Aloren were approaching, holding hands.

"What's he doing here?" Jacob asked.

Matt's mouth popped open. "Holy cow. I have no idea. Does he know about Eklaron?"

Jacob knitted his eyebrows and looked away when Aloren glanced in their direction. "He shouldn't, but how could he not? I mean, look at half the people here. They aren't normal. Unless she's about to tell him."

"So, that's Aloren's boyfriend?" Akeno whispered. He sat across from Jacob, putting his bowl and cup down. "He's here to meet Gallus. It seems he wants to date Aloren, but your parents told her it wasn't appropriate. Not unless Kevin got permission from her guardian. Gallus is the closest thing to a guardian Aloren has. He practically raised her." Akeno motioned to Jacob's parents. "I'm sure if they'd known she was Matt's sister—which, by the way, is absolutely insane—"

"Tell me about it," Matt muttered.

"They would've taken her in as well."

Jacob watched as Aloren and Kevin sat down near Gallus, disappearing from sight behind the heads of other people. He turned back to his food, trying it again, with better results this time. It wasn't bad, actually, if he thought of it as a cheesy-chicken soup.

A moment later, Gallus stood. "I'd like to take the opportunity to say a few things." He waited until every eye was on him—it didn't take long, since his voice resonated so well. "As is the custom in Gevkan, whenever young people wish to declare their engagement, the parents announce it first to all the loved ones and friends."

He motioned to where Jacob assumed Aloren and Kevin were sitting. "Aloren's parents aren't living, so they're not here to make the announcement themselves."

Jacob twisted, straining to see them. Aloren flushed and Kevin looked just as shocked as Jacob felt. The blood had drained from his face, and a greenish yellow—a color Jacob didn't see often, representing near hysteria—swirled around him. Jacob snickered. It seemed Kevin didn't know that by meeting Gallus, he was committing to a whole lot more than he thought.

"I'd like to let everyone know that I'll be conversing with Kevin throughout the party and, at the end, shall decide if I approve of Aloren's choice in marrying him."

18

M urmurs spread through the yard. Jacob's parents looked especially confused, and even the Makalos didn't seem to know what to do.

Aloren tugged on Gallus's shirt, pulled him down, and whispered something to him. He looked confused, gazing at Kevin. He said something back to the two of them, and they shook their heads emphatically. Aloren said something else to Gallus, and he righted himself, clearing his throat. The yard went quiet again.

"Excuse me, but I have misunderstood. It seems they aren't preparing for marriage, but are preparing for . . . for . . ." He turned to Aloren again, but it was Kevin who responded.

"We're dating."

A confused expression crossed Gallus's face, and loud enough for everyone to hear, he said, "What do you mean by 'dating?' You aren't planning on marrying Aloren? Why are you claiming her as your own, then?"

Kevin raised his palms, looking bewildered and embarrassed. Aloren, apparently having given up on the situation, put her head in one hand.

Gallus sat down. Jacob felt bad for him, and surprised himself when he realized he felt bad for Kevin, too. He pushed that away. Kevin had Aloren *and* varsity. That definitely made up for anything.

"Wow." Matt eyeballed the couple. "This, my friends, is an excellent example of cultures clashing."

"You're not kidding," Sweet Pea said. "Her boyfriend should've known better. *Aloren* should've known better."

Matt nodded. "Insane."

A short time later, everyone finished with the delicacy, and the adults disappeared to the kitchen and the grills to work on dinner. Amberly took the kids from Eklaron to the swing set in the back yard, and Jacob and Matt rounded the teenagers up for a game of basketball.

Jacob got his ball and took charge of the game—he wasn't about to let Kevin bowl everyone over at his own home. Kevin had also brought his ball. Jacob watched him carefully—he didn't seem surprised at all about the people around him. Or maybe he was hiding it, and Aloren still hadn't told him about Eklaron? No—that couldn't be the case. He'd be freaking out, trying to figure out who or what everyone was. But that meant she'd told him, and Jacob didn't want to believe she'd jeopardize everyone's trust like that.

He shook his head, putting the thoughts behind him for the time being. He could think about it later. For now, it was time to play.

They started with a couple games of eternal lightning, just to get the people from Eklaron used to how things felt. Jacob won both rounds of the game, with Kevin coming in second. That didn't seem to shock Kevin, and Jacob felt a ton of satisfaction.

Then Jacob split everyone into teams. Team Blue had Jacob, Matt, and Jaegar on it, and Team Red had Kevin, Sweet Pea, Akeno, and Aloren. The teams were evenly matched—

Aloren did well, but she wasn't athletic. Akeno had no coordination, but Sweet Pea was surprisingly good. Matt had played basketball plenty of times, so he made up for the lack of players on Team Blue and for Jaegar's youth.

The entire game was frustrating to Jacob. He tried not to show off for Aloren, but he couldn't help it. And, of course, he was disappointed when she didn't pay him any attention. She only had eyes for Kevin.

The first round ended surprisingly fast. Jacob's team lost. They lost! He glared at his ball, then called for a re-match with the same team members. This time he ignored Aloren, putting everything into it.

And they won. Jacob bent, hands on his legs, catching his breath. He straightened to high-five Jaegar and Matt, and squinted when sweat got in his eyes. He tried to wipe it away, but everything was too blurry. He squeezed his eyes shut, then opened them again.

The light around him changed, and he felt like the ground had been yanked out from under his feet. The sun raced backwards across the sky, followed by nightfall, then by daylight and nightfall again. He closed his eyes, willing things to go back to the way they were. A sensation of vertigo hit him. Jacob fell to the ground, palms over his face, trying to force the lights to return to normal. He looked up and watched stars appear and disappear each time the sun flew past. Hundreds, maybe thousands of people went by him, wandering in every direction. And animals, too.

What was going on?

Finally, the sun stopped at the midday position. Someone he couldn't see screamed, and he jumped up, yelling that he was okay.

Except, he stood next to his house alone. He walked forward, head tilted. Had everyone gone inside when he fell? The place looked different—very different. Fresh. New. His front door slammed open and Jacob jumped back, pressing against the side of the house. Then he realized one of the biggest differences—there wasn't a garage. Where was it?

A man stepped onto the porch, followed by a woman, and Jacob's jaw dropped. They were dressed like pioneers—she wore a long, faded red dress and a bonnet, and he wore brown pants and a loose button-up shirt. Kids poured onto the porch —at least five, dressed like their parents.

Jacob squinted at them, noticing the fear on their faces. He jerked around to see what they were looking at.

A man rode up the hill on horseback, waving his gun, hollering. The dad pushed his wife and children inside the house, reached above the door, and pulled down a rifle, then shut the front door behind him.

"Jimmy, what's going on?" he asked, his voice cracking.

Then the sun flashed across the sky several times, nearly making Jacob vomit. He wished he could go back to see what would happen with the pioneer man. The world stopped spinning with sunlight peeking across the mountains to the east, and he fell to his knees, trying to maintain consciousness. He looked around. A deer ran across the field near him, making him jump. He got to his feet again when he realized the house was gone.

The lights flashed, and the house was back. Only this time, it appeared to be sometime in the late afternoon. Dad pulled up in his silver car and got out wearing a suit and carrying a briefcase.

"Dad!" Jacob called.

He didn't answer. How could he not have heard? He was only a few feet away!

Except, Dad looked different. Younger—not so bald. And Mom came to the door to meet him, holding Amberly, who looked like she was only a year old.

Whoa. This wasn't happening—couldn't be.

The lights flashed across the sky again, and Jacob, falling to the ground, nearly throwing up again, called out, "Stop! *Stop!*"

And things obeyed him.

He tried to rub sense back into his eyes and heard familiar voices. Calling. Shouting. He could pick out Matt's and Aloren's. Aloren!

Jacob looked up. He couldn't see anyone. But he heard them—he heard them! How? That weird feeling in his heart hit him again, making it feel like he was having a heart murmur, and instead of shunning it, he concentrated on it.

Aloren's face appeared above him, concerned. He focused on her brown eyes, willing everything around him to calm down.

"I'm fine," he said, then turned to the side, coughing, his whole body shuddering.

Aloren pulled away, then walked to stand next to Kevin. He put his arm around her waist. Matt, Mom, Dad, and Ebony swarmed in, hovering over Jacob.

"Should we call 911?" Matt asked.

Dad shook his head. "No. It won't help."

Jacob had to agree. "I'm not sick."

"I know, honey," Mom said, "but we've still got to figure this out."

"I think," Jacob started, then paused, coughing again. "I think it's an ability. A power. I could almost control it this time."

"That's wonderful, son!" Dad said. "What did you do? What did you figure out? Can you try it again?"

Mom raised her eyebrows at Dad and he quieted down. She turned to Jacob. "You aren't to play around with this power—it's far too dangerous."

Jacob started. "Mom, I have to—things are getting out of hand."

"I agree with the child," Aldo said. "If he doesn't learn to control the hallucinations, they'll control him."

The Fat Lady nodded. "And it might help in our fight against the Lorkon."

Jacob slowly sat up. "Exactly. It's time for me to know more about this skill. And they're not night terrors. How long was I out of it?"

"About two or three minutes," Mom said. "Which was way too long. You really, really had us worried!"

"Three minutes? There's no way! It felt like fifteen, at least!"

Dad shook his head. "Mom's right. We'd barely come through the doors when you stopped shaking."

Jacob got to his feet, brushing himself off. "This is so weird. I don't know what to think."

"Don't stress over it," Ebony said.

The Fat Lady smirked, her eyes sparkling. "But figure it out, just the same."

Matt snorted. "He's going to freak out over it—that's how Jacob is. If he doesn't know what's going on, he focuses on it until he does."

With a sinking feeling, Jacob remembered that Kevin had witnessed the entire thing. He turned to see how the basketball player was reacting. He looked like he was trying not to run away.

"Sorry you had to see that," Jacob said.

"Nah, it's cool." The color around Kevin's face told Jacob it was anything *but* cool.

Jacob laughed. Then a thought hit him really hard. He looked at Aloren. "How much does Kevin know?"

The colors that made up the emotion of guilt flowed through the air around her. "Well . . . he knows I'm not from earth."

Jacob's mouth popped open. "So, you *did* tell him. Why?"

If the murmurs around Jacob didn't show the surprise of the adults present, the colors emanating from their faces definitely did. Most of them were shocked. The rest were upset. Really upset. Jacob understood—he was upset, too—but he couldn't figure out why they felt so strongly. Hadn't they gotten over it earlier, when Aloren and Kevin first showed up? Was it possible they'd hoped Aloren hadn't said anything to him?

Aloren rushed to explain herself. "I'd made way too many mistakes. Things didn't add up—he asked me all sorts of questions I couldn't possibly answer. Like, where my parents were, who I'd grown up with, my favorite things to do, favorite foods, who's my best friend. How could I tell him that Hazel is only two inches tall? And then he saw her! I tried to cover it—"

"She doesn't need to explain herself," Kevin said. "I believe her, and I won't spill what's going on and where she's from." The expression on his face, not to mention the colors, showed he was serious.

Jacob's parents looked at their son for confirmation. "He's telling the truth," Jacob said. "Or, at least, he thinks he is."

"When did you find out?" Ebony asked Kevin.

"This morning, when she invited me to come." He laughed. "She'd told me I was going to meet some pretty interesting people." He put his arm around her. "After the things she'd said, and after seeing Hazel, I knew she was being honest."

Matt snickered. "Yeah, well, did she tell you that none of our family, except for Amberly, are from earth? Not even our parents."

Kevin's jaw dropped. "What? Are you serious?"

"And what's more," Matt said, ignoring his parents' facial expressions, "my parents are royalty. My dad is the king of Gevkan, where Aloren is from, and my mom is the queen there. Oh, and Jacob and I aren't brothers. And Jacob has magical—"

"That's enough," Mom said. "You're saying way more than you've been given permission to tell."

Matt blushed slightly. "Sorry."

Kevin's mouth hadn't shut yet, and the bright yellow around his face showed he might not recover from his surprise for a long time. "I . . . I . . ." He looked at Jacob.

Jacob shrugged. "Yeah, it came as a complete shock to me, too. I've only known about all of this for a few months."

Kevin shook his head. He chuckled, apparently putting his disbelief away for the time being. "Clark, I always knew there was something wrong with you."

Jacob laced his fingers behind his neck. "You have no idea." It felt weird to joke with the guy.

Kevin laughed, then kissed Aloren on the forehead, and Jacob turned away to find his basketball.

"Okay, enough serious stuff," Mom said. "Time for dinner!"

Everyone cheered and returned to their seats to get their plates.

19

After dinner, Mom ushered everyone except the kids—who went to Amberly's room to play—into the large family room. Dad had insisted on adding it to the house several years back, wanting the extra space for watching movies and basketball games. It made Jacob smile now to think of how exciting America would have been to someone like Dad, who'd never seen an NBA game.

The movie started. After nearly ten minutes of blankly staring at the TV screen, the only thing Jacob knew was that it was an action film of some sort, shot in New York City.

He couldn't stop thinking about his "episode." Why hallucinations? Or were they closer to visions? Obviously, they weren't night terrors, as his mom had originally believed. And the fact that he'd seen his family in the *past* had to mean something.

He thought back on all the times he could remember it happening—whatever *it* was. The first instance had been while playing basketball in the orange gym. What had been unique about that situation? He remembered being tired—not having gotten much sleep the night before. Then there was the time when he'd woken up in the middle of the night to get a drink of water—maybe the episodes had something to do with sleep. Maybe his body was kicking him into a freakish sort of REM cycle.

But what about in the tunnel, when he was fighting the Ember Gods? He hadn't been sleepy then. Exhausted, yes, but not sleepy. And playing basketball earlier—he'd had plenty of rest the night before.

Jacob thought everything over. Was it the time of day? His temperature? Was he sick?

What if it had to do with the amount of danger he was in? Or, more concisely, the intensity of the moment? Fighting the Ember Gods was pretty freaky. And he was always super focused while playing basketball. But no—that time when he'd seen the Indians, he was staring out the window, and it didn't fit.

It wasn't due to location, or what he was wearing, or who he was with. Every episode was different from the others. Jacob sighed in frustration.

Then he decided to single in on the exact moment when the episodes started. Was there something smaller—much smaller—triggering them? He started with earlier that day, while playing basketball in the driveway with everyone. He'd had sweat in his eyes. He'd blinked to clear them, but couldn't, so he'd just squinted through the haze.

Jacob sat up in his chair, feeling like he'd just hit on something important. Was it possible? The episodes had something to do with his eyes? With squinting? Before the first hallucination, he'd been tired—tired eyes don't operate normally. And while in the tunnel with the Ember Gods, he'd been surrounded by fire and smoke, along with having sweat in his eyes. He had squinted in all of those situations. Then . . . while at the window. No squinting. But his eyes had been out of—

Jacob jumped from the couch when it hit him. His eyes had been out of focus! He'd been staring through the window, not really seeing what was out there, thinking about something else.

"Hey! Sit down!"

He didn't know who'd said it, but he popped back onto the couch, elation pouring over him. That had to be the trigger! Squinting was only a symptom, or a side effect of trying to get his eyes to focus. He'd figured it out. *Yes*!

He took several deep breaths, clearing his mind so he could put the theory to the test, then unfocused his eyes, gazing blankly at the TV. *Hallucinate*, he thought to himself.

Nothing happened.

Something wasn't right. What, though?

Jacob chuckled and nearly smacked himself on the forehead when he realized what it was. They weren't hallucinations, and his body wasn't going to obey an order it didn't understand.

He stared at the TV again, recognizing that the main characters were still in New York City, and unfocused his eyes, this time picturing the location where the movie had been filmed.

He stood on that exact same street. The sun was down already, but the road was still full of people. Everyone was wearing coats, but he didn't feel the cold.

"Yeah, I heard," said a sleek-looking woman with tall boots as she walked past Jacob.

A plump woman nodded emphatically. "And she's suing him!"

The two didn't even notice him.

Jacob felt a tight pain in his chest and he gasped, losing concentration. The pain dissipated and the scene changed back to the family room.

It worked! He'd done it!

He jumped to his feet. "I've figured it out! Turn off the movie! I gotta tell everyone something!"

Mom switched the lights on.

"What is it, son?" Dad asked after he'd paused the show.

Jacob felt himself flushing when every eye turned to him. He put his embarrassment aside. "I'm not hallucinating! I'm seeing other places and people! They're real, living people! I was sitting here, on the couch, practicing, and I ended up on that street in New York City!" He pointed at the TV.

Mom raised an eyebrow. "Are you sure, honey?"

"Of course! Here, let me tell you what's going on." He proceeded to explain his theories, along with the questions he'd considered, finally telling them about putting it to the test.

"Wow," the Fat Lady said. She turned to Aldo, who was sitting next to her on the last row of couches. "I suppose we shouldn't be surprised."

Aldo shook his head. "No, but I am, just the same."

"What are you talking about?" Jacob asked.

"What you've experienced is Time-Seeing," the Fat Lady said. "And it's incredibly rare for humans, which is probably why none of us considered it."

Dad nodded, putting his cup down. He was sitting in his usual spot—center row, center of the room. "And this is yet another reason you need to work with the Shiengols as soon as possible. They're also Time-Seers."

Jacob grinned. "Great! I can't wait!"

"Okay, so now that you've got this really super-freakin' cool ability," Matt said, "why don't you do something awesome with it?"

"Like what?" Jacob asked.

"Go see the pyramids!"

A few heads in the room nodded, and he was surprised to

see that even the adults looked interested in hearing the outcome.

"Okay, I can try." He cleared his thoughts and took a deep breath, then pictured Egypt in his mind. He looked ahead, unfocused his eyes, and concentrated specifically on the Great Pyramid.

The family room disappeared, replaced by a night-time glimpse of the pyramids. The scene was brief, and just as fast as it had come, left. Jacob found himself slumped on the couch.

"Dude, you totally fell."

"I know. That didn't last long. Let me go again."

He stood, trying to focus harder. This time he felt like he was actually standing there, in front of the huge pyramid. Wow. The pain in his chest returned, he lost concentration, and zipped back home, falling down again.

"I'm not very good at it."

"That's fine," Aldo said. "You'll have plenty of time to practice."

"No, he won't," Gallus said from the couch on the left side of the room. "This new ability is an extremely powerful one." He leaned forward. "Don't you all see? He could use it to spy on the Lorkon to figure out what their next plan will be. He needs to gain control of it, and fast."

Jacob glanced at his mom. How would she respond to that? She bit her lip, grimacing, then took a deep breath. "He's right." She pressed her hands against her cheeks, glancing apologetically at Jacob. "Honey, don't stress yourself, but continue practicing."

Jacob nodded, trying to keep from smiling. He couldn't believe Mom had actually agreed—she was always so overprotective! Being something more than an errand boy with a magical key was going to be great. Not only that, but this ability really did have some cool advantages—if he could figure out how to use them.

He glanced at Kevin and Aloren. He'd nearly forgotten they were there, sitting next to Aldo and the Fat Lady on the last row. Aloren was leaning back in her chair, hands behind her head. She gave Jacob an encouraging smile. Kevin gawked at him as if he'd turned into a new video game—awe, excitement, and a little nervousness flowing in the air around him. Jacob couldn't help but chuckle, wondering how long it would take for Kevin to adjust to this new knowledge.

Long after everyone had left, Jacob stayed in the family room, trying to Time-See. The best he did was to get brief glimpses at places around the world, but he had a lot of fun doing even just that. He could travel without going anywhere! It didn't take long for him to discover, though, that he felt sick if he didn't wait at least two minutes between tries. He took advantage of that extra time by pulling out some old encyclopedias and reading up on the places he was visiting.

During one of his breaks, a question popped into his mind. Before he'd known what this ability was, his body had sent him to some really random places. Why? And what had chosen those locations? Maybe nerve firings in his brain? The tunnel while fighting the Ember Gods had been really hot, and he'd gone to a snowy mountainside—perhaps to cool off? 'Course, that didn't really explain all the other places he'd been, but there might not be an answer for those occurrences.

Around one in the morning, his mom came downstairs and told him to get to bed. "You won't improve if you over-tire yourself."

"That might actually make it easier—"

Mom shook her head and pointed at the door. She waited for him to leave the room first before turning off the light and shutting the door behind them.

Jacob pulled himself up the stairs to his room. He'd been

so excited to practice that he'd ignored his body, and he was surprised to find that he really *was* tired. As he fell asleep, he smiled to himself. Today, he'd seen some of the coolest places in the world. Turkey, the Great Wall of China, the Pyramids, the Mediterranean, Hawaii, and he'd even visited ruins from the Incas, Aztecs, and Mayas. It was like using the key to get anywhere, only it wasn't illegal or off-limits.

This was going to be great.

20

J acob's parents decided that he, Matt, and Aloren would stay home from school Monday, Tuesday, and Wednesday the following week to help recruit Wurbies. Jacob couldn't believe they were actually in favor of that, but, after hearing Gallus's argument that there weren't many other people who could help in recruiting, it made sense why they'd say yes. Jacob was the only one who could use the key, Matt was as strong as an adult—none of the Makalos could keep up in that area—and Aloren knew Dusts really well. Apparently they were very similar to Wurbies.

Gallus was in charge of the trip, so naturally he was also going, along with Sweet Pea and Akeno. Sweet Pea because he was an experienced fighter, and Akeno because he could knock out creatures, light areas up, and sense living things.

At a meeting right before leaving, Gallus explained they'd be using Aloren's Minya, Hazel, to keep them in contact with Taga Village. He went on to say there would be a lot of dangers—getting to Ashay Hills wasn't an easy thing. "And we'll most definitely run into Eetu fish."

"Really?" Matt asked. "They live out of water, too?"

Gallus shook his head. "No, but to get to the mountains, we have to go through tunnels that run beneath Sonda Lake."

Jacob almost threw up, just thinking about going there again. His palms started sweating, and dizziness made it hard to see and hear. He breathed deeply, refusing to let himself think about the tunnels under Sonda Lake and all the things that could possibly happen.

"Why can't we just walk around?"

"The water is right up against the mountains, and since there isn't a gradual slope, it's impossible to get to the canyons of Ashay Hills by doing that. Onyev and the earlier humans and Makalos built tunnels a very long time ago to provide safe passage."

Aloren nodded. "They're not very safe anymore, as we've discovered. They'll be . . . let's just say, *interesting*. I've only been to the mouths of them—too creepy."

Gallus turned to Akeno. "Your father made more doors, correct?"

Akeno lifted his bag. "Thirty, at least. We'll be very well prepared."

"Good. Let's get going. Make sure you have everything you need. We'll stop by my shop to pick up extra supplies, then head to the castle."

Jacob and Matt had already packed their backpacks full of jerky, bread, a couple types of cheese, bacon, flashlights with extra batteries, matches, and anything else they thought they'd need.

They hefted their bags to their shoulders and Jacob keyed everyone to the shop in Macaria. Gallus gathered things from shop shelves, and Jacob assumed they had something to do with bribing the Wurbies.

When they got to the castle, Aloren led them to a different

section, away from where Jacob had been last time. Thank goodness. As Aloren crept around corners, keeping a lookout for Dusts and other dangerous creatures, Gallus explained that sometime in the last month or so, the earthquakes had stopped happening. That made Jacob even more relieved.

Aloren led them to a large door. It was locked, and Jacob used the key to open it. On the other side was a set of dark, rickety stairs. Aloren went first, leading the way, and Gallus took up the rear.

"My sister is freakin' cool," Matt whispered to Jacob.

Jacob chuckled. "Yeah, she is."

"It's 'cause we're related, you know."

"Whatever."

The group descended several stairs—at least 200. Jacob counted them until Sweet Pea broke through one of the steps and nearly fell. It was so dark, Jacob could barely see the hole the Makalo had created, and he stopped counting so he could concentrate better.

They finally reached the bottom. The air was musty, damp, and stale, and smelled of something Jacob didn't recognize. Something almost animal.

Gallus lit a torch and instructed Akeno and Sweet Pea to light their fingers. Jacob and Matt turned on their flashlights. Jacob strained to see ahead of Gallus, expecting a long expanse of passageway, but frowned when he saw that the way was rough-hewn and rocky—nothing like any of the tunnels he'd been in previously.

Gallus turned to face everyone. "From here on, things will be very dangerous. We're under the lake now, so don't touch the water or walls—even with your shoes—and do your best not to touch the ceiling. Most everything is moist, and we won't know which water belongs to an Eetu fish without finding out the hard way."

The group nodded.

"We'll be fine as long as we're careful." He turned to go, then looked back. "Eetu fish aren't the only pests that live around these tunnels. Keep that in mind."

"What else is here?" Matt asked.

Gallus tilted his head to the side and pursed his lips. "Critters—rats and such."

"Great," Matt grumbled.

They started slowly, then gradually picked up speed as the individual members of the group adjusted to the rough passage. Parts of the tunnel had broken away, revealing incredible depths of water—sometimes clear, sometimes dark and murky. Even in the clear waters, Jacob couldn't see the bottom.

"How deep in the lake are we?" he asked.

"Several hundred feet by now," Gallus called back.

Jacob pulled himself past a big rock in the middle of the way. "How is the tunnel not overflowing with water?"

"Magic," Gallus said. "It was built to be a passage, and a passage it will be."

Jacob nodded to himself. Makalo magic certainly was strong. How much of this sort of thing would Akeno be able to do, once he figured out his abilities?

He paused while Sweet Pea clambered up a huge rock, then grabbed the Makalo's offered hand and pulled himself up. His shoes slipped on the mucky rock beneath him, and he nearly fell against the wet stone.

The boys froze.

Nothing happened.

"That was close," Sweet Pea said.

Jacob nodded and turned to help Matt up.

During a particularly difficult section, Matt started muttering. Jacob chuckled, listening to his older brother.

"They call this a tunnel? Ridiculous. I've seen much better

ones before. Heck, *I've* made 'em better than this. And how did the rock get here, anyway?"

"The rock isn't suspended, you know," Gallus said. Apparently, Jacob wasn't the only one listening to Matt. "Yes, there's water below us, but this entire thing is attached to an overhang on the left. Above and to the right is water."

Matt sighed in frustration. "How much longer until the end?"

"No idea." Gallus grunted in exertion. "Don't expect it to be soon."

The group fell silent again. Jacob's hands got raw from grabbing the rougher sections of rock.

He jumped when Aloren's scream slashed the air, followed by a splash of water. He and Matt scrambled to catch up to her. She'd fallen into a puddle about a foot deep. Gallus and Matt pulled her up, then the group ran forward—climbing and crawling over the rock.

"Hurry, everyone!" Gallus called back. "If there was Eetu in that water, we need to increase the distance as much as possible."

But after a while it became apparent that nothing was chasing them, and they eventually slowed down. Gallus decided they needed to take a break, and he wrapped a blanket around Aloren's shoulders. Her face was white and she trembled, her teeth chattering. The air around her showed she was afraid—very afraid. Jacob didn't blame her. Matt approached and offered her his hoodie. She accepted it, and Matt put his arm around her once she'd put it on.

Jacob watched, helpless, wishing he could also do something to comfort her. He patted her on the shoulder.

It wasn't as cold down here as he'd expected. Maybe the Makalos had also set up a magical heating system. When Aloren had calmed down and everyone had the opportunity to eat, Gallus said it was time to start up again.

The next person who touched water was Jacob, and the group went through the same thing again, rushing forward as fast as possible, then taking a break when it was apparent nothing was following.

Matt flicked his flashlight on and off several times. "How do we know Aloren and Jacob didn't actually touch Eetu water? What if the Eetu are underneath us right now, waiting to attack?"

"If that were the case, we'd know. Eetu are incredibly fast and strong, and aren't conniving. They don't wait for the perfect moment to attack—they go in for the easy kill. Their strength and immunity protect them while they do it."

"Can we please not talk about this?" Aloren asked.

Jacob put his hands in his pockets. He thought it was fascinating, but could see why she wouldn't.

Something to the left of him scurried and he sprang from the ground, backing up against the other side of the tunnel. "What was that?"

"Where?" Matt asked.

Jacob pointed. "It was white and a foot long."

A movement at his side caught his attention. The biggest rat he'd ever seen clung to the wall right by his head. Where did it come from?

Its eyes were milky white, its body slimy, sleek, and hairless. Completely hairless. Jacob backed slowly away, then jumped when the rat leaped for him, landing on his chest. He freaked out, wiping at his shirt, trying to brush the thing off. The little beast clung tight, then squirmed, attempting to burrow itself in his jacket.

"Get off me!"

Finally, he grabbed the rat around the midsection. He almost dropped it when his brain registered the texture of the rat's skin—like a wet mushroom. He ripped its claws free and threw it away from him. He couldn't help the impulse to wipe his hands off. The feeling of a squirmy, hairless rat was too much.

Jacob turned to ask why no one had helped him and saw that they were all fighting to get rats off of themselves. The rodents were everywhere—jumping onto the group, climbing up legs, and scurrying around.

21

"Get moving, everyone!" Gallus called.

They bolted forward, shaking off rats as they went. It didn't take much to discourage the beasts from following, and after a moment, the group reached another wet section. The rats didn't pursue.

"Why did they attack us?" Matt asked.

"I suspect they were going for our clothing," Gallus said. "They don't find much material for nesting down here."

Aloren grimaced, curling her lip. "They're disgusting."

Jacob had to agree.

"Why couldn't Jacob just key us into the Wurby village?" Matt asked.

"Because that isn't polite," Gallus said. "You don't just barge into people's homes without getting permission from them first, especially when no one has talked to them in years and you want them on your side."

The group fell silent. They were passing over a part that had many holes, and they had to be careful. At one point, Jacob's heart nearly stopped beating when, while he hung over a huge gash in the stone, he saw a large, dark creature pass directly under him. He could've sworn it looked up at him and smiled. Could fish smile?

"We shouldn't be far from the end now," Gallus said.

Somewhere along the way, Matt had passed Jacob, and Jacob ended up in the back of the group. He didn't mind—he just made sure to be extra cautious. The idea that they were almost to the end of the tunnel gave him goosebumps. He couldn't wait to feel the sun again. It had been at least two hours since they'd last been out in the open.

He rushed forward, going as quickly as he could, shimmying underneath a large overhang of rock. Once on the other side, he pulled himself up, catching up with Matt.

Jacob was crawling across another hole when he misjudged his foot placement and slipped. Crying out, he grabbed at the rock all around him, attempting to stop his fall. He hit his head against the stone, scraped his hands and elbows, and knocked his knee really hard.

With a splash, he plunged into the dark water below him, wind whooshing out of his lungs. It was so cold! He panicked, flinging himself around. Which way was up? His foot kicked something in the water—something that wasn't rock. Something fleshy. He splashed around even harder, his fingers finally brushing the stone above him.

Hands grabbed him, pulling him out of the water. Matt and Sweet Pea.

He spluttered, coughing and gagging for air, doing his best to increase the distance between himself and the water. His lungs felt like they were on fire, and it was all he could do to control the spasms as his body expelled liquid from his airways.

"Hurry, Jacob!" Gallus called. "That may have been Eetu water!"

Jacob nodded, jumping to his feet.

Then Matt screamed, and without thinking, Jacob looked back.

The most awful, frightening thing he'd ever seen peered at him from the water. Spikes protruded from the sides of its pale face. Gills lined a thick neck. A webbed hand flashed forward and gripped his leg. Beady eyes intelligently bore into his, and the colors for determination flowed in the air around the creature.

Jacob tried to jerk away, but the grip was too tight. The Eetu fish shrieked. It opened its fleshy jaws wide and lunged toward him, holding his leg in place. Thousands of teeth lined three rows inside its mouth. Jacob screamed, yanking his leg as hard as he could, scrambling to get away.

Just then, Gallus jumped down, swung his sword, and struck the fish's arm. It shrilled loudly and dropped Jacob's leg, but didn't appear damaged. It jumped forward again. Gallus was ready. He struck the creature over and over again with his sword, but the fish ignored him.

Oh, crap.

Gallus pulled Jacob to his feet and flung him up toward Akeno and Aloren. Matt scrambled to help, and he and Jacob managed to get over a ledge to stand near the Makalos and Aloren.

Sweet Pea, Aloren, and Akeno pulled out their weapons, joining Gallus in the fight against the Eetu fish.

Jacob and Matt watched, their mouths open. The Eetu moved so quickly, Jacob could barely focus on it. It lunged through openings, trying to get to him, completely ignoring the people who were battering it. Its scales must've been made from something indestructible.

Jacob caught a brief glimpse of the eyes again. They were cold and green, staring into his with an amazing intelligence. It knew what it wanted. Almost mesmerized, Jacob didn't hear Gallus until Matt shook him.

"Jacob!"

He blinked, looking at Gallus.

"Run!" the black man hollered. "Matt, Akeno, go with him!"

"But—" Jacob started.

"We're not in danger. Jacob, it only wants you! Go! I'll alert the Makalos you're on your way."

Jacob's mind cleared, and just as if he were back on the court at school, he jumped into action.

"Come on!" he called to Matt and Akeno.

They dashed forward, guided only by the light of Akeno's finger. Matt and Jacob had both lost their flashlights—Jacob's was probably somewhere at the bottom of Sonda Lake.

They raced down the tunnel—scrambling past boulders and cracks in the rock like someone competing in the Olympics. Jacob winced when his wet clothes started chaffing. He forced the discomfort out of his mind, concentrating only on avoiding the water. No sense in having more than one Eetu try to kill him.

They hadn't been far from the end, and Jacob nearly collided with a metal ladder when he got there. He skidded to a halt and started climbing.

Inhuman shrieking and the sound of clanging swords from behind sent Jacob's hands and feet into frantic motion, and he climbed even more quickly. Akeno and Matt followed him.

His hands had been bruised and scraped from the rocks before, but now the pain tripled as he clung to coarse metal. The space around the ladder hadn't been chopped away very well, and several times Jacob scraped against the walls. He'd probably have scars.

A distant screaming reached his ears, and he recognized Gallus's voice. "Hurry, boys! It's heading your way!"

Oh, no! Jacob's legs cramped up and he lost his footing,

swinging into Akeno. The Makalo nearly fell off the ladder, but Jacob saw Matt grab him and pull him up.

Must climb faster. Jacob got back on the ladder and started counting rungs. He stopped somewhere around 448. They had to have gone up fourteen or fifteen stories by then.

He felt it when the Eetu fish reached the ladder. A clang vibrated painfully in his hands and he almost slipped again. The fish shrieked beneath them, and the ladder vibrated even more when the thing started climbing. Jacob pushed himself harder, wishing Hazel could come give him extra strength.

Finally, long after his hands had begun bleeding, Jacob reached the top. He pushed on the ceiling above him, sliding a slab of stone out of the way. Why couldn't it have been a door? He would have used the key to get them out of there faster.

He jumped through, then pulled out Akeno and Matt. He and Matt dragged the stone back into place, realizing it wouldn't do much good, but needing something to focus on while Akeno enlarged a door.

"Ready," Akeno said.

The door was barely three feet tall, but that was plenty for Jacob. He dashed forward, pulled the key from his pocket with some difficulty, and thrust it into the lock that appeared. Turning it to the left, he said, "Akeno's house."

Jacob pushed Akeno and Matt through ahead of him, then stepped across the threshold, turning in time to see the stone barrier fly away from the hole and the Eetu fish jump out. Jacob slammed the door shut right when the Eetu lunged for him, landing just two feet away. It screamed—an awful mix of a human scream and the sound an animal makes when it is in a great deal of pain.

22

The shriek was cut off when Jacob closed the portal, but he propped himself against the door just in case the link was still live. Nothing happened.

He slid to the floor, breathing so heavily he felt his lungs would burst. Ebony rushed over from where she and Kenji had been sitting at the table, Kenji following. They were both shaking.

Ebony pulled Jacob to his feet, throwing her arms around him. "We didn't know which door you'd go through, so we've been waiting near all those we thought you'd try. Your mom is at your house, Jaegar is waiting by the tree, and the Fat Lady at her place. Gallus and the others will be fine in the tunnel, so long as they don't touch water." She quieted long enough to notice the shape the boys were in. "And look at your hands! Thank goodness you came here—let's get you fixed up."

"I'll grab a Kaede sap package," Kenji said, leaving his wife's side.

Ebony got to work instantly, assessing the damage. "Broken fingers. You all have at least one broken finger. How'd you manage that?"

"Ladder," Matt said, still gasping for air. "My back—scratched up. Can you fix it?"

"Yes, of course. We'll get you all in good health."

Jacob inspected his arms while Ebony and Kenji mixed the sap. The index and ring fingers on his right hand were bent at weird angles. How'd he not notice the pain? 'Course, he was completely numb from the elbow down. His fingers were purple and blue with blood oozing everywhere. They'd never been this bad before.

Ebony had them sit at the table then started on Akeno first, working quickly. "Lucky for all of you, we won't have to set the bones. Kaede sap puts everything back into its proper form without much assistance."

Jacob relaxed against the chair when she worked on him.

"Hands first, then everything else later. Matt and Jacob, I'll have you go into a private room. Inspect each other and let me know what needs to be healed."

Jacob nodded. Ebony went on to Matt, and Jacob looked at the white cloth strapped to his hands, glad to have the bruises and scratches covered. They'd been so gross.

Kenji looked out the window. "If they find more water to replenish themselves, Eetu fish can track the scent of their water for twenty-four hours." He turned back to the room. "I'll have Early keep an eye on it. She can alert us if it gets close."

Jacob didn't want to hold on to the hope that the Eetu wouldn't find water on its way to him.

Ebony showed Jacob and Matt to a room. Luckily, only their backs were really bad, but they had a couple of minor scratches and bruises on their knees and shins, too. She insisted on fixing everything.

After half an hour, all three boys were at the table, attempting to eat soup. Their bandaged hands made it interesting. Jacob fought the severe exhaustion, focusing on getting the soup in his mouth one spoonful at a time.

Hazel flitted into the room, heading straight to Jacob. "Gallus says to send Akeno. The Eetu fish returned to the tunnel and jumped into the water, so we will be safe to continue, but we need Akeno to help set up doors."

Jacob nodded. It would only take a couple of seconds to key Akeno back. And perhaps doing so would confuse the Eetu fish, buying Jacob more time. He and the other two packed up their things and Jacob created the link.

Gallus waited on the other end. He stepped to the side to let Matt and Akeno through, then spoke to Jacob. "Taga Village isn't far enough away. The Eetu fish won't take very long to get there. Their magic is related to that of the Minyas —it finds the shortest, fastest distance to their prey as possible, and they run much faster than hu—"

With a flash, Early appeared next to Jacob. "It's coming! Now! It's coming!"

Jacob slammed the door to Gallus shut right as warning bells sounded over Taga Village. He looked at Ebony in shock —it had only been thirty minutes! How on earth did the fish get there that fast?

Kenji burst through the front door, making Jacob jump.

"The Eetu is almost to the entrance! It'll be able to break through your magic, Jacob! Go, quickly! To the Fat Lady's!"

Jacob grabbed his coat and bag and keyed himself to her cabin. He slammed the door behind him, the sound of the bells in Taga cutting off as he did.

"Is that you, Jacob?" the Fat Lady called. She rambled into view from down the hall. "Good. Figured it was you. You're the only one who has access without my password."

"Got a fish on my tail."

She nodded. "Those things are fast. Where are you headed next?"

"I'm thinking somewhere in my country."

"Be careful—there are many, many links between the different worlds accessible only to Eetus. Don't get comfortable in one spot for too long."

Jacob sighed in exasperation. How was he supposed to do that when he was absolutely exhausted? "That's not encouraging."

Early flashed next to him. "It'll be here in fifteen minutes."

"You've got Early—good. Keep her with you."

Jacob still held the key in his bandaged hands. The numbness was wearing off and they were throbbing. He needed sleep, but wasn't sure when or how he'd get it. The sap wouldn't fully heal him until he had some. He put the key into the Fat Lady's lock, glad it was attached to his pants with a chain.

"Guess I'd better get going."

"Guess so."

He said goodbye, then keyed himself to the first place that entered his mind—New York City.

23

The next several hours were long, exhausting, painful, cold, and tedious. It took hours for Jacob's clothes to dry, and when they did, they were stiff and uncomfortable. He keyed to many different locations around the world, only able to stay in each spot for a couple of hours at a time. He took naps where he could, and the pain in his hands gradually lessened.

He was so glad he had the key. Without it, there was no way he would have been able to stay away from the Eetu. It wasn't any wonder that no one had survived an attack. The fish found links in the most random and illogical places— through stone and small holes where its body couldn't possibly fit.

While in New York, he purchased several postcards depicting places around the globe and showed them to Early so she would know where to find him, in case they ever got separated.

The first time she gave him a report on the Eetu fish's whereabouts, she'd also thrown in a question regarding how he was feeling. That surprised him. He looked at her, eyebrow raised, wondering if she had ulterior motives. But then he realized she did it because she actually cared. From then on, she asked him all the time how he was feeling—if he was tired or hungry.

"Thanks, Early," Jacob said when she gave him the latest update.

She brushed his hand with her fingertips. "You're welcome. Do you need anything?"

A warm feeling started at the center of his chest and spread across him. He couldn't believe how much she'd changed over the last several hours. She was loyal and attentive now—constantly proving her value. It was completely different from the last time he'd spent time with her, and he was so grateful for the change. He wouldn't have been able to survive without her.

"I think I'm good. Thanks for asking."

"No problem!" She patted him again, then flitted away, staying within sight—a new development, considering how much food had been around them to tempt her. The only time he couldn't see her was when she was checking on the fish.

At her insistence, Jacob stopped by his house to eat and catch up with Mom and Dad. He was thankful for that—it felt good to relax, even if for only a couple of minutes. They reported that everyone was doing well and there hadn't been any more run-ins with Eetu fish. He breathed a sigh of relief, hugged them goodbye, then keyed himself to his next location.

THIRTY MINUTES before the twenty-four hours were up, Jacob decided to visit one of his favorite places on earth —Arches National Park. He keyed to a bathroom near one of the trails, holding the door open for Early. She zoomed past him, squealing in excitement, then did a few somersaults in the air. Jacob smiled at her enthusiasm. He couldn't figure out why she was so excited to go through links created by the Key of Kilenya—she'd acted this way after every one they'd gone through together.

Jacob wandered aimlessly. He made sure to stay within running distance of the bathroom door, in case the Eetu was lucky enough to find a link in time. Pausing on a bridge, he looked into the water below him, then absentmindedly picked at some fuzzies on the sleeve of his jacket. It was great to have the bandages gone from his hands—he'd removed them a few hours earlier when he got tired of getting strange looks from people. Residual bruises and a little tenderness were all that remained of the broken bones. The blisters and cuts were mostly gone.

He left the bridge and walked down the trail, following it as it led up a couple of short switchbacks and past a really large rock where tourists gathered to take pictures. He stepped to the side of them, not wanting to be part of their groups, and gazed at Delicate Arch, admiring the rugged beauty of the landscape.

Just then, someone screamed. Jacob whipped around to see why. The tourists were pointing into a gulch, yelling, panicking, some pulling out cameras.

Jacob climbed on top of the huge boulder and shaded his eyes. It only took him a split second to find where they were pointing. His stomach fell.

A huge fish was running on four legs through the gulch far below him, fins and tail flapping. Why hadn't Early warned him?

Just as soon as Jacob saw it, it saw him.

The Eetu went into a frenzy, scrambling up the side of the gulch. No way it could make it—the cliff was completely sheer. Jacob backed up anyhow, then jumped off the boulder and ran for his life. Literally. Maybe he could make it to the bathroom in time to key away.

Early appeared next to him and started crying. "I'm sorry, Jacob. I'm sorry!"

"No worries," Jacob said, pushing his shock away. "Where is it?"

She disappeared, then came back. "Almost to the top!"

More screams from behind, and Jacob heard footfalls as other people finally started running. Maybe they'd distract the Eetu?

He wouldn't count on that.

The switchbacks slowed him down. He took shortcuts wherever possible.

A moment later, as he crossed the bridge, he realized something: the fish wouldn't follow the trail. It would go straight down the hill. Jacob looked over his shoulder, trying to see where it was.

Just then, the Eetu jumped out of the water to the right of him. Jacob skidded to a stop so he could run the other way, but the creature tackled him, hissing loudly.

With a hard *thud*, he landed on his back on the wooden planks, people scattering and screaming around him.

The wind knocked out of him, he shoved and kicked, trying to get away from the fish, trying to push it away. Green, the color for excitement, flowed in the air around it.

The Eetu was incredibly strong. It repelled all Jacob's attacks. Faster than Jacob thought possible, the beast picked him up. It sung him into the air, mouth open, ready for a bite.

The fish went limp.

Its intelligent eyes appraised Jacob.

Then it dropped him hard on the bridge and jumped over the side.

Jacob gasped when the cold water splashed him. He

watched the fish swim leisurely away, then spring out of the water and run off the way it had come.

"Early? Early!"

"Here, Jacob!"

He rolled into a sitting position until he saw her floating above him. "It's gone? Did it . . ."

"It gave up! It lost scent of the water. You're okay! You're fine!"

Jacob slumped in relief, holding his knees to his chest. "Oh, man, oh, man, oh, man."

She patted him on the head. "I'll go watch it." She disappeared.

"Hey, dude, you okay?"

Jacob turned—a man in his thirties was staring at him. "Yeah, I think so. That was really close!"

"What on earth was it?"

Jacob shook his head, not sure how to answer, and the man pulled him to his feet.

"That was insane!"

"You have no idea."

"Are you sure you don't need anything?" The guy reached into his bag. "Here—my name's Jared." He handed Jacob a business card. Jacob looked at it. He was a photographer—that explained the huge camera hanging around his neck. "Please —call if that thing comes again or you need help in some other way." He peered down at Jacob. "Where are your parents?"

Jacob shook his head. "I'm not—I mean, they're waiting at another trail."

"I'll give you a ride."

"I think I'm going to be sick. I'll walk back when I can— when I . . ." He turned and stumbled to the bathroom, shutting the door behind him. Luckily, no one was inside. He took a few deep breaths, then keyed home.

JACOB'S PARENTS were understandably relieved at his return. Dad insisted he fill them in on all the details, then Mom insisted he sleep. He was glad for that.

When he woke, his mom said he'd been in the news and showed him the article. Jared, the photographer, had been taking pictures of the Eetu as it ran down the hill. The last shot was of the fish right as it jumped for Jacob. Only Jacob's back was visible, but the picture of the Eetu was pretty awesome. With all the eyewitness reports, authorities were looking into the event, though they doubted anything would come of it.

Jacob agreed.

He finished his breakfast, then pushed away from the table. "Okay, time to go recruit Wurbies!" He ran upstairs to grab his spare backpack, since the usual one was probably at the bottom of Sonda Lake by then, and dashed to the kitchen to stock supplies.

Mom was waiting by the counter. "Sorry, honey, but the meeting has already taken place."

"What? They didn't wait?" Disappointment flooded over him. "Why?"

"Apparently, the Wurbies found *them* and forced them to enter the village to talk. They had to negotiate terms for their release before the Wurbies would consider untying them."

Even though he was really disappointed to have missed it, Jacob couldn't help but smile at the thought of his friends being tied up by the Wurbies. He'd been in a similar situation once, but with Dusts. "What happens now?"

"They're waiting for you. The Wurbies wouldn't release anyone until they were promised you'd go meet them. And even though they've already discussed the upcoming war, they want you to make things official." She put her arm around him. "Go—make us proud. This is your first official act as prince."

Jacob felt a blush cross his face. He wondered if Aloren had been impressed. He could see himself striding into the village, commanding attention. But underneath the excitement was a nagging worry that they expected something from him he couldn't give. He'd never met Wurbies, after all. What would they want?

24

Jacob keyed to the door number Early gave him. Gallus was waiting on the other side and led Jacob back to the makeshift camp they'd set up.

"I wish you'd been here when we first arrived," he said, motioning to Jacob to enter a stick hut—obviously Akeno's handiwork. "It would've been much easier, actually, to get ourselves out of jeopardy."

Jacob stepped into the hut and found Aloren, Matt, Sweet Pea, and Akeno there, sitting around a small fire in the center of the space. He joined them, holding his fingers to the heat. "Sounds like you guys had a lot of fun."

Matt laughed. "Yeah, after everything you'd said about Dusts, I figured Wurbies would be easy." He shook his head. "They weren't."

Jacob sighed in disappointment. "Man, I hate missing out on things like this."

Gallus pulled up a log and sat. "From what we heard, you had just as much excitement as we did—probably even more."

Jacob nodded, then filled them in on what had happened.

After he finished, Gallus told him more about the Wurbies' desire to meet him.

"Fubble, the leader of the Wurbies, begged to meet you." Gallus shifted forward. "They'll recruit as many Wurbies as they can. They'll gather in their main village—the one we'll take you to—and in a year, will let us know they're ready. At that point, you'll key them to Taga, where they'll receive further training."

"So . . . we have at *least* a year before the war starts?" Jacob asked.

Gallus rubbed his forehead, then dropped his hand. "I hope we have more time than that, so we're better prepared."

"Sometimes it feels like it's on the verge of happening."

"I know. And either way, we can't count on anything, really." He got to his feet. "Let's get going."

Aloren rolled her eyes. "At least this time we'll have Jacob—they can fall to the ground in excitement instead of tying us up."

Gallus snorted—a half laugh—then got back to business and motioned for the others to gather their things. "Fubble has been waiting near the entrance to their village since we told him you were coming. It's farther up the canyon. I'll lead you there before coming back here."

"You're not coming?"

Gallus shook his head briefly. "No—I need to take note of everything that has happened. Besides, they don't see me as a leader, so it won't matter if I'm there or not."

Jacob watched the man carefully, waiting to see if he was disappointed or annoyed at all by this turn of events. If he was, he covered it very well—including masking his emotions, even the colors in the air. Maybe he really didn't care.

Jacob stepped out of the hut, taking a look around. The canyon had received a lot of snow since the last time he'd been there—everything was pristine. And the view of Sonda

Lake and Gevkan was astounding. The water was an intense shade of blue. Maivoryl City had the typical smudge over it, and Macaria was just as white and bleached as ever. Dunsany Mountain was covered with snow and looked very dramatic.

Just then, Jacob noticed that the forest surrounding him appeared to have burned recently. He glanced up at the sky. "What about Lirone? Has he come? Will he?"

Gallus shook his head. "We've been watching. According to the Wurbies, he attacks every three or four days. This one happened two days ago—right before we got here. The Wurbies have a warning system in place and we'll know when he's on his way. Frankly, I don't understand how they can live here, with him going on the rampage all the time." He reached into the hut and pulled his bag out. "The skies are really clear right now—the Wurbies say he's sleeping."

"So, you're telling me not to worry?"

"Exactly. Unless clouds form and you hear alarms going off."

Good to know. Jacob stamped his feet on the trail, trying to stay warm, while Akeno finished unfolding the hut, letting the branches go back to their normal position. Gallus looked at Jacob, who nodded.

"Okay, let's go see this Fub guy."

"Fubble," Aloren said.

"Your Highness, would you like to lead the way?"

It took Jacob a moment to realize Gallus was talking to him—the man had never referred to Jacob in that way before. He didn't know how to answer. "Uh . . . why?"

"Because you are the future king of this land. You need to get used to people following you."

Jacob felt his cheeks flush. He really didn't want to walk in front of Gallus. "How about I go in the back, and the rest of you act like you're escorting me or something?"

Gallus half-smiled. "As you wish. Though, let's have Matt

walk behind you. Let him get attacked by random creatures instead of you."

"Hey!" Matt said. "I'm his brother—doesn't that mean I should be treated better?"

Aloren jumped to Matt's side, linking her arm with his. "And I'm Matt's sister!"

Gallus only laughed, then turned and followed the trail in the snow. Aloren, Sweet Pea, and Akeno walked in line behind him. Jacob tried to see the expression on Aloren's face, but couldn't. He followed Akeno, with Matt bringing up the rear.

After five minutes of walking, Jacob heard a high-pitched voice up ahead.

"He coming? Coming? Where?"

Everyone stopped, and Jacob stepped into view. "Hi."

He saw a bright flash of blue cloth, then felt something pelt him in the legs, knocking him into the snow. "Whoa! Hello."

The short creature released him, then stepped back and pointed to himself. "Fubble the Wurby." He shook his hands in the air, an expression of intense excitement on his face. "So glad! So glad you here!"

Jacob swallowed his laughter. "Nice to meet you, Fubble."

"Sorry, sorry. Not Fubble. Fubble the *Wurby*."

"Oh, I apologize. Nice to meet you, Fubble the Wurby."

"Eeep!" Fubble's hands turned into a blanket, which he put over his head.

Jacob felt red creep across his cheeks and his ears burned. He smiled sheepishly at Gallus. The black man shrugged. Jacob would really need to get used to this treatment.

Fubble removed the blanket and jumped away, his hands returning to normal. "Come! See Wurb!"

"Wurb?" Jacob asked, but Fubble had already dashed off.

"A baby Wurby," Aloren said.

Gallus sighed. "They'll only help us if you see Fubble's baby. It's ridiculous."

Aloren frowned. "It's a sign of respect and mutual agreement to Wurbies and Dusts alike. The Wurbies show you their most beloved possession—something that symbolizes the future—and depending on how you respond, it seals whatever deal was made. It's a thing of trust."

"Sounds more like a way for them to go extinct," Matt said. "I mean, listen. How many babies have died after being shown to strangers who weren't really the good guys?"

Aloren's frown deepened, but Jacob could see his brother's point.

"Anyway," Gallus said, "the more support we show the Wurbies, the more support we'll receive. Go ahead."

He and Sweet Pea stayed behind while Jacob, Aloren, Akeno, and Matt rushed to catch up with Fubble. He waited near some stone ruins.

Jacob followed Fubble as he dashed under a half-crumbling arch, then stopped on a snow-packed road. Fubble motioned to the village around him, pride on his face, and Jacob's eyes nearly popped out as he took in everything that surrounded them.

The buildings were . . . *different*. That was the first word that entered Jacob's mind. Their construction was incredibly haphazard—nearly every kind of material he knew had been used. Stone, brick, wood, branches, rugs, tile, dirt, even plastic. How did they get plastic?

Everything was thrown together without an apparent plan, and many of the buildings had multiple items holding them together. Jacob laughed when he realized what must've happened—the Wurbies probably changed design a hundred times while working on the same project. It looked like they did the best they could, but he guessed their hands were like Dust hands—adapting to situations without the owner's permission, and thereby shifting the focus.

The result was a village that was visually pleasing while

also somewhat disorienting. Jacob wished he had his phone—he'd have to come back and take a picture sometime. He could stand there for hours, just looking at it all. One building was brick on one side, rope and branches in the middle, and what looked like a slippery slide on the other side. The brick was red and the slide bright blue. Another house looked like it had been built completely of leaves and banana peels.

Jacob jumped with fright when a Wurby rushed out to meet him, hands shaped like a spoon and a fork. He relaxed when he realized it must've been eating.

The next Wurby's hands were normal, but the third's were stuck in the hair of another Wurby . . . Jacob couldn't figure out why. All of their faces were flushed. Some touched their mouths, lowering their eyes when he looked at him. Then they bowed.

Fubble started forward again, and the other Wurbies fell into line behind the humans and Makalo.

Finally, Fubble stopped in front of an edifice that had been created out of old statues, some tarp, and carpet. The tarp looked suspiciously like something from Walmart, but Jacob didn't ask.

A female Wurby came out the door, one hand forming a blanket which was wrapped around a baby, the other tucked somewhere inside the cloth folds.

"My woman Wurby!" Fubble said, gesturing to her. "Her name are Tast!"

Tast bowed low. "Highness."

Jacob nodded at her, not sure what else to do. "And the baby? Is it a boy or a girl?"

"Boy!" Fubble said, jumping up and down with excitement. "He are Pug!"

"Like the dog," Matt whispered to Jacob.

Jacob waved his brother off, wondering what he needed to

do to show his respect and desire to "seal the deal." "Can I hold him?" he asked, reaching for Pug.

Fubble looked like his most favorite dreams were about to come true. "Oh, yes!" He motioned to Tast, and she handed the baby over. Jacob's face flushed when he saw that one of her hands formed the baby's diaper. His stomach flopped when he realized how much easier it would be to change the baby—she just had to wash her hand when the diaper was full. Disgusting.

Jacob gawked down at the ugliest baby he'd ever seen. Weathered-looking skin that was wrinkly and slightly browned; large, hairy ears; a nose similar to a pig's. It did have one redeeming quality, though—eyes that were the biggest and bluest he'd ever seen, lined by dark, long eyelashes.

Pug returned his stare, sucking a thumb that had swollen slightly to fit his mouth. Jacob almost gagged at the sight of the large thumb, but smiled instead, handing the baby back to Tast. He noticed that Aloren didn't seem as thrilled about the baby as he thought a girl would be. She probably thought it was ugly too. "He's a nice little baby."

"He are!" Fubble said, an expression of love on his face as he watched Tast and Pug go back into the home. He turned to Jacob, an expectant expression on his face. "You want something? Highness? What want?"

Jacob stammered when he realized this was the most important part of his visit to the village. "We . . . uh . . ." How was he supposed to sound official? He decided that being straight-forward was the best route. "Fubble the Wurby, we'd like your assistance in a war. Would you recruit Wurbies to help us?"

All joviality left Fubble's face. "Sir, yes. We will." He bowed low, swinging his arms to the side.

"Thank you. We . . . I look forward to our future communications."

Fubble grinned, nodding his head emphatically. Then he lightly pushed Jacob. "You are go to home now!" His grin disappeared. "You are *go* to *home* now. *Now.*"

Jacob blinked. That was abrupt.

"Whoa," Matt said. "Not one to beat around the bush, is he?"

Jacob opened his mouth, closed it, then opened it again. "Guess not." He shook Fubble's hand and said goodbye, then led the others away.

The Wurbies followed them to the city wall, cheering. Jacob glanced over his shoulder and waved back as he and the rest of the group trudged away through the snow.

After a few minutes, they caught up with Gallus and Sweet Pea, who were waiting near a door. The black man smiled at Jacob, and Jacob assumed it was because of the expression on his face, which was probably a mixture of shock, confusion, and surprise.

"So . . . what did you think?"

Jacob shook his head in disbelief. "That was interesting."

Gallus nodded crisply. "Yup. But they'll be a huge help in the upcoming months, possibly years."

Jacob raised an eyebrow. "How? You saw their city. It's awesome, but shows they lack concentration. They have almost no control over what their hands do, and they're practically incoherent."

Gallus glowered at Jacob. "Your Highness, you've got a lot to learn. A creature may not appear to be useful, but that doesn't mean you turn them down when they're excited and willing to be of assistance. Even the littlest, most *incoherent* creature can turn the tide against the Lorkon."

Jacob looked at his feet, feeling smaller at that moment then he'd remembered ever feeling before. He wanted to disappear. "You're right. Sorry."

Gallus clapped him on the shoulder. "We'll teach you to be a leader yet."

"Can we go home now?" Matt asked. "I'm absolutely starving. Not to mention freezing."

Gallus nodded. "Yes, we're done."

Jacob keyed Gallus back to his shop, where the black man's family was really happy to see him. He then took Aloren and the two Makalos to Taga, dropping them off at the tree, then he and Matt returned home. Jacob went straight to his room and shut the door, wanting some time alone.

Gallus was right. He had a lot to learn.

25

D ad called a meeting with everyone a few hours after the Wurby recruitment group returned. He started it off by having Gallus and Jacob report. He then changed the topic, a serious expression crossing his face.

"It's time to get the Shiengols out of August Fortress. Those who will be going are Jacob, Matt, Gallus, Aloren, Akeno, and Sweet Pea."

"Already?" Mom asked. "But they just got back!"

Dad nodded. "This is the best time to go. It's Thanksgiving weekend, which means the kids won't be missed in school." He ran his fingers through his thinning hair. "Now then. Before we get into logistics, I need you all to understand something. Your safety is more important than getting the Shiengols. They've been there for several years—a few more weeks won't make a difference. So, if anything happens, Jacob will key everyone home."

Jacob nodded. Hopefully that wouldn't be necessary.

"Your next priority is to ensure that Jacob gets to the fortress. I've got a feeling he'll be the only one able to open it up—he's gotten through other traps set by the Lorkon. Guard him, then help him in."

He looked Jacob squarely in the eye. "There's something you need to know about Shiengols. They're dangerous, and they have varied and hard-to-predict emotions. They'll be rude one minute, then nice the next. Expect it."

Kenji laughed. "I remember my first encounter with a Shiengol. He slapped me when I asked his name."

Dad chuckled. "Yes—didn't he say it was none of your business?"

"That was his excuse. Who knows the actual reason."

Dad turned back to Jacob. "Just be polite and you should be fine."

Jacob bit the inside of his cheek. "And don't ask them what their names are, right?"

"Right." Dad leaned back. "Tomorrow is Thanksgiving Day. We'll eat dinner around eleven in the morning. I'll send Jacob and Matt to Taga Village at one."

Everyone stood to go, but Dad put his hand up. "One last thing." He motioned to Aldo. "Will you take the group to your lookout point and show them what they'll be up against?"

"THIS WAY," Aldo said, gesturing to the left of the door they had all just come through. The door overlooked August Fortress and the valley, and was one of the ones the scouting group had placed right after exiting the infected forest. "It's a bit of a walk, but nothing you can't handle."

Aldo led the group along the top of the hill. They were careful to stay away from the branches of the infected forest and were mostly successful. After walking for twenty minutes, he took them around some dense bushes near the edge of a sharp drop-off, then hiked up when the hill rose steeply in front of them. After nearly ten minutes, he had them stop. They'd reached the pinnacle of the hill.

Aldo then pointed out where their sense of sight would be taken away, also showing them the location of the Argots. He continued, pointing at the outer wall of the fortress. "You'll lose your next sensation there—feeling."

Gallus stepped up between Jacob and Aldo. "We plan to bring a potted plant. Akeno will use it to see living creatures, since that ability doesn't have anything to do with physical senses."

Aldo nodded. "Good. Once you enter the township, you'll need to remember the following: walk thirty paces. Turn right. Walk seven. Right. Walk fifteen. Left. Walk twenty-seven. Left. Walk one hundred and thirty."

A roar echoed through the valley, originating from somewhere near the fortress. Jacob looked out, but didn't see where exactly it had come from. He gnawed on his lip and turned back to Aldo. "Uh . . . could you repeat that?"

"Yes," Aldo said, and he gave them the numbers again. "And I'll write it down for you, too. These are according to my footsteps."

Matt frowned. "Why'd you memorize them?"

"I figured the Lorkon would do something to prevent people from entering the area, and I wanted to know how to get to the fortress from the entrance, just in case."

"Impressive," Sweet Pea said. "I wouldn't have thought of that."

"It's what I'm paid to do." Aldo turned to Jacob. "I'll expect a bag of cash from your father as soon as possible." The twinkle in his eye let Jacob know he was kidding, and they chuckled together.

Aldo then compared the length of his stride to the others,

finding that Jacob and Matt were the closest. Jacob sighed—he should've seen that coming. Gallus was too tall, and Aloren and the Makalos were too short. Because of Jacob's abilities, Aldo and Gallus decided he would take the lead. But that just meant Jacob would be in the most danger. As he'd thought earlier, he should've seen that coming.

Aldo put his hand on Jacob's shoulder. "Remember to walk naturally. Don't run, don't make your steps bigger than usual, and you'll be fine."

"What if we get chased?"

"You won't be—not while you've still got your hearing. After your hearing leaves, you'll be dealing with something else entirely." He looked back at the city. "And I hoped we'd see it from here. We might not."

"What is it?"

"A Cerpire. Similar to a dinosaur."

Matt raised his eyebrows. "You're kidding."

Aloren looked confused. "What's a dinosaur?"

Matt cleared his throat, putting on a comical, professor expression. "Prehistoric creatures, which have been extinct for tons of years and roamed the lands of my world until they were destroyed by a meteor or something."

"Most of them were dangerous," Akeno said.

Jacob looked at Aldo. "How on earth did the Lorkon get one here? And how will we know where it is if we can't hear, see, or smell it?"

Aldo folded his arms, grimacing at the fortress. "Cabins eat breakfast foods on Wednesdays," he started. "Oh, excuse me." He took a deep breath. "I would assume they brought the creature here from another world. And you'll have to count on other senses—yours and Akeno's, to be exact."

Another roar echoed across the valley, and recognition showed on Aldo's weathered face. "He's still there."

Matt held up his hands. "Wait. That sound was it?"

Aldo motioned to the forest. "Maybe he'll show himself."

The group waited, but nothing happened.

Aldo sighed. "Either way, I'd better describe him to you. He's about as tall as a Sindon—maybe taller, with a large tail. Walks on two feet and has long arms lined with spikes. He might be hungry. It's possibly been quite some time since he last ate."

"This is insane!" Matt said. "There's no way. We can't possibly fight a dinosaur without any of our senses!"

Gallus nodded. "I agree. How are we to defeat a creature that large and dangerous without being able to protect ourselves?"

"Well, you won't be completely alone," Aldo said. "I'll camp out here and keep an eye on you with my telescope while you're traveling. I'll pay special attention to you once you're inside the fortress walls. Early will deliver frequent messages to me, and I'll tell her how to help you. We've hired another Minya named September. He has agreed to be with me for the duration of your trip. He'll take frequent updates to the village and your families." He paused—his forehead creased—obviously thinking. "Oh, and also, Early will be able to increase Jacob and Akeno's magical abilities."

Jacob looked out at the valley. "And she could help us run faster."

"Exactly." Aldo said. "She'll help you, even when you don't know what's happening, and your abilities will be hugely beneficial to the entire group. Akeno will be able to sense where the creature is, and Jacob, you can see emotions. You should be able to see the Cerpire's."

"But sometimes I can't see them when they're coming from animals."

"Could you see the Eetu's?"

Jacob nodded.

"Then it will work out. The Cerpire is as intelligent as an Eetu fish—"

Aloren gasped. "You've got to be kidding!"

"—but not as advanced. It has magic, but can only use it to benefit others. Like to give power to other, dangerous creatures. And remember, Cerpires, like Eetu fish, go for the obvious, easy kill. When Kelson and his group were there, the Cerpire didn't sneak around, but jumped out right in front of them. Also, its size is against it—they're not fast." Aldo put his hands behind his back. "You'll be fine. You've got things Kelson didn't have. And don't forget your abilities—*all* of them."

"I hate to be a downer," Matt said, "but this is a death trap, regardless of our abilities. The chances of survival are zero, and I don't know about any of you, but I want to live. I just found out I have a sister. *Another* sister. I want to keep getting to know her before we die."

Aloren nodded, sending a grateful expression to Matt.

Aldo put his hand on Matt's shoulder, looking concerned. "What other choice do we have? The Lorkon will win unless we release the Shiengols. Without the training they'll provide Jacob, we can't do anything. Besides that, they're incredibly powerful, and if the Lorkon hadn't caught them by surprise, they wouldn't be trapped now. You can bet they'll never let it happen again. Having them on our side will most definitely turn the tide against the Lorkon."

"What if we don't care about the Lorkon?" Matt asked. "I'm sorry—I don't want to offend anyone, but what if Jacob and I go back home and forget about all this? Aloren, you come too. Don't get me wrong, Aldo—I'm usually up for a challenge, and I think you all know that. But this isn't a challenge, it's suicide."

"We'd allow you to do that, if that's what you choose. Not having grown up here, you're not emotionally attached to this world, not really. But what about earth? As soon as the Lorkon realize Jacob can Time-See, they'll be doubling their efforts to get their hands on him. They want him! They want the other key—the Key of Ayunli. And I promise you, they will succeed. They'll find Jacob, enslave him, and eventually destroy your world as they are trying to do here."

Matt's shoulders slumped, and Jacob felt bad for him. Heck, he felt bad for himself. They were basically sacrificing themselves for every living person on both planets. Jacob looked at the others in the group. Aldo was the only one who didn't look devastated.

Jacob shook his head, realizing he had to say something. They couldn't leave the next day feeling like this about their mission. He took a deep breath.

"All right, everyone. We know what we're up against—at least partially. And it isn't going to be easy, but Aldo is right. It has to be done. Think about it this way—even if something terrible happens, even if we die, we did it trying. Sacrificing ourselves for innocent people, and that's not so bad, is it?" He paused, staring at the fortress. "It's a noble thing to do. I know I've got royal blood—I'm a prince. But in my eyes, you're all nobility. You've proven yourselves over and over again. You're loyal, hard-working, charitable people. I'm not saying Kelson wasn't, but Aldo is right—there are a lot of things we have that Kelson didn't. We *will* succeed."

Jacob looked each person in the eye until they nodded. Gallus held his gaze the longest—finally, the black man inclined his head.

Aldo smiled affectionately at Jacob. "Yes, you will succeed. And you won't be as alone as you think you are now. Kelson didn't have a Minya—you do. Possibly two, if Aloren brings Hazel. They aren't affected by Lorkon magic." He pointed back over the landscape. "After you've defeated the Cerpire, you'll head to the fortress. Your senses will return once you get there. Then Jacob will find a way in while the rest of you set up a door for your escape."

Aldo motioned for everyone to follow him, and they headed back. They were quiet the entire way. And no wonder, considering what lay ahead of them.

26

Jacob returned everyone to their homes, experiencing feelings of dread and despair, but also determination. He believed what he'd said earlier—they *could* do this. He just wasn't sure they would succeed on their first try.

He had strange dreams that night of blind dinosaurs trying to sell him reca flowers. When he finally woke the next morning, he had a headache and sore joints from tossing and turning. He took his time showering and dressing, then finally headed downstairs to see if he could help Mom.

She was making gravy while Dad carved the turkey, separating the white and dark meats onto two platters. Neither looked up when he entered, and they didn't respond when he asked if they wanted help. He sat on a barstool and watched instead.

Mom kept her back to him, busy at the stove. Jacob frowned when he heard sniffling noises coming from her direction.

"Mom? You okay?"

She didn't answer, but after a moment, she came over and

hugged him. He patted her arm, not sure what to say. Then she pulled away, clearing her throat.

"You'll be fine, Jacob. I can feel it."

"I hope so." He kicked himself mentally. He was supposed to be encouraging and uplifting his mom, and here he wanted comfort from her, when she was clearly suffering. She might be losing two of her children over the next few days, not to mention some very close friends.

He wrapped his arms around her tightly, not wanting to let go. He felt like a little boy again, running to his mom after falling off his bike.

Dad came over and hugged them both. Jacob enjoyed the feel of having his parents close. It didn't happen a lot, since they were all so busy. Matt came downstairs, looking for Jacob, and Mom pulled him into the embrace too.

She finally extracted herself, sniffling and laughing. "We're all such babies!"

"With good reason, honey," Dad said. He put his arm around her and she snuggled up to him.

Thanksgiving dinner was much more relaxed than Jacob had thought it would be, considering the trip he and Matt would be taking soon. Matt and Amberly teased and joked with each other, and Jacob found himself following their conversation closely, enjoying it more than he normally would.

Mom beamed at her kids. "I have one thing to say." Everyone looked at her. "I'm so very proud of our family—of our children. Jacob and Matt, you are growing into fine young men, and Amberly, you're a sweetheart—an example to all of us."

The color flowing around her face was a very light blue-green, the one for peace, and Jacob felt his mood shift to match hers. She knew the danger of the next few days, but she chose not to dwell on it, instead focusing on the love their family shared.

"Yeah, Mom, we love you and Dad too," Matt said. "Even though you never told us you were a king and a queen."

"And I'm a princess!" Amberly said, her face rosy.

She'd always said it—since she could talk. Jacob half smiled. She'd been right.

JACOB WISHED he could rewind the day and spend time with his family over and over again. That wasn't possible, though, and he before he knew it, it was time to go. He and Matt got their things together before meeting in Jacob's room.

"Matt, I'm so glad you're coming. I . . ."

Matt laughed, clapping Jacob on the shoulder. "Yeah, man, I know. You'd all die if I stayed home."

Jacob snorted, deciding not to disagree. They walked downstairs together, giving Dad, Mom, and Amberly goodbye hugs. Mom made them promise to send a Minya back with messages as often as they were able.

After Jacob could no longer stand Amberly's pleas for them to stay, or Mom's tears, he opened the connection between his home and Macaria.

Dad poked his head through the door, calling to Gallus and offering last-minute advice. "Use the Minyas! Don't touch the ground near the Argots!"

Gallus laughed. "Don't worry, Your Majesty. I've got things covered."

After one last goodbye, Jacob shut the door to his home and keyed himself, Gallus, and Matt to Taga Village, where Aloren and Sweet Pea waited.

27

G allus didn't want to spend a lot of time in Taga, so after everyone there had said goodbye, Jacob keyed Aldo to the door near the infected forest, where Aldo would oversee everything. Then he turned around and keyed the group to door number twenty-four. It was the last one he and the others had placed while scouting out the area around the fortress.

"How are we going to get across the Argots?" Matt asked after they'd closed the link behind them.

"Don't worry," Gallus said. "I've got a plan. Let's talk about it for a minute before getting started." He dug through his bag, pulling out bananas. "Is anyone hungry?"

Matt and Sweet Pea each took one, commenting on how weird it was not to be able to taste them, and Gallus continued, putting his food knapsack away and opening his utility bag. "The plan involves Minyas and Akeno and lots of other things." He held up a megaphone and a ton of rope, then motioned to Sweet Pea's bag, which was full of more rope, wood, leather straps, and nails.

"What are you going to make?" Aloren asked.

"Well, first we need to figure out where the Argots start." Gallus shaded his eyes, looking in the direction of August Fortress. "My theory is that you won't lose your eyesight until you're a good way across them already. Otherwise the trap wouldn't work. You'd just back up quickly and be out of danger."

"They won't chase us?" Jacob asked.

He shook his head. "Argots are pretty much stuck where they're planted."

"What if we run fast?"

"If what Aldo said is correct, the area they inhabit is big enough where that wouldn't be possible. And once you've lost your eyesight, you won't have any idea how much farther you've got to go. Not only that, but their backs are very rough. You'd feel like you were running through brush and big boulders, and it'd be very easy to trip and fall."

Aloren knit her eyebrows. "If we can't see anything, how are we going to know when we've made it all the way across?"

Gallus put his hand on her shoulder. "Aldo said the land they live in ends near the fortress wall. And don't worry. My plan takes all of this into account—we'll be fine."

Matt snorted. "That doesn't make me feel very safe. Plans can fail."

Gallus nodded. "True. We'll have to be extremely careful as it is. And the risks are high—very high."

Sweet Pea tossed his banana peel aside. "What do they look like?"

"Nothing you can imagine," Gallus said. "No arms or eyes or legs. Just one huge mouth—and a torso, which you wouldn't normally see." He slung his utility bag over his shoulder. "I was a member of an exploratory group several years ago—we pulled an Argot out of the ground. It was disgusting. Not pleasant. Not pleasant at all. Their innards are visible through their skin. They live underground, tightly packed together to protect their organs."

Jacob turned to look ahead. Aside from the emotions coming from the fortress, he couldn't see anything. "Are they intelligent?"

"Nope. Not at all. They live to eat and eat to live. Just like chickens."

Sweet Pea laughed. "Minus the eggs and delicious meat, though, right?"

Gallus looped his thumbs in the front pockets of his pants. "No, nothing about them is edible. The only muscles they have are used in the digestive—"

"Disgusting," Aloren said.

"—and eating process. Their mouths are incredibly large and strong."

Matt shook his head, an expression of displeasure on his face. "You know, normally I'd ask to see one . . . but I think I'll pass this time."

Gallus chuckled. "You wouldn't see it anyway—your sight will be gone."

Matt nodded.

"Any more questions?" No one responded, and Gallus grinned. "Good. Let's get going!"

He told them what to look for—smaller, oddly-colored bushes, stones that didn't really look like stones, and other such things.

The group spread apart by five feet and started forward through the forest, walking slowly, watching where they placed each step. Occasionally, they called back and forth, checking up on one another when the undergrowth got too thick to see each other.

They didn't make much progress. Jacob assumed everyone felt the way he did—terrified to be trapped by the creatures.

What would it be like to step on them? *Springy*, Gallus had said.

After around fifty feet—nearly long enough for him to have forgotten they were in danger—he noticed a bush that had leaves on it. Leaves—green, and natural-looking—but leaves nonetheless. It was November, and all the other plants had already lost their foliage.

"Got something here!" He wasn't worried about the Argots hearing, since Gallus had said the creatures didn't have ears.

"Same!" Aloren responded.

"I've also found signs of them," Gallus called. "Let's regroup."

Jacob backtracked a few feet, staying away from the edge of the creatures, and joined the others. He looked around. "Where's Matt?"

"Here! I need some help," Matt called from somewhere up ahead. "I think I might have gone too far. Oh, whoa! Something's moving under me!"

Jacob and Gallus rushed together through the brush toward the sound of Matt's voice. Gallus put his arm out and stopped Jacob from going onto the Argots when they saw Matt. He stood frozen, one foot ready to take another step, several feet past the line where the Argots started. He was just outside of grasp.

"Don't panic!" Gallus yelled to him.

Jacob figured he meant well, but how was that supposed to keep Matt from freaking out?

"And don't put your foot down. Hold still. They know you're there, but they might be waiting for you to do something."

"How do I go back?"

Gallus looked around the group. "Give me a second."

Just then, the ground around Matt rippled. Aloren screamed, catching up with Gallus and Jacob.

"I didn't do anything! I swear!" Matt shouted, struggling to hold his balance and keep his foot in the air. "Tell me what to do!"

The brush and boulders moved and huge pits appeared around him, razor-sharp teeth growing from the edges.

Jacob's jaw dropped. The teeth were growing? How was that possible? "We've gotta get him out!" He spun. "Where's Akeno?"

Akeno pushed through the group, rushing forward. He held his arm out and picked Matt up.

Matt disappeared just as one of the huge mouths closed around his leg. He reappeared with Akeno, a little smaller than his normal height. They fell into the grass, both screaming in pain.

Everyone dashed to them—Aloren got there first. She dropped to the ground next to Matt. "His leg! It's bleeding and cut all over!"

"Kaede sap!" Sweet Pea yelled, ripping off his backpack. He pulled out a package and a bowl. "Fast! Help me!"

"I need a package too!" Gallus called, pulling Akeno away from the feet rushing around Matt.

Sweet Pea handed one to Jacob, who tossed it to Gallus, then fell at Matt's side, helping separate the cloth while Aloren pulled Matt's shoe and sock off and Sweet Pea mixed the sap.

It wasn't until Jacob was putting strips of sap-saturated cloth on Matt's foot that he realized the implications of Gallus *also* needing a Kaede sap package. Had Akeno been injured too? He put the last strip on Matt, then jumped to join Gallus.

28

"What's going on?" Jacob asked.

"My arm . . ." Akeno gasped. "My chest—it hurts. Everything hurts."

Akeno's bag was open near them and Gallus was mixing a second package of Kaede sap, the first near him, ready to be used. "I don't know what happened—maybe Matt was too close? Too heavy?" He looked up at Jacob. "Go back to the door and get Ebony—she's the only one who can diagnose this."

Jacob rushed through the forest, trying to remember where the door was. He nearly ran into the tarri, but saw the door just in time, veered for it, and keyed to Kenji's house.

Ebony jumped up from the table. "What's wrong? What happened?"

"Akeno—come!"

Ebony raced through the door and followed Jacob. She fell to her knees, and her panic was replaced with urgency and determination. No wonder she was good at this sort of thing. She poked and prodded at Akeno through his shirt, checking his skin first, then the bones.

"Several broken ribs, a broken collarbone, shoulder, and his arm bones," she said. "There are probably other things broken—in his legs. Too bad he can't shrink himself to be put in a Minya container."

Akeno moaned. "Sorry, Mom . . ."

She brushed his hair off his forehead, a tender expression crossing her face. "Rest, love. We'll do our best not to cause you any more pain." She turned to Jacob and Gallus. "Help me take his shirt and pants off. Jacob, tell Aloren that she might want to stay away since he'll be nearly naked."

Jacob relayed the message to Aloren, then he, Gallus, and Ebony quickly removed Akeno's outerwear. Jacob couldn't help but notice that Akeno was wearing Batman boxers. He did his best to put that fact out of his mind, helping Ebony mix three more packages of Kaede sap.

They got to work covering his entire body with the strips, being careful to put them under him as well. It took ten minutes, at least, and they used five Kaede sap packages—everything Sweet Pea had in his knapsack.

When they finished, Ebony got to her feet and helped Gallus spread a blanket over her son. "He'll be fine now." She wiped moisture off her face. "What happened?"

Gallus explained, and Jacob looked at the Argots. They were back to bushes and boulders, as if nothing had taken place.

Ebony shook her head. "This is why we've always warned Makalos about shrinking big things, and then enlarging them again. Akeno hasn't had a problem with it for a while—he must've been completely panicked."

Jacob tilted his head. "He was panicked when Aloren and I fell into the mud bubbles, and he didn't get injured *that* time."

She tucked a strand of hair behind her ear. "Makalos have to be completely in control of their emotions—they struggle with it at first, and most struggle their entire lives." She looked at her son. "But he doesn't normally have those problems."

Jacob looked at Akeno as well. He didn't know the Makalo could even make a mistake in that area. "Why did his bones break?"

"Akeno's arm and body couldn't hold your brother's weight. But the magic is stronger than bones—Matt would've come to him, regardless." She walked to Jacob's brother. "How *is* Matt?"

"Asleep," Aloren said.

"Good. He'll need the rest." She lifted a piece of cloth to inspect his ankle. "How bad was his leg?"

"Not terrible—just a few cuts from the teeth."

Sweet Pea joined them. "Did you see how the Argots' fangs grew when their mouths opened?"

Gallus nodded. "The teeth are kept inside the jaws until they're needed, and then they extend like cat claws. They can be several feet long, depending on the age of the Argot."

Jacob shook his head. "We barely got Matt out in time."

"He wouldn't have lasted another few seconds. Oh, and another thing about these creatures is that they share their meals—what one of them eats gets spread through them all."

"Okay, I've learned enough about them," Aloren said.

Sweet Pea laughed and started to say something, but Ebony glared at him. His mouth slammed shut.

"I don't know, Gallus," Ebony said, turning to the black man. "Should I come along?"

They'd gone over this a lot during the last meeting. Ebony had opted to stay home since Echo, her baby, still needed her. But she was the only one who really knew medical things inside and out.

Gallus blew out a breath. "It's up to you. However, as we'd already said, we won't be able to see or feel or hear anything. We won't know if we're injured, and neither will you—you won't be able to help us." He put his hand on her shoulder. "You can come, or we can stick to the original plan."

She sighed. "We shouldn't change course now. I . . . I just hate feeling helpless."

"I know it sounds abrupt, but you'll be helpless anyway. How about you stay until we're ready to cross? Make sure Akeno really is okay?"

She nodded. "I'd feel much better about that."

"Okay, good." Gallus motioned to Matt and Akeno. "How long until they wake?"

Ebony shook her head. "An hour for Matt, possibly several hours for Akeno. It depends on how much damage there is. Luckily, Akeno is a Makalo and will heal much, much faster than a human would. Kaede sap works best on Makalos."

Gallus sighed. "Okay, let's get to work while waiting." He separated everyone into groups, leaving Ebony to watch over the injured people. Gallus and Aloren went one direction, and Jacob and Sweet Pea the other. Gallus had them work on clearing a long strip of land that ran parallel to where the Argots lived.

Clearing the underbrush wasn't easy. Jacob and Sweet Pea talked while they worked, using machetes Gallus had given them from his duffel bag.

Jacob and Sweet Pea first talked about school, then basketball, movies, and music. Jacob's machete got dull, and he was tempted to pull out his sword to chop with instead. He knew better than to use it on weeds, however. Having it in its scabbard, by his side, was oddly comforting. He wasn't used to fighting with it, but at least he felt like he could seriously injure . . . a defenseless evil creature. He smiled. He still needed a lot of practice.

After nearly an hour, Gallus called everyone over for a rest. Jacob was happy to see that Matt was waking up, and that he felt well enough to get to work. Gallus soon ended the break.

Jacob teased Matt about being shorter than him. "You're the little guy now!"

Matt rolled his eyes, snorting. "My muscles still work fine, and it's only by a few inches. I could still beat you at football."

Jacob grinned at his brother, then got back to work.

After another thirty minutes, Gallus declared everything good and had them all return to where Akeno slept.

"Now what?" Jacob asked.

"We wait until Akeno wakes. There isn't anything else we can do until he's better."

"It shouldn't be much longer," Ebony said. "Assuming he didn't have internal injuries, that is."

The group settled themselves in for a long wait. Three hours later, when the sun was ready to set, Akeno woke up. Ebony checked him out, declared him healthy, then had him get dressed and eat.

When he was finished, he jumped to his feet. "All right, I'm ready to put Matt back to his normal size."

Gallus held his hand up. "Don't—let's figure out the next step first. You're going to need to shrink someone. Preferably one of the stronger guys who can tie knots."

"Me!" Sweet Pea and Matt said at the same time.

Gallus looked at them. "Matt. You're taller than Sweet Pea."

Sweet Pea scowled. "What does that have to do with anything?"

"Because he's taller, he'll ultimately be bigger than you."

Matt laughed at Sweet Pea's disappointment. "Maybe next time, dude."

Gallus addressed Akeno. "Shrink Matt, then enlarge him on top of the wall." He pointed to the stone wall dividing the forest from the city. It wasn't very close—perhaps a hundred feet away. Parts of it were crumbling, but it was in good shape otherwise. A large arch was flanked by ornately embellished lamp posts with old, ragged flags attached to them. The flags were really big, deep red, and had a design on them that looked like a trident spear with a sun on it.

Akeno's mouth popped open. "He'll be huge if I do that—like, really, *really* huge."

"Exactly," Gallus said. "And make sure you put him nearer to the entrance, by the lamp posts."

A panicked expression crossed Akeno's face. "But enlarging him that big might cause damage—it could kill him."

Ebony put her hand on Akeno's shoulder. "We'll make sure you're able to concentrate."

"It has to be done," Gallus said. "Otherwise we won't make it across the Argots."

Uncertainty remained on Akeno's face. "You're sure?"

Gallus nodded. "We need him on the other side to tie ropes to support the plank. Take a few deep breaths, then go when you're ready."

Akeno hesitated, then finally turned to Matt. "All right. Walk over there." He pointed to the place Sweet Pea and Jacob had cleared. "It might hurt a little when I pick you up. It's hard for me to tell if I'm holding too tightly."

Matt ran to where Akeno had pointed and turned, a huge smile on his face.

"For Narnia!" he yelled, fist in the air.

Jacob snorted—his brother was so ridiculous.

Akeno reached out and Matt disappeared, reappearing in the Makalo's palm. "Did I hurt you?"

"Not at all! Wow! You guys are *huge*!"

"Matt—listen closely," Gallus said.

Matt stopped grinning and straightened. "Listening."

"Akeno is going to put you on the wall. Don't squirm or step backward—it would be disastrous if you fell off."

"Okay."

"You won't be able to see anything, but you'll still have your hearing, which is why I brought this." Gallus pulled the megaphone from his bag. "I'll be calling instructions to you, and we'll have Early come back to help if it doesn't work."

Jacob scanned the air—he hadn't seen the Minya in a while. She was probably exploring.

Gallus motioned for Akeno to proceed. "Remember—next to the pole."

Akeno nodded, reached out, and gently released Matt. Matt disappeared, reappearing on the wall. He nearly lost his footing and swung his arms out, yelling. His left hand struck the lamp post, though, and he grabbed it, steadying himself.

"I can't see anything!"

Using the megaphone, Gallus called to Matt, "Get comfortable—sit down, if you can. This next part will take some time."

Matt nodded and Gallus turned to Akeno, handing him a long, very thin piece of wood with a small claw attached at the top. There were little metal loops drilled into the wood on both ends, each with leather straps tied through them.

"Keeping the claw facing down and away from you, enlarge the board, making it as long as you can—at least a foot wide, preferably more. If my measurements are correct, once it's that big, it should be long enough to go from here to the wall."

Akeno walked to one end of the clearing, and Gallus had everyone step back so they wouldn't get hit when the wood fell. The Makalo reached out, squinting an eye shut. He released the board, and it appeared in front of the group, filling the entire length of the clearing.

"Now then," Gallus said. "The hard part."

29

"We have to swing the end with the claw to Matt and get the claw to hook on to the other side of the wall so it's lying on top of the stone. If it's close enough to the lamp post, Matt will be able to tie it in place."

Aloren looked at Gallus with doubt. "How are we going to do that?"

The black man pulled out ropes and pulleys. "With these, and all of us helping." He gave a pulley and some of the rope to Sweet Pea. "Tie this to the board and climb that tree," he pointed to a very tall maple, "then hook the pulley over the largest, highest branch you can find and thread the rope through."

"Why didn't we just have Akeno send a door over with Matt?" Aloren asked.

"I'd thought of doing that originally," Gallus said, "but opening and closing the door on top of a wall would have been dangerous—there's nothing to secure it to there."

After Aloren showed she understood, Gallus motioned for Sweet Pea to proceed.

Sweet Pea scampered up the tree. When he got down,

Gallus had him tie another rope to the board and climb up a tree on the other side, doing the same thing.

Gallus had Ebony and Aloren stand at the foot of the board to steady it, and he pulled on one of the ropes while Jacob and Sweet Pea took the other. They practiced for a while, trying to figure out who had to pull the hardest and at what time. It got tangled in branches, and the group slowly maneuvered it just right to get it untangled. Luckily, the foliage where the Argots lived was short and stubby.

Gallus called to Matt to be ready as the board neared him. Matt reached out, feeling blindly, and grabbed the board, pulling it toward himself, then hooked the claw in place so the board went all the way across the wall. He tied the leather straps to the lamp post.

Everyone cheered when he called out, saying he was done. They now had a plank of wood that completely crossed the Argots.

A businesslike expression crossed Gallus's face and he addressed the group. "One last thing. Remember, we'll be losing our sight halfway across. We need a rope to hold on to." He turned to Aloren. "I'm sorry, dear, but you're the most nimble."

Ebony cleared her throat. "Actually, Gallus, it would be better if I went—I'm smaller, and it'll be easier for me."

Gallus nodded. "Oh, yes, of course. I hadn't thought of having you here to help."

He tied one end of another rope about six feet up a tree, then handed the rest to Ebony. "Take this across and have Matt tie it to the pole as high as he can."

Ebony wrapped the rope several times around her arm, then started across the board. Like when he'd first seen her fighting, Jacob was surprised at how quickly and gracefully she moved—like a dancer.

About halfway, she paused, her legs wobbling. "Whoa. My eyesight just left."

"Hold on to the board and use it to guide you," Gallus called.

Ebony lowered herself, then crawled forward. Everyone waited, watching. Finally, she made it to the wall. Matt helped her to her feet and took the rope from her, tying it well above her head. With Gallus guiding him, he tightened it so it would be firm enough to provide support, but loose enough for everyone to hold on to at the same time.

Then Gallus had Ebony untie the ropes Sweet Pea had attached to the board for the pulleys. When she finished, Akeno picked her up, momentarily shrinking her before enlarging her on this side of the Argots. She returned, giving the ropes to Gallus while Akeno put Matt back to his normal size.

"Let's eat, then set up a door near here," Gallus said.

The group sank to the ground, eager for a break. Jacob wished he could taste the beef jerky, fruits, and veggies, but his stomach loved the food, and after a moment, he felt mostly satisfied.

Ten minutes later, Gallus got to his feet and had Akeno enlarge a door. Matt and Jacob put it in place.

"Time for us to cross." Gallus held up the rope. "But we need to tie ourselves together first."

"You've only got probably half an hour left until it's dark," Ebony said, motioning to the setting sun.

Matt laughed. "We'll be blind anyway, so it doesn't even matter."

Ebony chuckled. "Good point."

"We'll set up camp just inside the arch," Gallus said, making sure everyone tied their knots securely. "Hopefully we'll find a spot before we lose the sensation of touch." He turned to Ebony. "Jacob will need to take you back now rather than later."

Ebony nodded. She turned to her son, holding him close for several moments, then gave everyone else hugs and last-minute advice, including not to die or get hurt. Jacob opened the door to Taga, let her step through, then shut it.

Gallus lined everyone up—Jacob first, then Akeno, Aloren, Matt, Sweet Pea, and finally himself. He had Early let Aldo know they were about to start across the Argots.

Jacob could just picture the old man—he'd probably keep his face glued to the telescope the entire time the group was on the board. Even though Aldo couldn't do anything to help, just knowing he was watching brought Jacob a sense of calm.

Gallus looked Jacob in the eye, blue—the color for peace—swirling in the air around him. "It's up to you now. You and Akeno are the only ones who'll be able to help us, and I've got a feeling you'll be better at this next part than I will. Maybe one of your gifts will surprise us."

Jacob took a deep breath. He hated having pressure placed on him like that, but he agreed with Gallus. He was still adjusting to the fact that he could do things other people couldn't.

He faced the fortress, squinting against the bright emotions emanating through the stone walls, concentrating on picking out individual sources. He raised an eyebrow when he noticed something.

"One of the Shiengol's emotions is brighter than the rest."

Gallus shrugged. "Wouldn't surprise me."

Jacob turned to him. "What do you mean?"

"I can't tell you without causing offense."

"To whom? The Shiengols?"

"This particular Shiengol, yes."

Jacob found himself wishing he were on a different mission. "Great. We're about to rescue temperamental, powerful beings with lots of emotional baggage. Just what we need."

He looked up in shock when the emotions of the brightest Shiengol flashed from anticipation to annoyance. Whoa. Had it heard him? How was that possible? He hesitated, watching. When nothing happened, he turned to Gallus. "Are we ready?"

Gallus nodded. "Yes."

30

J acob put his foot on the plank and looked up to find the rope. It was level with his head, which would make things more difficult. It was at that height for a reason, of course. Sweet Pea and Akeno wouldn't be able to reach it if it was higher.

His hands were still sore from using the machete. He should've taken the time to fix them with Kaede sap. No chance to do that now.

Jacob walked slowly, looking back occasionally to check on the progress of those behind him. The emotions emanating from them were surprising. Everything from nervousness to fear to excitement and even slight boredom— that one was Aloren, of course. But no, Matt's emotions showed some indifference too, along with his excitement. Why was he bored? Then Jacob smiled when he remembered all the rope courses his brother had completed over the past few years. He wasn't really afraid of these sorts of things.

He felt a tug in the rope around his waist when he was at least fifteen feet across and turned to see that Gallus was just getting on the plank. Jacob took a deep breath. The entire group was on the board now. If they fell, no one would be able to save them.

He continued onward, trying not to think about that.

A moment later, everything went black. He gasped, pausing. It was the weirdest thing ever—as if someone had turned off the sun and the lights, with no action on his part, and no residual vision. He'd never been in such complete blackness.

Jacob shuffled forward, feeling with his feet, making sure he knew what was under him before stepping.

Akeno practically freaked out when he went through the trap, and Jacob instinctively looked back to see what was wrong. He nearly stumbled in surprise at what he saw. "I can still see your emotions!"

"That's wonderful!" Gallus said.

"Yeah! I'll check on you guys every few steps."

"Good. You're about twenty feet from the wall."

Jacob nodded, knowing Gallus was watching. He counted the steps in his head, listening as the others went through the trap one at a time.

He'd nearly reached twenty when he felt a strong lurch in the rope tied around his waist, causing it to dig sharply into his stomach. His sword shifted, its weight knocking him off balance, and he lost his footing, holding onto the line above as tightly as he could while his legs swung out from under him. The board banged sharply against his shins, and his hands burned from the friction. He slid backward down the line by what felt like a couple of feet, bumping into Akeno, who cried out.

Everyone yelled in shock, and the line bounced Jacob up and down. He scrambled back onto the board, wishing he could see what he was doing.

"Quiet!" Gallus said. "Who fell off the board first?"

"I did," Sweet Pea said. "Lost my grip. I'm holding on to the board. I . . . I think I can pull myself up."

Jacob heard grunting, and the rope dug into the skin of his waist, making him wince from the pain.

"Careful, Sweet Pea," Gallus said. "I've got you."

The rope slackened and Jacob faced away from the others, toward the wall again. He held tight to the line above. "Is everyone okay?"

"Yes, we're all on the board again," Gallus said. "Keep going."

"That was really close," a little voice said near Jacob's ear, making him jump.

Jacob looked and saw a tiny spot of green—her emotion, representing happiness. "Early! Where have you been?"

"Watching and visiting Aldo—I would've come to help if you needed it."

"Okay. How far from the wall am I?"

"Close. Very close."

Jacob scooted forward, feeling the board with every step, making sure not to put his foot down without being confident he wouldn't fall off the side. How would they do stuff like this without the sensation of touch?

Then his foot found nothing. He shuffled to the side and felt solid stone. Great! "I've reached the wall!"

"Wonderful!" Gallus said.

Jacob found the lamp post and clung to it for support with one hand while helping Akeno off the board. The wall was fairly wide on top.

"Gallus, now what?"

"Um . . ."

Jacob frowned, hoping Gallus had thought this far in advance.

"I need you to climb past the pole, then drop to the ground in the middle of the archway. Aldo said the wall is about ten feet tall. Don't go into the city and don't exit—stay right in the middle of the archway. From what Aldo mentioned, we'll have around six feet of area under the arch to work with."

"Okay."

"And I'll help you!" Early said.

"Thanks, Early. You totally rock."

He felt his way around the pole, then paused. "How am I going to drop to the ground without pulling all of you with me?"

Silence. Then, "Good point. Untie yourself. The rest of us will stay together and undo ourselves one at a time. When we join you, we'll do up the knots again."

Jacob untied the rope and continued with Early guiding him.

"Just a little farther," she said. "Just a little farther. Stop. You've reached the arch."

Jacob sat on the part of the wall closest to where the stone rose, then twisted and lowered himself until he was hanging by just his hands.

"How far is the ground from my feet, Early?"

"A little less than you are tall."

Just wonderful. He pulled himself back up to talk with the others. "When you come around the pole, find the spot where the wall meets the arch—Early will help you—and lower yourself with your hands. I'll be below, trying to guide you. The drop from the wall to the ground is more than ten feet. I'll do my best to catch you. Luckily, I can still see your emotions, so I'll know where you are."

The others acknowledged that they understood, and he watched the colors of their emotions brighten, reflecting anticipation, panic, confidence, and fear. No boredom now.

Jacob took a deep breath and wiped his sweaty hands on his pants. After a moment, he lowered himself once again, took another deep breath, then let go. The wind rushed by him, tickling his ears.

The fall was over and he landed, stumbling a bit, then righted himself. He froze, waiting to see what happened. No pain! The tension he'd felt earlier dissipated—being an athlete had its perks. And he definitely still had the sensation of touch, thank goodness.

"I'm ready for you, Akeno."

Akeno's emotions showed he was about to go hysterical. "All right," he squeaked.

"If you get hurt, we have plenty of Kaede sap. You've got to calm down. It's going to be okay. "

"I'm fine."

Jacob narrowed his eyes when Akeno's colors didn't change. "Seriously, Akeno. I can see your emotions, remember? You aren't relaxing. Just breathe."

Gallus chuckled. "He's probably not going to feel better until he's on solid ground again."

Jacob agreed, and changed tactics. "Just take your time. You're light enough—I'll be able to catch you. Sack of potatoes, remember?"

Akeno laughed, a bit of yellow coloring the air around him. "Yeah, I remember." He paused. "Okay, I'm coming."

Jacob watched the emotion come closer. He was going to have to get used to this. There wasn't a real shape, and the color faded in and out—stronger in some areas than others. It was interesting to see it without Akeno's face. And it was even stranger to realize Jacob saw it without using his eyes.

While waiting, Jacob glanced in the direction where he imagined the fortress to be, and sure enough, the strong emotions were still there. He detected slight movement and figured the Shiengols were restless. He would be too, after being trapped for over sixteen years.

Jacob looked back and saw Akeno's color lowering. He wasn't sure if it was around Akeno's head or his torso at that moment, but at least it gave Jacob an idea of the Makalo's position.

He reached up on tippy toes, but didn't feel anything. "Are you hanging by your hands yet?"

"Nope. Give me a minute."

The deep yellow lowered even farther, then Akeno said, "Now I am."

Jacob reached up again, swishing his hands through the air, and finally his fingertips brushed the bottom of the Makalo's shoe.

"Whoa," Akeno said. "Was that you?"

"Yeah. I can't really reach your feet."

A pause. "I guess I'll just let myself fall, then."

"And I'll do my best to catch you."

"On the count of three. One, two—you're still down there, right?"

"Yes, Akeno."

Another hesitation, then, "Three."

The emotion rushed down to Jacob and he put his arms out, trying to keep them below Akeno.

31

With a loud *umph* and a painful kick to his face, Jacob caught the Makalo.

"Sorry! I felt that! Was it your head?"

Jacob put Akeno down, his cheek smarting. "I'm fine." He rubbed where he'd been kicked, hoping it wouldn't bruise too badly. It sure hurt! His eyes watered. He blinked several times, then shook his head to clear it and called up. "All right, Aloren, we're ready for you."

Aloren didn't hesitate before coming. That wasn't surprising—she'd had a lot more practice doing insane things.

Determination was the emotion that guided Jacob. The colors flowing around her were red and green—anger and happiness. He'd been surprised a couple of months ago to figure out that determination was closely related to anger, but a determined person would face their problems with a positive attitude.

The tinted air showed Jacob when she'd reached the edge and had lowered herself. He stretched up and felt her ankle.

A blush crossed his face, and he was very glad no one could see it. Except Early, who probably didn't care. Speaking of the Minya . . . she was most likely observing and making sure no one got hurt. Jacob hoped so, anyway. He couldn't see her emotions right then.

"Okay, I'm dropping now."

Jacob caught her smoothly, enjoying the feeling of holding her in his arms, knowing his blush was spreading. He put her down quickly, then froze when she kissed his cheek.

"Thanks," she whispered. The red in the air around her dissipated, overpowered by green. Did she like him? Had she been hiding it all that time? No—she'd also had those feelings toward Kevin. Maybe the stress of the current situation made her like Jacob more?

Her emotions showed her moving away, and he brought a hand to his face. She'd kissed the same cheek Akeno had kicked. He sighed, then realized Matt was trying to talk to him.

"Hello? Are you ready for me?"

"Huh? Oh, yeah. I am."

Matt's typical emotions of excitement and happiness marked his progress, and Jacob guided him without a problem. Matt didn't want to be caught when he dropped, and Jacob was grateful for that. His brother was heavy.

When Sweet Pea's turn came up, Jacob had everyone lock hands, forming a sort of trampoline where Sweet Pea could land. It worked perfectly. They put him down and moved back when Gallus said he didn't need any help. Jacob breathed a sigh of relief. There was no way he and the others would be able to support the man's weight. He was much taller than anyone there.

Jacob watched Gallus's emotions descend as the man lowered himself. When he dropped, he stumbled, and Jacob reached out to steady him. His hands swept through empty air. The swish of cloth and a thud, followed by a sharp smacking sound, let Jacob know Gallus had fallen. The black man cried out in pain.

"What happened?" Akeno asked.

Gallus only gasped in response.

"Everyone stay where you are." Jacob got to his hands and knees and carefully approached Gallus's colors. "Gallus fell. I'll inspect him—we don't want anyone to stand on him accidentally."

Gallus moaned. It looked like he was trying to get to his feet.

"Don't move."

Gallus stopped and Jacob found the man's foot, glad the man wasn't thrashing. "I need Kaede sap," he called over his shoulder.

"I'll get it!" Akeno said.

Jacob turned his attention back to Gallus, feeling around until he located the man's shoulder. "Gallus? Are you okay?"

Gallus gasped. "My knee . . . my knee . . ."

"Ouch. We'll take care of you." Jacob turned. "Akeno? The package?"

Akeno's voice sounded very small. "Um . . . my bag's open and mostly empty—no sap. I . . . I think it fell out while we were crossing the Argots."

Jacob growled in frustration. "Anyone else have some? Check your bags, even if you don't think you do."

He was glad Mom and Ebony had packed the bags for the group. They'd come up with the idea to separate everything into different categories, using cloth for the food, paper packaging for the Kaede sap, plastic for hygienic items. Of course, this would only work before the trap that removed the sensation of touch.

"I *had* a ton of it," Sweet Pea said. "But we used it all on Matt and Akeno."

The others reported they didn't have any sap either. Gallus

groaned, then gasped out a couple of words. "Pain" and "hurry."

"How is it possible that Sweet Pea and Akeno were the only ones carrying it?" Jacob asked. He bit his lip, frustrated. They couldn't continue without Gallus, and they couldn't leave him here like this. That left only one other option. Jacob had to get more sap. "Aloren? Where are you?"

One of the emotions stepped forward. "Here."

"Come watch over Gallus and make sure he's comfortable. I'm going to Taga Village."

Aloren gasped. "You can't go back!" she said. "What happens if you fall? The key will be lost, you'll die, and we'll be stuck here forever."

Jacob shook his head, not wanting to answer.

"I'll go," Akeno said. "It's my fault we lost the sap."

"Let's both go," Jacob said. Two would be better than one. "Okay, let's get going."

"Jacob," Aloren started.

Jacob glowered. "What else can we do? What are our other options? Leave him, and continue onward? Stay here, hoping someone comes and finds us? There's nothing else." He hated talking to her like that, but she was usually tougher than this.

"This is insane."

"Yeah, I know. But I have to do something."

"What about setting up a door here and going back that way?"

Jacob did his best not to sound exasperated. "Because Akeno can't see to enlarge anything, and even if he could, there isn't enough space under the arch to make the door big enough."

"Go, Jacob," Gallus gasped. "I'll be fine . . . while you're gone."

Jacob turned to scan the skies before remembering he couldn't see anything. "Early? Are you there?"

A spot of green flitted near him. "Here, Jacob!"

"Tell Aldo that Akeno and I are heading back, then please stick very close to me in case anything happens."

Early agreed, and Jacob put his hand on Aloren's arm before getting to his feet. "We'll be careful, I promise. We'll come back."

She released a long breath of air. "Okay."

Careful not to bump into Gallus, Jacob scooted a couple of feet away—clearing himself from the man's legs—then got up. He unbuckled his sword, laying it down against the wall of the arch. He didn't want it to knock him off balance while crossing the board.

"Early, would you be able to give us a boost? Like you did while I was fighting the Ember Gods? I don't know if it would help or not to weigh less while climbing the wall, but it could be good."

She didn't answer for a moment, then, "This is different—I don't know if I can do it."

Akeno's voice sounded close to Jacob. "She would have to exert a lot more energy to keep us moving in the same direction," he said. "Gravity doesn't affect her, but it affects us. And her energy boost might shoot us off into Argot territory."

"But when I was fighting the Ember—"

"That was different. You were on your feet, and could somewhat control where you went. Honestly, I'd rather she didn't help us."

Jacob raised his eyebrows. Earlier, Akeno had been so afraid of falling, he'd taken a very long time getting off the wall, and now he was turning down assistance? "All right. I'll go first."

Early guided them back to the correct place near the arch, then Jacob climbed. The going was difficult—he had to feel around for hand and footholds without relying on sight. A moment later, however, he reached the top and turned to help Akeno.

After Akeno was up, Jacob stepped past the lamp post, then found the line and the board.

He felt like kicking himself when he realized he and Akeno hadn't tied themselves together. "Akeno, is it possible for you to latch your arm through the strap of my bag so I can keep you from falling? It'll help me know if you do fall."

"Sure."

Akeno did so and Jacob took a deep breath, holding tightly to the line above. "Here goes."

They started forward, Jacob going as quickly as was safely possible. He'd always been afraid of heights, but thankfully, this was different. He couldn't see how far they'd fall if that happened, and the dizzy attacks didn't come. He felt Akeno's movements behind him and was glad his friend held tightly to his bag.

As he moved forward, he looked at the ground instinctively, then nearly stopped in shock at something he hadn't noticed before—there were faint white lines tracing patterns through the space below them. Were his eyes playing tricks on him? Did the patterns mark where the ground was, or were they floating in the air? And what were they?

Jacob and Akeno were at least halfway when Akeno gasped, then yelled, and the line above jerked, followed immediately by weight on Jacob's backpack. The increase in weight knocked him off balance, and his hands slipped off the rope. He spun to the side, the board scraping his leg, then smacking into his rib cage as he flipped over. He tried to grab it, but Akeno's weight pulled him down farther, and he plunged, landing hard on the ground below, Akeno beneath him.

32

The air knocked from his lungs, Jacob couldn't move at all. His frantic mind only focused on one thing—the faint white lines were brighter and somehow attached to the dirt.

Early freaked out, squealing and shouting. "Get up, Jacob! Get up!"

Jacob gasped for air, finally raking in a breath and able to move again. He pulled Akeno out from under him. A deep rumble below made him freeze. "Oh, no!" There was no way they could escape!

"*Get up!*" Early shrieked, the colors swirling around her showing hysteria.

Jacob felt a spot on his shoulder heat up—Early was giving him energy! His mind cleared and he remembered something very important. The Argots hadn't done anything for several moments when Matt had started crossing them. Did they always take so long to react? And would it be enough for Jacob and Akeno to get to safety? It had to be! He held on to this hope as tightly as he could and grabbed Akeno, throwing the Makalo over his shoulder, then lurched to his feet.

"I'll guide you!" Early squealed. "I can see them!"

Jacob dashed forward, realizing he would probably trip over rocks and bushes, but he wouldn't allow himself to be devoured by monsters. It would be so much easier if he could see their emotions.

Early's directions came fast. "Side-step to the left! Jump forward! Go back a foot! Side-step right! *Run*! *Fast*! Left! Back again!"

Jacob felt a pinch on his pant leg. He jerked free.

A moment later, sight returned. The light from the moon nearly blinded him and he shaded his eyes with his free hand. The edge of the Argots wasn't far, but Early led him away from it.

"Early! The forest is right there!"

"Ignore it! Obey me!"

He took a deep breath and continued running, following her directions. She'd kept them alive this long and deserved his trust.

Akeno screamed, but Jacob didn't risk looking back, preparing instead to follow his instincts and jump to safety in a spot between some pink shrubbery and yellow boulders.

"No, Jacob! It's dangerous there! This way!"

Irritation flooded over him and he growled in frustration, but he continued following her anyway. After a moment, he saw the wisdom in Early's choice. Several jaws opened in the crevice he'd been running toward, and it quickly became apparent that the Argots exploited the self-preservation instincts of their prey.

Then something else dawned on Jacob as he paid closer attention to Early's directions. Yes, she took him much farther from the edge of the forest than was comfortable, but she wasn't choosing the path arbitrarily. She was having him follow the brightest of the faint white lines. And as he watched, he quickly figured out they marked where each Argot started and ended, like boundary lines.

Panting in exhaustion, he said, "Brilliant!" He smiled in excitement. "I see! I see where you're leading us!"

"Good!" Early cried. "Keep running."

A new burst of energy slammed into Jacob and he dashed forward, following the biggest of the lines, no longer needing Early's directions.

"I'm going to warn the Makalos!" she said after making sure Jacob was really going the right way. She disappeared with a flash.

"No! Early!" Akeno screamed. "We need her!"

"It's fine! I can see where to run!" Jacob dodged some rocks, then jumped around a little tree.

"How?"

"The lines!"

"What lines?"

"Never mind." Jacob focused on running and skirting obstacles.

The line led him along a haphazard path—taking him in a ridiculous course around bushes and brambles and rocks. The springy ground under his feet continued rumbling and shifting, and except for a couple of times when his pant legs got snagged, he remained clear of the sharp teeth.

Finally, they reached the edge of the forest, and he stumbled to the ground when his feet met solid earth once more. He released Akeno, gasping, trying to catch his breath.

"Jacob? Jacob!" Aloren's voice called through the megaphone.

Jacob got to his feet and yelled back as loudly as he could, "We're fine! We made it! We made it!"

He heard faint cheering and grinned. He'd done it!

Early reappeared, reminding Jacob that they still had a mission to accomplish. "They're waiting!"

"Let's go! And help us find the door."

"Yes! Yes!"

The two boys took off at a run, following Early through the forest.

They reached the door and Jacob keyed them to Taga Village, where the Makalos waited anxiously on the other side.

The increase of sensation nearly knocked Jacob over. The smell of roast beef and potatoes assailed him, and his mouth instantly watered. The light burned his eyes and he covered his face. Ebony shoved Kaede sap packages into their bags, which, thankfully, hadn't gotten lost when the boys fell.

"You're ready," Ebony said a moment later. "Did you set up a door near the arch?"

"No," Jacob said. "Akeno can't see, so he wouldn't be able to enlarge anything."

Ebony nodded, then turned to Akeno. "Do you still have your potted plant?"

He shook his head. "I think I lost it when we fell off the board."

"I'll get him another one," Kenji said, stepping into the back room. A moment later he returned, holding a bright blue pot with a scraggly plant in it, around four inches tall.

"Are you sure that's going to make it through the entire trip?" Jacob asked. "It looks like it's about to die."

Ebony chuckled. "It'll be fine. It's a type of evergreen—though it doesn't look it. They're hardy little things." She put it in Akeno's bag.

Jacob nodded, swinging the backpack over his shoulders. "We'll send Early later when we've finished working on Gallus."

They said goodbye, then keyed back to the door and crossed the board with no problems. They dropped to the ground under the arch and Jacob pulled a package out of his backpack, giving it to Akeno to put together.

Jacob got to his knees. "Can we use Gallus's pant leg instead of the cloth in the package?"

"No," Akeno said. "It has to be completely clean."

"Well, we can't afford to cut his pants." Jacob carefully inched up to Gallus, making sure not to bump the man. "It's too cold for him to walk around in shorts. And it'll be too painful to take them off."

"Let's roll up his pant leg as far as it'll go," Aloren said. "Then reach up the rest of the way."

Jacob agreed, and he and Aloren soaked the cloth strips in the mixture while Akeno and Matt readied Gallus. It was oddly comforting, being this near the people he cared for most. His hand brushed against Aloren's several times and he thought over the kiss she'd given him on the cheek earlier. He sighed inwardly—she'd obviously done it as a way to say thanks and nothing more. She wasn't the type of person to cheat, and he knew she really cared for Kevin.

Jacob turned his thoughts back to the task at hand, finding it required more concentration when he couldn't see what he was doing.

Within a couple of minutes, Gallus's knee was covered, and the man's moans had stopped.

"Thanks, Jacob," Gallus murmured.

"We need to get you to shelter. It's too cold for us to be out in the open."

"Tent. In my bag."

Jacob pulled the bag out from under Gallus and rummaged through it, trying to figure out what everything was. "Gallus, I don't know—"

Someone took the bag from him. Either Aloren or Akeno —he couldn't tell.

"Here," Aloren said.

Something heavy was placed in Jacob's hands. "Push this button when you're ready to open the tent."

Gallus sighed. "It's large—you'll need space." He took a deep breath. "Put it closer to the fortress than to the Argots."

Jacob got to his feet and helped everyone move to the other side of Gallus. After they were safely out of the way, Jacob put the folded fabric on the ground, making sure the opening was nearest him. He pushed the button and jumped back.

A *whoosh* rushed through the air, followed by several clicks and the sounds of cloth being tightened quickly. When everything was quiet again, Jacob stepped forward and found the door of the tent.

"Okay. Aloren, you first. We'll give you the far corner."

He grabbed her hand, leading her around Gallus, then helped her into the tent. Good—her emotions were visible through the thick material. This meant that others' emotions would also be visible through the tent, which would come in handy in case they had visitors during the night. Jacob shuddered at the thought.

"Matt, Sweet Pea, Akeno—I'll need all of you to help me pull Gallus inside." He guided them to Gallus's shoulders and feet, then on the count of three, they half lifted, half dragged the nearly unconscious man into the tent.

After she was finished delivering messages, Early said she'd spend the night at the foot of Jacob's sleeping bag, which was fine with him. He found his sword, pulled it into the tent with him, then closed the flap.

"Aldo said we wouldn't be bothered by animals, right?" he asked.

Early didn't respond, and Gallus only sighed. Jacob didn't press either of them. They both needed sleep after the busy day.

33

Sometime in the middle of the night, or what Jacob assumed to be the middle of the night, he was awakened by something shuffling outside the tent.

He bolted upright in his sleeping bag and grabbed the tent zipper, holding it down.

The shuffling stopped. Jacob couldn't see any emotions through the fabric, so whatever it was must not have been intelligent. He didn't know if this made him feel better or worse.

A moment later, the shuffling started up again and gradually got quieter until it disappeared.

Jacob waited several minutes longer, still holding the zipper. No one else had been disturbed by the sound, so why had it awakened him? He finally snuggled back into his sleeping bag, completely exhausted, but so wired he doubted he'd be able to fall asleep.

Sure enough, after what seemed like an hour of trying, he gave up. He decided to use the opportunity to practice Time-Seeing into August Township. Maybe his ability would allow him to see through the Lorkon traps.

He'd found a while ago that it worked best when he unfocused his eyes and told his body where to go and when. He did that now.

At first, he couldn't see anything, so he concentrated, ignoring the chest pains that started. It seemed like he was standing near a tall wall, but he couldn't be sure. A bit of light appeared to the side of him. He focused on that—it looked like the sun was rising. Excited, he turned back to the city, eager for the light to brighten the mass in front of him. But everything was so smudged and unnaturally hazy, he couldn't make out any shapes. Nothing at all. He wasn't even sure if the mess of rock and wall in front of him was part of the actual city. He frowned, perplexed. Had the Lorkon figured out his ability? Did they do something to make him unable to Time-See? Or were the traps powerful enough that he couldn't pierce them?

The pain in his chest increased until he couldn't ignore it anymore, and his body jerked him back to the present like a rubber band.

He fell asleep quickly after that.

ALOREN'S VOICE pulled Jacob out of his dreamless sleep.

"All right, everyone. *Get up*. I'm tired of waiting." A smile tainted her rushed words, and the emotions surrounding her were impatience and excitement. Jacob also thought he detected a bit of gratitude, then realized she probably didn't think they'd make it through the night. "It's morning now," she said. "Let's go."

"How can you tell it's morning?" The question came from Matt, his usual color of happiness, which green, was tinged with a slight yellow—suspicion.

"My body says it is. We need to eat and get our things together."

Matt sighed in exasperation, his green turning to a light pink. "Who died and made *you* queen?"

Jacob laughed, then jerked to a sitting position when the word "died" entered his brain. "Gallus? Are you awake?"

Gallus chuckled, probably at the panic in Jacob's voice. "I am."

"How are you feeling?"

"Much better—completely back to normal."

Jacob breathed a sigh of relief. "Oh, good."

"Yes, I'm pretty relieved myself. Thank you for what you did last night."

Jacob felt his cheeks flush and he turned to roll up his sleeping bag, nearly forgetting that Gallus couldn't see his face anyway. He smiled at himself—those habits wouldn't go away so easily.

He shoved his bag into the largest pocket of his backpack, hearing the others cleaning up as well. His thoughts turned to the upcoming traps. Loss of hearing and loss of touch. How long would the traps last, and would they be all-encompassing?

Jacob decided to voice what was on his mind. "I can't help but wonder how much losing our sense of touch will affect us. I mean, the more I think about it, the more I realize I depend a lot on what I can feel. I know I'm kneeling now because my shins feel the ground beneath me, and the skin on the back of my knees is pinched. I know what my hands and arms are doing—also thanks to the sense of touch."

Silence for a moment. The colors swirling around the others changed to an orange-yellow for concern, and for a moment, Jacob felt bad for having brought up something that would potentially worry or depress them. But he recognized it was important to consider these things.

Gallus let out a long breath. "Yes, I've been pondering similar points." His color moved to the tent door, and Jacob backed away. "And I don't have an answer. The best we can do is be ready for anything. We'll have to figure things out as they come." He paused. "Luckily, the sense of hearing will be last to go. We'll be able to communicate even after we've lost the sensation of touch."

"And we're sure there won't be any creatures or animals out there? Aside from the Cerpire?" Jacob wondered if he should mention what he'd heard last night. He decided not to—either they'd get attacked or they wouldn't. Being paranoid would only make things much, much more difficult.

"Not entirely. We're going off what Aldo said, of course. He doesn't think big creatures would be able to cross the Argots. Small creatures are rarely dangerous."

"And do the Argots surround the city?"

"Probably not. The fortress is right up against the mountains. The volcano eruption from a hundred years ago made the land impassible. The Shiengols never had animal problems before. I assume it's still the same."

Jacob thought over this for a moment. "I've noticed something. The inhabitants of this world like to have only one point of entry for their castles. Even Macaria Castle is up against the lake."

"Your world is the same," Gallus said. His voice was muffled because he'd just stepped outside the tent. "Moats and walls and mountains and lakes. It's a defensive tactic."

Jacob nodded, then realized Gallus couldn't see it, and laughed at himself. Of course, this made the others ask why he was laughing, so he told them what he'd done. "It's frustrating, not being able to see."

"I'm almost used to it," Matt said, "but I can't wait to get my taste back. I'm starving, and the food I've eaten isn't doing anything for me. It's like eating cardboard!" He paused. "I think."

"Speaking of food," Gallus said, "come out of the tent so I can pack it away. When I'm done, I want each of you to eat as much as you can handle. When we next get hungry, we probably won't be able to feel our teeth and tongues, which could be quite dangerous. You never know if you're biting your tongue off or not."

Jacob and the others filed out, and Gallus somehow packed the tent up without seeing what he was doing. They sat in a circle and Gallus had Jacob divvy up the food, since he knew where everyone was sitting.

"I wish I had a Braille watch," Matt said. "Oh, and I wish I could read Braille."

Sweet Pea laughed at him, but Jacob could see his brother's point. It sure would've made things more convenient.

"So, what's the plan?" Akeno asked.

Gallus's deep voice reverberated in the small space between the walls. "Akeno, make sure you keep your plant in your hands at all times. And we'll need to be attached to each other again—in a row, with Jacob in the lead. Jacob, you remember the footstep sequence for how to get to the fortress, right?"

Jacob ran through it in his mind. "Yes, I do."

"Good." Gallus's emotion colors rose, showing he'd gotten to his feet. "Let's get going."

As soon as everyone else was ready, Jacob put them in the same order as before, then he and Gallus tied them all together.

"Whatever happens," Gallus said, "Keep moving and keep talking, if you can."

Jacob agreed. How they would make it out of this, he didn't know. He raised his face to search for their Minya, again out of habit. "Early? Are you there?"

A flicker of green—the color for happiness—flitted next to him. "Yup!"

"Does Aldo have any last-minute instructions?"

"Let me check." A minute passed, then her tiny voice returned. "He hasn't seen the Cerpire for a long time, but doesn't think that means it's not here anymore. He also says you've done very well so far, and he'll be giving me orders every now and then to help, but that you probably won't know it once you're in all the traps."

Jacob nodded. "Okay, well, stay close. I might need you and Aldo to help me find the way if I get disoriented. Remember this: straight for thirty, turn right then walk seven, right and fifteen, left and twenty-seven, left and one hundred thirty."

"Will do!"

Warmth radiated through him at the tone in her voice. She was a great messenger. "Is everyone ready?" he asked.

A chorus of yeses surrounded him and he faced forward, glad he had a good internal sense of direction. "Oh, and Akeno—are there any living creatures out there?"

No response for a moment, then, "Nope. Just the Argots. The area in front of us is empty of anything living."

"Okay, then. Let's go. Straight for thirty."

Jacob started forward, making sure he took normal-sized steps.

At five feet, the next trap made its presence known.

34

Jacob stopped. He couldn't feel the ground beneath his feet. He couldn't feel himself swallowing. He couldn't feel the rope around him any longer, and it was almost as if he were naked because he couldn't feel his clothes. It was like he'd spent the day at the dentist's, and that numb sensation had enveloped him completely.

He could, however, sense his movement. He lifted his hand, and knew his arm was rising. He could tell which way was up, and that he was standing. His body still knew its directions.

"Just entered the next trap," he said.

"How is it?" Gallus asked.

"I can't feel anything. But I know I'm standing, and I know when I'm moving."

"Excellent." There was a pause. "Can you sense the rope?"

"No. Or my clothes."

Matt snickered.

"Wait until you're here," Jacob said. "You won't be laughing anymore."

"Yeah, I'm sure. But it's funny. What if you *aren't* dressed anymore?"

Jacob snorted in response, but an insane desire to back up and check nearly overwhelmed him. He didn't want to lose his place, though. "Going forward. Each of you say something when you enter the trap."

Jacob continued, counting out loud. His legs knew how far to go—at least, he trusted they did. "Six. Seven. Eight."

After Akeno had gone through the trap, Jacob asked him to check again if there was anything living around them.

Akeno didn't respond for a moment, then he said, "Oh, weird. It's hard to find the plant when I can't feel it. I know I'm touching it by the visions that enter my mind. And no—there's still nothing."

Jacob breathed in relief. "Good." He continued walking forward.

One at a time, the rest of the group announced when they'd entered the trap. By the sound of the others' voices, they were keeping up with Jacob just fine.

"Coming to the first turn," he said. "We're going right. The rest of you count your steps so you know when to turn."

Jacob didn't pause, trusting the others to follow his instructions. He kept an eye on the Shiengols' emotions, making sure they were in sight as much as possible. They helped him know where he was in relation to the fortress. He announced the next turn, then followed it.

So far, so good.

Forward fifteen feet. Jacob wasn't able to move any longer. He turned, putting a mental bookmark in his place in the footstep sequence. "I've stopped."

"Me too," Matt responded.

"Is it because of me?" Gallus asked, his voice sounding muffled. "It feels like it might be me."

"Aldo says Gallus is stuck behind a broken door," Early said, her green emotions floating near Jacob's head.

Jacob nodded. "Gallus? Did you hear that?"

"Yes. Early, can you guide me?"

"Yep!" Early said. "Step to the right. One more step. There."

Jacob noticed that Gallus's colors got brighter, probably because the door had partially blocked them from view.

"Everyone ready?" he asked. "Gallus, you should be able to continue." Jacob faced forward again, glad when he felt himself moving. "Okay, we're turning left now. Follow me, same as before. One, two . . ."

He kept track of the numbers as closely as he could, concentrating on their shapes in his mind—picturing them—and giving them colors just to help make them different from each other.

"Wait," Early said. "Gallus—you're off track again."

"Oops. I apologize."

Early guided the man back in line with the rest, and Jacob smiled at her emotion. "Thanks, Early." He resumed walking. "Twenty-one, twenty-two, twenty-three—"

He paused when the emotions of the Shiengols appeared to his left, much brighter than before. His heartbeat doubled before he remembered it was them. He hadn't noticed their colors disappear. It must have been very gradual, because their abrupt reappearance freaked him out.

He took a deep breath. "We're coming up to our last turn. And the path leads directly to the fortress—the emotions of the Shiengols are especially strong right now."

"That's excellent," Gallus said.

Jacob got to the corner, then paused. "Early, does Aldo have any last-minute advice? Pretty soon, we won't be able to hear anything, so he should give it now."

No response. Then, "He says you're doing fine and that

he'll have me help you with a boost of magic if you need one. Your families all send their love."

Jacob nodded. "Thanks. Akeno, would you check the area?"

"Yes." The Makalo didn't say anything for a moment. Then, "Jacob? I can sense the Cerpire. Not to scare you or anything, but it's . . ." His voice cracked. "It's really, really, *really* big."

The others in the group moaned in dismay, and Jacob looked back. He wasn't surprised at the fear and panic flowing in the air behind him. He nearly gave in to the panic himself, but he felt the weight of the responsibility he held. It was up to *him* to make sure they made it out safely. He took a deep breath, trying to calm himself before addressing the others.

"Guys, we'll be fine."

"You don't know that," Sweet Pea said.

"At least we won't feel pain when we die," Matt said, his voice strong.

"Hey!" Jacob said. "No one's going to die!"

"Again, you don't know that," Sweet Pea said, his negativity surprising Jacob. "And you can't say anything to make us feel better. Either we'll make it or we won't."

Gallus sighed loudly. "Sweet Pea is right. Honestly, we just have to keep going."

Jacob nodded, taking a deep breath. "I'm going to need everyone's help to remember what number I'm on—one hundred and thirty is too large to track, especially if anything distracts me. If you count with me, that would be great."

"Do we know when the Cerpire will attack?" Akeno asked.

"No, we don't," Gallus said. "But the fortress is one hundred and thirty feet in front of us now, so we can assume it will come sometime before then."

Jacob checked that everyone was still in line. "I can see your emotions—I'll make sure you're not going off to the side.

And it's a pretty straight shot—the Shiengols are directly in front of me. As long as I can see them, we should be okay."

"Let's go, then," Matt said. "Take us to safety, fearless leader!"

Aloren giggled and Jacob shook his head, smiling. "One, two, three . . ."

The others chanted with him. Then, when he reached fourteen, they stopped counting. The silence was very unnerving. "Uh . . . guys, are—" He slammed his mouth shut. He couldn't hear himself! He might not even have said anything, since he couldn't tell what his mouth was doing. He still felt like he'd spent the day at the dentist's, and not being able to hear himself made it worse.

He took a breath. "Okay," he said, hoping his mouth was obeying his brain, "I've entered the last trap. Um . . . I'm just going to keep walking. I'll keep track of the numbers in my head. Do the same, so you know where we are."

The strong sensation that he was going mad filled his chest. He was talking to himself, but couldn't hear it; walking forward, but couldn't feel it, and leading people he couldn't see. An appreciation for what Kelson and the others had gone through flooded over him, along with the need to say thanks to Aldo for the information he'd given Jacob and the others before they left.

There wasn't a pause behind him, so he continued forward, counting out loud even though he couldn't hear himself.

"One hundred one. One hundred two. One hundred three." Almost there! Where was the Cerpire? "One hundred four. One hundred five."

Jacob paused when he sensed something he hadn't felt in weeks—the ability to discern others' magical powers. He hadn't even realized this gift disappeared after he fought the Ember Gods a few weeks ago.

But now he felt it. And something was nearby. Something with a very strong, very large, very old magical pulse. He hesitated. The magic felt . . . distracted. Like it was being used up. Worn out. Exhausted.

Jacob realized what this meant. The Cerpire was nearby. And it was tired. Could that help him win the fight? It felt like the hair on the back of his neck rose, but he couldn't be sure.

The emotions of the Shiengols disappeared. Jacob stopped in surprise, unsure what to think. Had they turned their feelings off? If so, how? He blinked several times, trying to clear his eyes, then looked up and nearly fell backward in shock.

The brightest red he'd ever seen hovered about twenty feet in the air above him.

The Cerpire had made its presence known. And it was *very* angry.

35

Jacob felt himself slide backward and couldn't tell what had caused it. The Cerpire? Akeno?

There was a flicker of movement in front of him, and he blinked. It was almost as if something had pierced his blindness, returning his sight for just a moment. But only in fragments. He squinted, trying to see.

Another flicker.

A third flicker and the entire Cerpire shifted into view, though very hazy. Jacob could see it! He froze, completely unable to believe his luck. Was this like in the cave, when he'd fought the Molg? Akeno and Aloren hadn't been able to see it until Jacob touched it. The Molg's features had been easier to see, but at least Jacob wouldn't lose track of the Cerpire.

Faint—very faint—details appeared. It had scales, as Jacob had expected, but fur as well. That was weird. The image flickered, and Jacob caught the color of the scales—bright blue-green.

Jacob stared up at the beast, at its emotion, its indistinct shape, wishing he could see the dinosaur's face.

It didn't move. Had it lost sight of Jacob and the others? He itched to turn to see the emotions of the rest of his group, but he knew that doing so would be disastrous.

He waited longer. The Cerpire still didn't do anything. It could probably smell its visitors, though, right? If it was hungry, why didn't it attack? Or . . . maybe its only job was to keep people from going to the fortress. Did that mean if they turned around now, they would be safe?

Jacob pushed that idea away and frowned, concentrating. He needed to come up with a plan, and fast. His first priority was to live—for all of them to make it. And he wasn't completely helpless like he'd thought he'd be. He was able to sense the magic of the dinosaur. He could see its outline. He could see its emotions. And Early would help wherever possible—he knew it.

Turning back was pointless. They'd just have to make the entire trip again. No, he had to get them all to the fortress. They'd also have their senses returned and would be able to fight with him against the Cerpire. They only had twenty-five feet to go, and the traps ended *before* the fortress started.

But how to do it safely?

Jacob watched the dinosaur, sifting through his memory of every movie and book he'd read, trying to think of something that would help. He wished Aldo and Early could communicate with him.

Then he remembered another ability he'd recently discovered—the ability to mold air, like he'd done in the tunnel with the Ember Gods. Would that work now? Could he do that and create a shield to protect himself and his friends long enough to get to the fortress?

Moving slowly, keeping his eyes on the beast and hoping the others wouldn't do something stupid, he faced his hands forward, raised them a few inches, and concentrated on molding the air in front of him. He nearly jumped in surprise when he felt his palms heat up. Of course he'd feel it! It was magical warmth, after all.

But nothing else happened. At least, he didn't think so.

A spot on his back heated up. Early and Aldo must have figured out what he was doing! He sensed Early's energy rush through his hands and felt the heat bursting from his fingertips.

A sheen appeared in front of him—sparkly and milky white. He could see it! He couldn't help but smile in excitement. This would work!

Jacob concentrated all his energy into the sheen, watching it start to grow, turning into a shield that stretched farther and farther.

When it was tall enough to protect him if the Cerpire attacked, he glanced back to judge how far it would need to go to cover the rest of the group. Only a few feet longer. He exerted as much energetic pressure as he could until the sheen had grown to completely cover everyone's emotions.

Okay. Ready.

Trusting Early, his instincts, and his abilities, he raised the shield higher, careful to keep the others and the Cerpire in sight. He stepped to the right.

Nothing happened.

Then the dinosaur attacked fast and hard, knocking Jacob to the ground, momentarily exposing the rest of the group. Jacob jumped up, putting the sheen over his friends again. Had they been injured? No way to know. He continued walking, bracing himself for the next attack.

It came swiftly, followed by several shorter, smaller attacks. Jacob fell to the ground again, doing his best to keep the sheen in place as the dinosaur repeatedly hit the shield, biting, then swiping it with what appeared to be its forearms.

Jacob shook his head. The slow-and-sure method wasn't

working. He needed to get himself and the others to the fortress as quickly as possible.

He sprang to his feet, then lurched hard toward the fortress, straining against what he assumed was the rope, holding the shield between his group and the dinosaur. He kept his legs bent and crouched over so that when the next burst of attacks came, he would be ready.

The attack didn't come, though, and like a pop of electricity, Jacob burst through the end of the trap, his body flooded with sensation—light, sound, touch. The sun burned his eyes, and he instinctively raised his hand to block the brightness. His shield disappeared.

Remembering the group, he whirled in time to see Gallus fall. The Cerpire was no longer in view. Had it left? Putting aside his surprise that he could see into the traps, Jacob pulled hard on the rope, yanking Akeno forward.

The Makalo gasped as he came through the end of the traps, then turned to help Jacob pull the rest of the group through. The others stumbled out, crying with surprise when the sunlight hit them. Gallus was the hardest to pull, and Jacob felt bad about dragging the man on his knees—his poor knees.

The group took stock of themselves. Miraculously, only Gallus had been injured. Akeno and Aloren jumped to help him.

Jacob hesitated, though. Where had the dinosaur gone? He couldn't even see its emotions anymore.

A slight movement to the right alerted him to a creature there, stepping out of the trap. Jacob shook his head. How could this be the Cerpire? It was much, much smaller than he'd seen in the traps—barely five feet tall. It looked like a miniature Allosaurus—one of Jacob's favorite dinosaurs— only, its forearms were much longer and were lined with spikes. Like the Allosaurus, it stood on its hind legs. Fur and scales covered its body in randomly placed patches.

The creature didn't let its size deter it. It burst forward, incredibly fast, roaring the roar of a huge monster. He stared at it in shock. It sounded like something forty feet tall. But it wasn't.

"*That's* the Cerpire?" Sweet Pea said. "I could crush that tiny thing with just my beard!"

The creature jumped forward to attack Gallus, Aloren, and Akeno. Sweet Pea lunged at it, sword in hand, shrieking.

Momentarily distracted, the dinosaur turned to Sweet Pea, who danced away, dodging attacks, leading the creature to the side of the fortress.

Jacob dropped his bag near Gallus. "How's he doing?" he asked Aloren. He jumped in surprise when Sweet Pea screamed.

"Something's wrong! I stab it and it keeps going!"

"We're coming!" Matt yelled. He, Jacob, and Akeno pulled their swords out and dashed to join the fight.

Then Sweet Pea fell silently to the ground, even though the dinosaur hadn't made a visible movement.

Lure it back into the traps.

Jacob stopped, almost dropping his sword, confused by the sensation of foreign thoughts invading his mind. The last time this had happened was in the Lorkon castle, when he hadn't known where to go to find the key.

Shaking his head to clear his thinking, he jumped forward, swinging his sword at the dinosaur. Just like Sweet Pea said, though, it didn't feel right when his weapon connected with the dinosaur's side. It felt off, but he couldn't figure out why.

Lure it back into the traps!

The idea hit him so strongly, he was absolutely positive it hadn't come from himself. But no way was he going to obey the thought! He'd stay out here where he could see, thank you very much. He kept fighting and cried out when Akeno fell to the ground. He and Matt jumped together, ready to defend each other to the death, if need be.

Trust your abilities.

Who was talking to him? He looked up at the fortress. The emotions were so close, he felt he could reach up and touch them. The Shiengols had to be just on the other side of the wall.

Go.

Were the thoughts coming from the Shiengols? Were they somehow able to communicate with him? Should he obey?

Jacob parried with the beast, frustrated when it didn't seem to get hurt. The creature roared again, and he had to resist the urge to cover his ears. He should obey the thoughts —he hadn't been led astray before.

Trust.

So he did. "Matt, help Gallus—I have to fight this thing by myself!"

"No! I'm with you!"

Scanning the air, Jacob searched for Early as he dodged the Cerpire, running around it in circles, trying to avoid being struck himself. "Early! Come to me now!"

She flitted to his side, her colors showing she was both hysterical and excited.

"Help me like last time—give me power!"

She disappeared, and he felt the familiar sense of warmth spread through him from behind.

"No, Jacob! You can't!"

He ignored his older brother and jumped away from the dinosaur, entering the traps.

36

Jacob's world fell down around him. The feeling of numbness was just as powerful as the return of sensation, if not more so. His body now sluggish, he almost froze in a stupor of thought. Another burst of warmth flooded over him—Early must have given him extra juice—and his thoughts became crisp again.

The outline of the dinosaur reappeared—much, *much* larger than what he and his friends had been fighting. Jacob looked up. The bright red emotion was twenty feet, at least, in the air. Why had it looked so short and weak before?

Then it dawned on him—there were six traps, not five. The very last trap wasn't the loss of hearing. It was their senses being distorted. Everything they felt and saw was a lie. They'd been given a false sense of superiority and in turn, it made them much more vulnerable.

The dinosaur advanced on him and he backed up quickly. The sensation of falling hit him—he must have walked into a pit of some sort. He felt it when he landed—he was no longer standing. Jumping to his feet again, he hefted his arms—his right was heavier than the left. Good. He still had his sword.

He drew a little power from Early—not too much—and molded the air around him with his left hand, creating another shield.

The dinosaur pounced at him, pushing him to the ground with the force of the strike.

"How do I defeat it?" he yelled, getting to his feet and dodging the next attack.

The emotions of the Shiengols in the fortress didn't change, and there was no response.

Jacob swung his sword at the Cerpire's leg. As expected, it didn't do anything to the beast. "Come on, Shiengols! I know it was you!"

One of the colors burned redder.

"Oh, sure! You're angry about this? Me demanding help instead of you offering it? Ridiculous!"

Several of the other emotions changed to a bright red.

He backed away from the Cerpire, holding the shield in place, repairing the damage the beast had done to it. He was careful with the amount of power he pulled from Early. He couldn't have her go unconscious—that would be really bad.

The dinosaur lunged, and Jacob barely got out of the way. It was so tall, it hurt his neck to look up at it, and he had to keep an eye on the long forearms as well as the huge jaws.

The Cerpire bit at the shield again. Jacob repaired it. He couldn't do this forever. He ran between the creature's legs, banged into something hard—probably a wall—and fell to the ground, then rolled to avoid being hit by the long tail he could barely see.

Jacob jumped up, whirling to face the Cerpire.

He decided to try a different tactic with the Shiengols.

"You obviously want out of the fortress—otherwise, you wouldn't have helped me earlier. I'm the *only one* who can get you out. So, I ask again. How do I defeat the Cerpire?"

No response, then finally, *The side, below the arm, is the soft place.*

Relief—along with some irritation at how petty the Shiengols were—flooded over Jacob. "Thank you!"

He realized this would probably be the only help he'd receive from the temperamental creatures, so he put them out of his mind and concentrated on the task at hand. The spot they'd mentioned was fifteen feet high. How would he get up there, especially without his vision and the sense of touch?

The Cerpire batted him with its long arms, and Jacob again dodged the attacks.

He raised his sword and charged the dinosaur, running between its legs at the last minute. Knowing it wouldn't work again if he failed, he let the shield flick away and grabbed the creature's tail, then pulled himself up. He hung on as the beast whipped around, trying to find him. He couldn't feel his sword in his hand, but knew it was still there by the weight on his arm.

Jacob climbed, making sure he kept the fingers of his right hand tight, hopefully around the sword's handle.

The Cerpire figured out where he'd gone and flipped its tail back and forth, but by then, Jacob had already reached the beast's mid-section. He held on as tightly as possible, inching farther whenever he could.

Finally, he made it high enough. His first attempt to stab the Cerpire failed, and he nearly dropped the sword. The creature tried to knock him away, but he held on. The dinosaur's emotions were so bright, Jacob would have shut his eyes if he'd had his normal vision. The red swirled around, confusing him.

A spot on his shoulder heated up—Early! Yes! He didn't even realize she'd released her magic from earlier.

A violent tremor passed through the creature. Had it just roared? Jacob didn't know, but he was glad he couldn't hear.

He told his left fingers to hold on to whatever they could

find. It was impossible to know if they'd grabbed anything, but he didn't fall, so they probably had. He swung the sword as hard as he could with his other arm. It met some resistance at first, then a sucking sensation reverberated through the handle to Jacob's arm, and the sword drove faster for a moment before abruptly stopping. Jacob knew he'd reached his mark, and he cringed at the idea.

Nothing happened.

Then Jacob felt himself falling. The Cerpire flickered in and out of view underneath him. An immense jolt shocked him through—they'd hit the ground. He tried to move, but didn't feel his limbs obey. Had he been trapped somehow? But the Cerpire was under him!

Panic flooded through his mind—he'd be stuck there forever! No one would be able to find him! He pushed the hysteria away when he noticed something about the Cerpire below. With fascination, he watched as its emotions faded slowly. The creature's outline dissolved along with the bright red, then both disappeared completely. It was dead! It was dead! *Yes!*

He struggled even harder to move, but something about his position wouldn't allow him to do so.

All of his sensations were returned with a rush—sight, sound, smell, touch.

Jacob screamed when the pain hit him. It flooded over his whole body, enveloping him like scalding bath water.

He looked down—he'd been slashed across the stomach. And his leg. It was broken. No wonder he couldn't move! There were gashes on his arms, too. He watched the blood seeping through the fabric of his clothes. He was losing too much blood. He needed help now!

"Hello!" he cried out. "Early? Someone! Help me! I can't move—I'm hurt! Bad!"

A dizzy spell hit him and everything turned black.

37

J acob woke up, surrounded completely by darkness. Not again. He groaned in frustration, realizing the traps must have been sprung once more. But did that mean the dinosaur was alive? Looking for any visible emotion, he sat up in terror and cracked his head against something solid above him. He fell back. That hurt.

But wait. It shouldn't have—not if the traps were in place.

Hesitantly, he reached out. His hands met a hard, smooth surface above him, and below was a soft, cushy fabric. He could feel!

Then it dawned on him that he must have been in a Minya container. He'd been saved!

Preparing for the rush of light, he reached up to push the top open, squinting against the brightness.

"Jacob!" Aloren said, her head—much larger than normal—appearing next to him. "You're awake!"

Jacob laughed. "Yeah, and please don't yell. It hurts."

"Oh, oops. Sorry." She jumped to her feet. "He's up!"

Jacob heard a chorus of exclamations of joy and was surrounded by giants. He could only see their knees.

"Akeno? Are you there? Can you enlarge me?"

"Sure!"

One of the giants—Akeno—reached over and picked up Jacob, held him out, and dropped him.

Relief rushed over him when he saw that his hands and arms were back to normal. He stretched, enjoying the pops in his joints, breathing deeply, the smell of the nearby forest rushing through his nostrils. The clouds above were fluffy, partially covering the sun. Rays of light streamed across the sky, and a slight breeze lifted the hair off his forehead. He'd never, ever take these things for granted again.

Before returning to the others, he took stock of the area around the group. August Fortress was to his left, with the emotions of the Shiengols showing impatience, happiness, and of course, annoyance. He smiled, shaking his head. Thank goodness they'd helped him.

Only a part of August Township was close to the fortress. Huge, towering walls and volcanic rock marked the boundaries between most of the city and the Shiengol stronghold.

Early flitted to his side, tumbling and doing somersaults in the air. "You're alive, Jacob! You're alive!"

He laughed with her. "Yes, I am."

They headed back to the group, more relief washing over him when he saw that everyone looked healthy, safe, and happy.

Gallus stepped forward and shook Jacob's hand. "Well done, Your Highness. Well done." He grinned broadly. "Thanks to you, and of course, Aloren, we all made it out okay."

"What happened?"

Gallus motioned to a bunch of logs set up around a campfire. The tent was situated a few feet away.

"Let's have a seat." He nodded to Akeno and Sweet Pea.

"Would you grab us something to eat? I'm sure Jacob is starving." Then he pointed to Aloren. "She can tell you everything that happened—she's the only one who didn't get injured."

Guilt crossed Aloren's face. "I'm really sorry about that. I—"

Jacob shook his head. "Someone had to stay in charge of the situation."

She thought about that for a moment, then nodded. "You're right." She sat down.

There were two free seats, and Jacob summoned the courage to take the one nearest her. It felt good to be that close.

Aloren took a deep breath. "While you and the others attacked the Cerpire, I worked on Gallus. He was really badly injured, but Akeno helped fix him up after you went back into the traps." She frowned at Jacob. "Which was absolutely insane, by the way."

"Yeah, I know. Sorry."

She continued. "Anyway. Akeno had a concussion and a cut on his head. He worked through it all, helping me keep Sweet Pea alive while you were fighting. Sweet Pea ended up getting shrunk too, and put in Hazel's container. I left him in Akeno's care so Matt and I could find you."

Jacob held up his hand, swallowed, then asked, "How *were* you, Matt?" He couldn't imagine what life would be like if Matt had been killed.

Matt shrugged. "All of my sores were superficial and easily treated. They could've been much worse."

Aloren nodded. "Yeah. And Jacob, when we found you, we weren't even sure you were still alive. It was insane! You'd fallen into a tunnel-type thing—Matt said it probably used to be a main line for sewage—and the Cerpire was dead underneath you. At first, it looked like you'd stabbed yourself with your sword." She pointed at Matt. "He sprained his ankle jumping down to get you."

"It's still sprained, actually," Matt said, holding up his wrapped ankle. "We ran out of Kaede sap trying to keep you and Sweet Pea alive."

Aloren gave Matt a glance of pity. "I do feel bad about that, you know."

Matt snorted. "Whatever. You're just glad Jacob didn't die."

Aloren flushed slightly, and Jacob didn't need to see the colors around her to tell him she was embarrassed. She apparently chose to ignore Matt's comment.

"I hated leaving you there on top of that disgusting thing, but we worried it would kill you to be moved, even just to put you in a Minya container. So, I cleaned you up there, and Jacob, it was awful. Absolutely awful."

Jacob finished his apple and peeled the banana. "I can imagine. I must've lost a ton of blood."

"You did. Aldo helped a lot."

Jacob perked up. "Aldo? He's here?"

He looked around, then jumped to his feet when the old man stepped out from the tent, a big grin on his face.

"Surprise!"

Jacob quickly stepped to Aldo and they embraced.

Aldo grabbed Jacob's cheeks with both hands. "You scared me, boy."

Gallus chuckled. "Apparently, when you went back into the traps, Aldo figured you'd lost your mind. He deserted his post and charged down the hill, deciding he was willing to risk the tarri, blindness, and loss of sensation and hearing to help."

Aldo turned to Gallus and pushed a bit of wild gray hair away. "Yes, but by the time I got off the hill and into the forest, you must've killed the Cerpire because the tarri were running around, trying to get away. Sick of being stuck there, I'm sure."

Jacob raised his eyebrows, munching on his banana. "So it's true—all the traps are undone?"

"We think so," Gallus said. "You probably noticed that your senses returned when you killed the Cerpire."

Jacob nodded.

"We're thinking the beast was the magical source for everything. Once it died, everything else did too."

"That makes sense, actually," Jacob said. "'Cause I could feel its magic, and it was spent. Tired. Like it had been used too much."

Aloren cleared her throat. "I'm not done telling what happened."

Everyone turned back to her, amused, and Matt snorted, muttering something about her being a drama queen who wanted all the attention.

She playfully narrowed her eyes at him, then continued. "Luckily, Aldo had no problem crossing the board and getting down the wall. Early helped him. He arrived while we were cleaning you up. He had you drink an entire package of Kaede sap. Said it would completely burn your mouth up, but it was the only way to keep you from dying. He was right. It worked on you from the inside while we focused on your external wounds."

Jacob's mouth had a slightly rubbery taste and was a little numb, but other than that, it was fine. He ate the last of his banana, and started on the beef jerky next.

"We decided it was safe to shrink you and put you in a Minya container. And then we hung out, waiting for you to get better."

Jacob looked at Matt. "Did you let Mom and Dad know what happened?"

"Yeah. Early sent messages all over for us. She's really been great."

Early hovered down and stood on Jacob's knee. "Your family was worried, but they're fine now that you're awake and okay."

Jacob felt an urge to pet her in appreciation, like he would Tito, his dog. He refrained, figuring she wouldn't respond well to it. But she'd definitely earned his respect all over again with everything she'd done over the past few days. He looked back at Aldo. "I'm assuming it was your idea to have Early help me form the shield when we first got to the Cerpire?"

Aldo laughed. "Was that what you were doing? I couldn't tell. I saw you hold your hands out and concentrate really hard. I figured it would only make things easier if Early pitched in."

"Yeah, it did. The shield didn't come until I drew on her magic." He took a drink of water. "What did it look like from far away?"

"What?"

"The shield."

Aldo shook his head. "Couldn't see it."

"Really? I could."

"You weren't using your normal vision—you were seeing it in a magical sense."

Jacob nodded. "I guess so." He turned to Aloren. "How did you know the traps had been sprung?"

Aloren's face lit up. "It was really awesome! All of a sudden, everything went up in flames. Not real flames, I don't think, but bright blue and green ones, with a whooshing sound. Matt figured something had happened and went to find you."

Matt raised his chin and thrust his shoulders back. "What can I say? It pretty much made me the hero of the day." He laughed, dodging Aloren's hand as she tried to slap him. "After Aloren, of course."

Aloren leaned back in her chair, and Jacob felt her eyes on him. He glanced her way and she smiled. "It's great to have everyone healthy again," she said. She bent forward, scrutinizing Jacob. "Hey. Has anyone told you that you have very pretty eyes? I've never seen eyes that light blue before."

He blushed, looking away. Yes, many people had said so. He didn't understand what the big deal was.

Gallus chuckled, shaking his head. "Aloren, how many pairs of eyes, other than brown, have you seen in your life?"

She knitted her eyebrows, tapping her cheek. "One or two." Her face lit up. "But Jacob's mom has blue eyes too—not as light as his, though."

"Amberly's got them too," Jacob said.

Matt groaned in exasperation. "No offense, but things have been seriously boring over the last couple of days. And now that Jacob is better, can we do something exciting? Like get the Shiengols out of the fortress?"

Gallus stood. "Yes, it's time to work, and quickly. You kids missed school today."

Jacob did the math in his head. He'd fought the dinosaur on Friday, so it was now Monday afternoon. He'd been unconscious for three days. Matt and Gallus were right. The group couldn't afford to hang around anymore.

He looked up at the wall above him, sending another mental thanks and a sorry-for-the-wait to the Shiengols. He half expected a response, and a small twinge of disappointment hit him when he didn't receive one. Oh, well.

"But before we leave," Gallus said, "It wouldn't be fair to our families if we didn't allow them to talk to us in person. They've been begging to see for themselves that we're all safe." Gallus nodded at Jacob. "We'll make it fast. You've got the key still?"

Jacob nodded. "Where's the door?" He spotted it, leaning up against the wall of the fortress. "Let's set it up. I'll go right now."

Gallus and Matt propped the door between two large rocks and Jacob pulled the key out, noticing with dismay that the chain had been broken sometime earlier, possibly while he'd fought the dinosaur. He'd have to get that fixed when they returned. Luckily, the key hadn't fallen out of his pocket.

As soon as he created the link to Ebony's door, Mom and Ebony rushed through.

Mom flung her arms around Jacob, holding him tight. "Oh, my son, my son."

"I'm fine, Mom."

She reached out for Matt, grabbed his shirt, and pulled him into the hug as well, then buried her face into Jacob's neck. He patted her shoulder, feeling the blush cross his face when he realized Aloren watched him with a smile.

Finally, Mom released them. Ebony had just finished fawning over Akeno, and an older woman Jacob hadn't noticed let go of Sweet Pea.

Ebony restocked their Kaede sap supplies, then the mothers left, and Jacob shut the door behind them. He created a link to Gallus's house, and after Gallus had hugged his wife and kids, Jacob looked at Aloren. "Want to see Kevin?"

She held her hands loosely behind her back. "It doesn't matter. We've been talking through Hazel nearly non-stop for the past three days."

Jacob nodded, pushing his feelings of disappointment away. What did he expect? That she'd ditch Kevin that quickly?

He squared his shoulders and looked up at the fortress. "All right, everyone." He glanced at the group. "Are we ready?"

"Definitely," Gallus said.

38

J acob sighed in exasperation. "What if we don't find a weak spot? I won't be able to get us in."

Gallus wiped sweat off his forehead. "I don't know. Maybe we could break through one of the walls. Use explosives."

Jacob nodded. They'd need to do something. He'd been searching all over the fortress, trying to find a way into it for several hours. And the thing was *huge*. Lots of bends and corners and a ton of rock and stone, covered with the symbol he'd seen on the flags outside—the trident with the sun on it.

His throbbing, blistered hands would be scarred for life. They already would have been scarred if it weren't for the sap.

He paused, a thought occurring to him. He spun, nearly running into Matt and Sweet Pea, who were still trailing him long after the others had wandered away.

"I need something to stand on so I can check the stone above, too."

The guys nodded, and Jacob followed them. So far, he'd only checked everything within his own reach. They found a couple of old wooden crates—still in fairly good condition—

in an abandoned building and hauled them back to the fortress. Jacob got on top of one of them, feeling around as far as he could.

It didn't take long for him to find the point of his searching. "Aha!" he said, putting his hand on the warmth. "Got it!"

Sweet Pea, Gallus, and Matt cheered, causing Aloren and Akeno to come running from the tent to join them. Aldo had gone off to explore the town.

The group watched as Jacob warmed, molded, and peeled away the stone like putty. It was hard work. The rock was very thick—much more so than Jacob had thought it would be —and after three feet, he still hadn't made it all the way. Also, he'd expected to go straight through, but he ended up forming a somewhat winding tunnel as he encountered stone that wouldn't mold.

After fifteen minutes, Aloren and Gallus left to find Aldo, wanting to see what he'd been doing. Jacob figured they were bored and didn't want to say so.

Forty-five minutes later, Jacob was pulling out some loose and still-warm rock when he noticed a pear-shaped burst of flame that lasted only a second or two. It was about ten feet away from him and five feet above ground.

"Did you guys see that?"

"See what?" Matt asked.

"Something small on fire over there." He pointed.

Sweet Pea and Akeno shook their heads and left to investigate while Jacob thought it over as he continued working. The last time he'd seen a fire hovering in the middle of the air had been when he'd seen a fire beetle. But the flames weren't the same—they were a different color and shape.

The others returned, and Aloren insisted Jacob take a break to wrap his nearly-mangled hands with Kaede-Sap saturated cloth. Grateful, he climbed off the crate.

While resting, he ate roast beef that Akeno had put on the fire several hours earlier. It was delicious, and Jacob found, to his delight, that Akeno had also prepared potatoes just the way Jacob liked them. He thanked the Makalo over and over again, savoring the rich flavor of the gravy and spices. After a while, he decided his hands were fine, then resumed the work.

Only a few minutes later, he felt the last layer of stone give way, and a draft of musty, gross-smelling air—like rotten cucumbers, dead wood, and melted plastic—rushed past at the same time a very bright light from inside nearly blinded him. Did the Shiengols have electricity in there? He squinted, trying not to look directly into the beam, and worked harder, enlarging the hole enough for someone Gallus's size.

Strong arms yanked him through the tunnel into the fortress, and Jacob yelled in alarm. He heard Aloren and Matt freak out, then his attention was taken away by the very full room in front of him. The person who grabbed him stepped back while others moved behind him, forcing him to roll away from the tunnel.

The light was much more blinding inside, and he raised his arm to shield his face.

"Shut your eyes!" a man's voice said.

Jacob's were already shut, but he noticed that the light disappeared. He peeked through his lashes, only to discover that the command had been for everyone else in the room. All the Shiengols stood motionless, eyes shut, hands behind their backs.

At first glance, using the filtered light through the high windows, they looked like humans—especially from his peripheral vision. But when he looked at them directly, it was obvious, in a not-so-obvious way, that they weren't. They were skinny—almost too skinny. Or maybe they were too tall? They were taller than him, at least, and proportioned differently from a human—fewer curves, more straight from the shoulders to the feet. Jacob slitted his eyes, still trying to figure out why they looked so slender compared to humans. Maybe it was their long robes, in bright shades of red, blue, purple, and green.

He started when he realized all of them had markings on their faces that looked like the trident with the sun on it. These markings purposely drew attention to their eyes, and he could tell the Shiengols were proud of this feature. He found himself impatient for them to look at him so he could examine their faces more fully. Similar trident and sun markings were on their robes.

"Uh . . ." Jacob started. He clamped his mouth shut, though, when several of the Shiengols shifted positions a few times.

They moved gracefully. Like Ebony, when she was fighting, only more fluid. It was like a dance—one movement leading naturally to the next.

Remembering how temperamental they were, he honed in on their emotions. What he saw surprised him—they were irritated. Very irritated. At what, though? Was it because of him? How could it be?

Anger, frustration, the pains and stress of the past few days —all of it—boiled inside Jacob. He jumped to his feet, not caring anymore what these creatures thought of him. He'd just risked his life again and again for them! "Why are you all so annoyed? Is it with me? And if so, why? That doesn't make any sense!"

Their emotions flickered quickly to red—anger—and the Shiengols opened their eyes, gazing at him. He gasped in shock at the light of their diamond-like eyes. It felt like he was staring into a billion LED flashlights. He raised his arm and looked down, surprised to see that his whole body was glowing.

One of the Shiengols stepped forward. Jacob assumed it

was a man, though he couldn't tell. His hair was long, dark brown, with part of it braided on one side.

"Who are you?" the person demanded in a deep voice— definitely male.

"I'm Jacob."

The Shiengol grabbed Jacob's arm, flinging him against a wall, the others parting to make room. "You are *lying*." He scrutinized Jacob.

Lying? How could he be lying? And ouch! "Let go of me! I'm telling the truth! My name is—"

"I know what *they* call you," he motioned to the hole, still blocked by several Shiengols, "but who are you *really*?"

Realization hit Jacob. "Oh . . ." He squared his shoulders and raised his chin. "I am Danilo Leontii. Prince of Gevkan, son of Dmitri and Arien, king and queen of Gevkan." He frowned. "But you knew that."

"Prince Danilo?"

"Yes."

"*Good*." The Shiengol released his hold on Jacob and folded his arms. "I am Azuriah, leader of the Shiengol people." He peered into Jacob's face, but didn't say anything more.

Jacob blinked a couple of times, expecting the brightness of Azuriah's eyes to burn his own eyes, surprised when it didn't. He raised an eyebrow in suspicion. How had he adjusted so quickly? Moments ago, he couldn't even look in the faces of the Shiengols, but now, doing so didn't bother him at all. He stared back at Azuriah, holding the Shiengol's gaze without flinching.

Azuriah's emotions were stronger and brighter than the others. He felt determined. Jacob knew this Shiengol meant business.

Apparently satisfied, Azuriah pulled back. "How have you broken into the stronghold?"

"The fortress? Are you asking how we got through the traps, or how I got through the stone itself?"

"Yes."

"Uh . . ." Jacob looked back at the hole, hoping that at any instant Gallus or Matt would push the Shiengols aside. He couldn't figure out why Azuriah was asking questions he already knew the answers for. Maybe the Shiengol was just messing around.

Azuriah noticed where his attention had gone. "You'll see your friends again. But not now." He snapped his fingers and said something in a different language. Jacob rolled back on his heels. He'd only heard English since coming to Eklaron, except when the Molg and tarri had spoken. Hearing the Shiengols speak in their native tongue was cool. It sounded like German mixed with Japanese and Latin—or, how Jacob assumed Latin sounded. Kind of Spanishy and Italiany.

Azuriah said something else and the Shiengols broke into a cheer and rushed around the room, gathering things. Swords, poles, clothing. At first, Jacob had a hard time distinguishing the females from the males since they all had long, dark hair, but once he got past their emotional state of extreme excitement, he could see that the females were exceptionally exquisite. They had medium-toned skin, like someone from an eastern European country. Beautiful. They reminded him of a person he'd seen or met before, possibly an actress from a movie, though he couldn't remember which.

The Shiengols escaped the fortress through the hole, and soon only Jacob, Azuriah, and a female Shiengol remained.

She put her hand on Azuriah's arm and Azuriah smiled—smiled!—at her. She said something in that strange language, then followed the rest.

Azuriah turned back to Jacob. "We have much to do."

"We . . . we do?"

Azuriah motioned to the hole. "They just left to seek the

Shiengols in other parts of Eklaron. Danilo, you have mere months until you must defeat the Lorkon."

Jacob was stuck on the idea that there were more Shiengols out there, and it took a moment for his mind to switch to the other thing Azuriah had said. "I thought I was only supposed to *help* do that."

Azuriah gaped. "You're the only one who *can* do it. Why do you insist on saying so many ridiculous things?"

Jacob's mouth popped open. This Shiengol wasn't nice. He tried to control the disappointment that rushed through him, but he couldn't. He'd heard so much about Shiengols and had looked forward to meeting them for a very long time. And they were jerks! He thought of many retorts, but held them back, realizing this being in front of him was powerful. Very powerful.

"Explain to me the talents you've uncovered so far. In your own words and your own understanding."

Jacob pushed his negative thoughts away, figuring he'd get answers to his questions eventually. "I can sense weakness in things—that's how I got into the fortress."

"Do you know how this works?"

Jacob shook his head. "I just hold my hand over the spot that feels warmest and encourage it to get warmer. Then it becomes moldable."

"You are exhibiting a partial response to the Rezend that was put in your body."

"How do you know—you were stuck here when that happened."

Azuriah raised his eyebrow and stared at Jacob. "Do you *have* to ask?"

Jacob shrugged.

"I see the Rezend in your body. Do you not see it?"

Jacob shook his head.

"You will someday. *If* you learn to control your abilities." Azuriah walked to an alcove, beckoning Jacob to follow, and they sat on a window seat. Awkward—sitting so casually next to the very touchy, grouchy leader of the Shiengols. "The Rezend would have given you control over living things. However, due to the Lorkon blood in you, and the fact that you aren't a Makalo, it had an opposite effect. You are able to sense weakness in things that are dead."

Whoa. That was insane. "Really? Cool." Sensing weakness in dead things. He couldn't wait to tell Matt.

"What other abilities have you learned to control?"

"Well, I can see emotions—I can see yours, and it's . . ." He paused at the expression on Azuriah's face, and decided against saying which emotion it was. This guy was super intense! And scary. Jacob hoped he'd adjust to the mood swings. "I, uh, know the creature or person has to be intelligent—meaning, able to think on their own or something. I can't see the emotions of rats. But I could see the emotions of the dinosaur and the Minyas and the Eetu fish."

"Dinosaur?"

"The thing we just had to fight—the one outside the walls."

"Cerpire."

"Yeah, that's what I meant."

"The evil and good inside you are constantly working against each other to achieve separate purposes." Azuriah motioned to the wall Jacob had come through. "You could see the Cerpire and the Molg because of the evil inside you."

"Evil inside me?" Jacob choked on the words. "I can see evil things, but that doesn't make me evil."

Azuriah rolled his eyes. "I didn't say you were *evil*—I said evil was *inside* you. They're completely different."

Jacob hesitated, thinking that over, then nodded. Then something Azuriah said earlier sank in. "Wait. How'd you know about the Molg?"

Azuriah glared at Jacob.

"Never mind." Jacob bit his lip, deciding then and there

never to ask Azuriah another question. This guy was ridiculous.

Azuriah watched Jacob for a moment, his emotions changing, and Jacob did his best to ignore them. Obviously, the man didn't believe his feelings were Jacob's business.

Azuriah closed his eyes, making darkness fall upon them. "Do you understand what I've explained so far?"

"Yes." Jacob had known for a while now that the Lorkon tried to change him into a tool—it would make sense they'd also tried to turn him evil.

Azuriah got up and paced. "And do you know why you can see emotions?"

Jacob shook his head. "Not a clue. Because the Lorkon gave me the ability?"

"*No*, they did *not*. For now, just know that some of your abilities—the purer, more intelligent ones—were inherited, not administered via Rezend or Lorkon."

Shocked, Jacob stood. "Inherited? From whom?" And why hadn't he been told? He crossed his arms. This secret-keeping was really getting on his nerves.

Azuriah grunted in annoyance. "Never mind that."

Jacob almost clenched his fists. Instead, he ran his fingers through his hair. At least he was getting information—he figured it was better not to press his luck. He glanced over, realizing no one was guarding the hole. Why hadn't his friends come in? "My brother . . ."

Azuriah seemed to know what Jacob was thinking. "Is fine. We'll join them shortly."

Jacob nodded.

"What else?"

"You mean, about my gifts?"

The Shiengol didn't answer.

"Well, sometimes I can sense the abilities of other people. Though that seems to come and go."

Azuriah nodded. "It isn't necessary at all times, and will fade until it needs to be used again. Of course, it would be ridiculous to expect to tap into it whenever you feel like it."

Jacob couldn't see why such an expectation would be so ridiculous—all his other talents were available whenever he wanted them. He brushed that aside. "Okay. I can also Time-See."

"Time-See?" Azuriah sat down. "You mean, you can 'gussam?'"

"Huh?"

Azuriah waved his hand dismissively, an impatient expression on his face. "Time-See is fine. Describe it to me."

Jacob stood to pace, hoping Azuriah wouldn't get mad about him doing that too. The Shiengol didn't say anything, so Jacob continued. He took a breath. "It's my newest thing. I used to think I was hallucinating, but then I discovered I could control it. I have to concentrate really hard, but I'm able to see different places."

Azuriah cocked his head, an expression of pleasure on his face. "How far have you developed this ability?"

"I've tried to see one place for longer than a couple of seconds, but I haven't been successful. It's pretty painful to do it."

Azuriah jumped to his feet. "We shall practice now."

"Wait, what? You're going to practice with me?"

"Yes. Come."

Jacob followed and stopped in the middle of the room when Azuriah turned to face him.

"Show me."

"All right." Jacob paused. "How?"

Azuriah tapped his fingertips together. "Just Time-See, and I'll watch what you do."

Jacob closed his eyes, trying to think of a place he hadn't gone yet. He decided to Time-See his high school.

He stared ahead, unfocused his eyes, and concentrated on a mental picture of the school. The room around him changed, and he was in the orange gym. Kevin was there with Coach, shooting basketballs.

The pain in Jacob's chest pulled him back to the somewhat dark interior of the fortress.

Azuriah was still watching him. "Well, that was interesting. Have you no control *whatsoever* over your body?"

Jacob held back his response because he was sure it would make the Shiengol upset. How was he supposed to focus on controlling his body while he was trying to see a different place?

"You went somewhere in the present. Have you tried seeing in the past?"

"Only a little. Time-Seeing hurts."

"Well, of course it does." Azuriah's tone sounded like he was talking to a child. "Do it again. Time-See to when your mother was kidnapped by the Lorkon."

Jacob nodded. He concentrated on the event, not sure how to tell his body to take him back that far. Things around him flashed over and over again, then stopped, and he saw a younger Princess Arien with a large belly. A feeling of nostalgia flooded over him—he missed his mom!

The pain in his chest stung, but he wanted to see what happened next, especially when someone—a Lorkon—stepped up behind her. He was hit by an overwhelming desire to cry out and warn her, but he couldn't stand the sharp burning any longer, and lost focus. He was whipped back to the present.

"That was ... disappointing. Danilo, you *must* try harder."

Jacob bit his tongue. Danilo might be his name, but it was really starting to annoy him. He'd much rather be called Jacob. And he was tired of being pushed around by this Shiengol. "Fine."

He concentrated more. The room around him vanished, replaced again by the one where his mother had been. It looked like her personal quarters. There was the Lorkon, reaching a gloved hand around Arien's face—

The pain in his chest was just too great. It felt like his heart was going to explode. With a rush, things popped back to normal and he fell to the ground.

40

"Get up. Now."

Jacob scrambled to his feet.

"That was *pathetic*. Is this how it has always been?"

Jacob nodded. "Before, when I wasn't in control, it lasted a lot longer and there wasn't pain. Why does it hurt now?"

"Because your body is feeble when you're in control. It's using a muscle you've not exercised." Azuriah strolled around Jacob, hands behind his back. "You must focus on the pain. Concentrate on it. Force it to expand and envelop you."

"That's crazy! Why would I do that? It'll kill me!"

Azuriah stopped in front of Jacob. "No, it won't. It'll make you stronger. Do it now."

Jacob's shoulders slumped. Practicing with Azuriah was the last thing he wanted to do, but it seemed he had no choice. He doubted he'd be able to escape, and he didn't want to argue or fight the Shiengol. There was no way he'd win. Azuriah's presence was commanding, and he could really whip someone verbally. And even though he was skinny, he didn't look weak.

"Get on with it."

Jacob nodded. He took a deep breath and concentrated again on the place he wanted to see, but now he focused on the pain in his chest, willing it to grow.

With a jerk he was in his mother's quarters, but only momentarily before flipping back to the present. Jacob held up his hand, not wanting Azuriah to say anything, and tried once more. He concentrated on the burning and felt a corner of it sliding to his lungs. Jacob tried to hold it there, but something snapped him back. He scowled, annoyed at his inability to do something which, to Azuriah, was so simple.

"This is ridiculous," he said.

Azuriah frowned. "You *must* master this!"

Jacob realized he'd forgotten his earlier vow not to ask any more questions. He didn't care anymore. "But right this second? Before we can even go home and eat?"

"*Yes!*" Azuriah shouted.

Jacob clapped his hands over his ears. Azuriah's response had been so loud—almost like a gunshot—it made Jacob's ears ring. How did he have so much volume?

"All right. I'll try again."

And he did, going from a different angle. Instead of focusing on the pain first, he Time-Saw to his mother's quarters, held himself there, closed his eyes, and *then* honed in on the pain. Instead of forcing it to grow, however, he willed it. He poked and prodded at it gently, requesting it to grow. He felt it start to spread, ignoring the pain. It reached across his torso, up his neck and over his head, then down his arms and legs.

The agony was so bad he felt like he was on fire, as if he was being covered head to toe with hot oil.

But then . . . it dissipated. With a gasp he opened his eyes, and things were different. His body tingled, but no longer hurt. The residual soreness in his chest went away.

He watched as the Lorkon put a handkerchief around

Arien's face. She screamed, almost staring right at Jacob, then collapsed. He rushed forward and tried to beat the Lorkon off his mother, but was powerless. His swings hit empty air. The Lorkon hoisted Arien, carrying her from the room. Jacob followed, unable to believe he was still there. He hadn't been whisked away yet!

The Lorkon strode through several rooms and halls, then down a series of stairs. He entered a huge room with ornately carved doors on the opposite end.

Where was everyone? The place was completely empty.

The creature swung the doors wide open, revealing a group of Dusts, a Sindon, and two other Lorkon practically on the front porch of the castle. All three Lorkon conversed for a moment in hushed tones, then together raised Arien to the back of the Sindon, where she was placed inside a coach-type thing. It was then that Jacob noticed each Lorkon wore gloves and was careful not to touch her skin. What would have happened if their blood had gotten on her? She probably would have died.

The three Lorkon took hold of the Sindon, and with a loud command from the one who had kidnapped Arien, the huge, four-legged beast got up and rambled away from the castle. Jacob followed on foot, but at the sound of a whip, the Sindon unrolled its long arms, reached forward through the trees, and zoomed away, leaving Jacob in the dust.

He growled in frustration. He couldn't possibly keep up! Then he realized something, and felt like slapping his forehead—he wasn't really there. He didn't have a body and shouldn't need to walk or run to Time-See. Right when he figured this out, his sight zipped forward, making it seem like he was floating in the air alongside the Sindon.

He glanced around, surprised at what Maivoryl City looked like before the Lorkon took up permanent residence. It was magnificent. Tall stone buildings, flagpoles, rich draperies in nearly every window, ornately carved bas reliefs on the walls. Definitely worthy of a king's city.

After only thirty seconds of charging, the beast stopped near the shores of Sonda Lake, and Jacob realized that the stone wall wasn't there. He quickly looked back at the Lorkon and watched as one of them pulled a strange-looking creature with many arms and legs from a bag. He set it on the ground and said something in a different language.

With a rush, the thing scurried off, up over the hill.

"*Jacob Clark!*"

The sound of his name freaked him out and he gasped for air, feeling like the oxygen had been ripped from his lungs. Everything around him flashed and he returned to the present and the musty fortress.

Azuriah stood before him, the colors around him showing he was annoyed, but also pleased. "Very well done."

"Why'd you bring me back? That was interesting! I was about to—"

"Yes, you were learning things, but they are things you don't need to know right now. There will be opportunities in the future to figure it all out. If I'd let you stay longer, it would have killed you."

"What? How?"

Azuriah motioned with his hands. "As I said before, you're employing muscles you've never used before, which are being forced to facilitate the magic they were designed to use. Just like learning to fight with a sword, you must allow your body to heal between each practice."

Azuriah looked expectant, but Jacob didn't say anything. This made sense, even though it was disappointing that he hadn't been able to watch the wall get constructed.

"Did it hurt this time?"

"Only a little—at the beginning." He checked to see how his body felt. Exhaustion fell over him. "Whoa. I'm so tired!"

Azuriah nodded. "That will eventually go away with practice." He sighed. "You don't respond to the name Danilo." He looked at Jacob disapprovingly. "That needs to change. And you must have someone near you when you practice to keep track of how long you've Time-Seen. You went for five minutes, which is way too long. Have that someone clock you for two minutes, and then gradually add ten seconds every following instance. Have them call your name to bring you back."

"Why can't I just keep track myself while I'm doing it?"

Azuriah watched Jacob for a moment. "With practice, you'll be able to do that." A glint of happiness colored his emotions.

Jacob felt his legs turn to jelly underneath him. The exhaustion seemed to keep piling on him. It was so overwhelming, he felt like he was about to faint or something. Azuriah put his hand out to steady him.

"It will get better."

Jacob nodded.

"With practice, you'll learn to master this ability, and then you'll be able to take your Time-Seeing to the next level: Gussar. I suspect you'll refer to it as Time-Travel."

"Wait—did you just say time travel?"

"Of course. I'll teach you how. Don't try to figure it out on your own—there are many, many rules you must follow that will keep you from killing yourself." Azuriah strode away, sweeping his robes behind him. "We'll go now." He paused near the hole, motioning for Jacob to go first.

Relief flooded through Jacob at the idea of going back to his house. The new information he'd received in the past half hour had turned his brain to mush, and he couldn't wait to get home and into his warm, comfortable bed.

41

The sunlight burned Jacob's eyes as he wriggled out the other side of the tunnel. He had to be careful that his sword didn't get caught on the rock.

"Oh, thank goodness!" Gallus said. He reached to help Jacob down to the crate. Matt, Sweet Pea, and Aloren watched, worry written on their faces.

"Jacob, what on *earth* were you doing in there?" Matt asked. "We were freaking out—we couldn't follow you into the hole, and then the Shiengols came out, but you still didn't come, and they were seriously the biggest jerks I've ever met —wouldn't let us go in after you—and . . . whoa. Who's that?"

Azuriah had just climbed through the hole. "None of your *business*, human."

Matt's eyebrows raised. "Oh, uh . . . Okay." He looked at Jacob, who shrugged.

Aloren gave Jacob a quick hug, then stepped back. "We were really worried about you. What took so long?"

Jacob wasn't sure how to answer, and when Azuriah spoke, he breathed a sigh of relief.

"We were practicing. But now we must go to Taga Village

to speak with the king and queen and the Makalos." He turned to Aldo and shook his hand. "Thank you for sending Danilo."

Aldo inclined his head slightly. "Don't thank me—thank Arien. She was the most adamant about getting you out."

Azuriah nodded, and his eyes sparkled. "Of course." He turned to Jacob, his emotions changing to show intense excitement. "Take us to Taga."

Jacob started, then fumbled in his pocket, grabbing the key. Everyone followed him to the door and he opened it to Kenji's house, unsure if that was what Azuriah wanted. He pulled back, letting the others go ahead of him.

He heard Aloren say something about being really excited to see Kevin again. Jacob rolled his eyes. He hated to admit it, but that hurt. How many times did he need to save her life before she actually decided to like him?

Azuriah was last. As he reached the threshold, he turned to Jacob. "Don't forget what you've learned and what we practiced."

Jacob sighed in exasperation. "Okay, I won't. Let's go."

Azuriah gave Jacob a nod, then turned and walked through the door. Jacob stepped to follow him, but an arm reached through a crevice between the frame and the supporting rock and grabbed him. He struggled to get out of the grip and through the door, but it slammed shut. In his scramble to get away, he dropped the key.

No!

He saw a shadow as someone came up behind him, and everything went black.

JACOB JERKED TO A SITTING POSITION, groaning when pain split across his skull. He rubbed his temples, trying to make the throbbing go away, then remembered what had happened. He'd been knocked out!

He looked around, automatically feeling for his sword, which wasn't there. He was in a stone room with a window and door. Was he back in the fortress? He got off the cot, being careful not to make his headache worse by moving too fast, and tried to open the door. It was locked. He fished in his pants for the key, then, with a sinking feeling, remembered he'd dropped it.

"Let me out!" He pounded on the door.

Jacob pressed his ear up against the wood, listening for any sign of someone approaching. Nothing. He jumped on the cot and looked out the window. Relief rushed over him when he recognized the township below—he *was* still in the fortress— but he must've been put in the tallest tower. He was several stories above ground.

He had to get out. Obviously, it was the Lorkon who'd trapped him. Who else would?

Gratitude for his talents flooded over him. He could mold a hole in the wall, then sneak away.

He started by the door, but jerked away when he felt a slimy texture on the stone. Disgusting! A brownish-green film covered his skin. What was it? He shivered when possible answers flew through his mind, and wiped his hands off on his pants.

But then he set his mind to the task. He had to get out— he'd touched many disgusting things before, including the faces of dead people, and there wasn't any way he'd allow himself to be trapped there.

Jacob took a deep breath, put his palms on the walls once more, and worked on finding warmth in the stone. His headache slowly left as he worked. Possible solutions to his entrapment crossed his mind, and he quickly realized that if he were to escape, it would all be up to him. His family wouldn't be able to help without use of the key to get them. 'Course, they could always ask the Fat Lady to come . . . but she lived several days' travel away.

He'd finished checking all the walls except the one with the window in it when he heard tapping at the glass. Jacob jumped back onto the cot. "Early!"

She waved at him to open it, but he couldn't find a lever anywhere. It wasn't the opening kind, so he hit the frame and glass several times with his fists, but nothing budged.

"I can't open it!" he mouthed to her, then motioned for her to come into the room through the door. She shook her head. Had she tried already? Was someone standing guard? That seemed likely.

Stepping off the cot, Jacob searched the room for something to break the window, but stopped when he heard footsteps coming down the hall. He motioned frantically at Early to go away and lay on his cot, trying to look innocent.

Voices sounded outside the door, then it swung open, and Jacob sat up.

A Lorkon stepped through the door, but it wasn't Keitus. Obviously, visiting a prisoner was below Keitus's "station."

"Come with me," the Lorkon said, light purple-blue—the colors for boredom—floating in the air around him.

"Why?"

Bright red immediately replaced the more calm colors, and the Lorkon lurched toward Jacob, slapping him across the face. Jacob collapsed on the cot. He brought his hand to his cheek, gasping at the pain that pulsed through his head. His eyes smarted, and he glared at the Lorkon and the two Molgs behind him.

"Save your questions for Keitus," the Lorkon said, growling. He grabbed Jacob's arm and dragged him to his feet, pulling him through the door.

Jacob struggled to stand on his own, but the Lorkon

continued to drag him. "Okay, it's not like I'm going to run away. Let me walk."

The Lorkon released his grip, allowing Jacob a second to get to his feet, then continued down the hall. The Molgs prodded Jacob from behind with something sharp and he yelped, jumping to follow the Lorkon.

The group walked through several rooms and corridors and down a few flights of stairs. Something about the place felt off—different. It took Jacob a moment to put his finger on what. There were no doors anywhere, which made sense. The Lorkon had removed them to prevent anyone from keying into the fortress.

They finally entered a large room. Jacob almost snickered when he saw the makeshift throne in the middle, along with thick curtains on the walls. What was Keitus's deal? Was he seriously that ridiculous? Couldn't feel like he was in charge without a stupid chair and some curtains?

Speaking of Keitus, he sat on the throne, watching Jacob. A flash of green—excitement—swirled in the air around him, but it was quickly replaced by a light pink. Keitus was cranky, albeit somewhat excited to see Jacob.

Jacob's sword leaned against the throne, and his hands ached to hold its comforting weight. He wasn't very good with it, but at least he'd feel less exposed.

The Lorkon shoved Jacob to the center of the room, near a table and chairs. Jacob straightened, ignoring the urge to sneer at Keitus.

Keitus said nothing, and Jacob waited. He wasn't about to break the silence.

While waiting, he took the opportunity to glance around. Bright sunlight filtered through several windows, and Jacob wondered why Keitus hadn't used the curtains to cover the glass. Didn't he dislike the sun?

The Lorkon who'd brought him there joined the other

two, standing in a line behind Keitus. Molgs guarded the corners and doorways, watching him with their large eyes. They looked like they were in pain—the colors definitely showed how irritated they were—and Jacob wondered if it was from the sun, since they usually lived in caves.

Keitus cleared his throat. "Danilo, is it?"

"I go by Jacob. You already know that."

"Drop your insolent attitude, boy. I have no patience for stupidity." Keitus glared, his face nearly completely masked in shadow.

42

Jacob stared at the Lorkon's mouth in disgust—the teeth were dark—and he opted not to respond. It wouldn't matter anyhow. Everything he said would come out as "insolent."

Keitus beckoned for Jacob to come closer, and Jacob took one step. The Lorkon blew out a breath in exasperation.

"Come on, Jacob, let's not play games. We have things to discuss."

"Why would I want to talk with you?"

"Because I hold the key to your freedom."

Jacob looked closely at Keitus's hands. He couldn't see the Key of Kilenya there. "What do you mean?"

"Isn't it obvious? One word from me and you're dead."

Jacob held back his retort. That was one of the most over-used threats in movies and books. He didn't think Keitus would respond well to the remark, though, and his head still hurt from the earlier punishment. "What do you want from me?"

"You ask ignorant questions, son. You already know what I

want—I can see it in your eyes. I seek the power I gave you. It's rightfully mine. And *you're* rightfully mine."

"I don't belong to anyone."

"I created you."

Jacob scoffed. "No, you didn't—you tried to destroy me."

Keitus took a deep breath. The colors swirling around him flickered from red to blue, showing that he was trying to stay calm.

The Lorkon didn't speak for a moment. Then, "Sit down; eat," he said in a much more conciliatory tone. "I insist."

He waved to a table loaded with food. Jacob approached cautiously, expecting an attack at any moment. When one didn't come, he sat at the table and regarded the food. He hadn't realized how starving he was until the smell of rotisserie chicken and warm bread flooded into his nose. "Did you poison it?"

"If I wanted you dead, you'd be that way already."

Jacob grunted impatiently. "Yes, I know. But did you put something in it that'll make me talk? Like a truth serum?" He knew Keitus hadn't read modern earth fiction, so the *Harry Potter* reference would be lost on him.

"Oh, no. I expect we'll have a very open, honest conversation."

"Fine." Jacob decided to eat. He was so hungry he didn't think he could wait any longer. And if Keitus had done something to the food, he'd find out sooner than later.

The food was wonderful. Breads and soups and salads of every kind. Fruits and vegetables and meats. Jacob ate the rotisserie chicken first. He couldn't tell what kind of meat most of the rest were, but he opted to eat the fish and chicken, because he knew what they were. He didn't want to eat something disgusting. Like human. Gross.

When he'd finished drinking everything down with a tall

glass of fruit juice, he leaned back in his seat, sighing contentedly.

"Better already." Keitus said. "Walk with me, Jacob."

"Uh . . . okay." Jacob got to his feet and followed Keitus down the hall. They entered a longer hallway lined with paintings of many different kinds of Shiengols.

"How did you get in the fortress?" Jacob asked.

"You do know I am the one who sealed it before, right? Don't you think I could unseal it?" Keitus motioned to a painting of Azuriah. "You've met him now." A statement, not a question. "He trained you to see into the past." Keitus turned to Jacob. "I know he did—you can't deny it." He bent over, looking into Jacob's eyes.

Jacob backed up against the wall. His stomach turned, having Keitus that close. The Lorkon reeked of mold and blood and sweat.

"And you will now use that ability to help me achieve my ends."

Jacob scowled. "You think I'm going to help you? After everything you've done to me and my family?"

Keitus sighed. "You are an impertinent little cub." He walked several paces, then paused again, examining another painting. "I expected more of you."

Jacob clenched his jaw. How much longer until the guy actually got to the point? Keitus glanced at Jacob, then indicated the painting with his eyes. Apparently Jacob was supposed to look at it. He took a breath to calm himself, then did as was expected.

It was a woman. A beautiful woman, and breathtakingly so. Dark hair like the rest of the Shiengols, a partial smile that was familiar, mocking. In fact, *she* was familiar, and he looked at her with his brows knit, trying to remember where he'd seen her before. She wasn't the woman who'd earlier put her hand on

Azuriah's arm—he was sure of it. And he was sure Keitus wanted to be asked who she was. Well, Jacob wasn't about to give him the satisfaction of knowing he'd piqued Jacob's curiosity.

Finally, Keitus turned to Jacob. "Your parents were meant to marry each other."

Jacob raised an eyebrow. "Are you taking credit for that, too?"

"Of course. And I'll even take credit for your grandparents' marriage. None of it would've happened without me."

Jacob snorted. "*You* planned it? How's that possible?"

Keitus's hands twitched. Red flashed in the air around him. "I've been alive for a very long time, Jacob."

"Oh, yes. Lorkon are immortal. How'd I forget?"

"The point is, I *bred* you. Your abilities are because of *me*."

Jacob gawked at Keitus, not wanting to believe him. It was too great a stretch of the imagination to think that Keitus had actually arranged for his parents and grandparents to meet each other. And even if he had, why go to all the trouble? Jacob deflected the comment by saying, "I already know you poisoned me when I was little."

"I didn't poison you." Keitus paused, as if to think before he spoke. "I tried to make you into a Lorkon. My own blood went into you."

"Wha—" Jacob's mouth popped open. A Lorkon? Jacob almost became a *Lorkon*?

"Yes. You're surprised? Hadn't heard that before?" Keitus laughed. "Don't think for a moment that your parents and your precious little *Makalos* actually know what I was intending to do with you. They can't possibly see that clearly."

Jacob couldn't help himself, even though he'd vowed not to show curiosity. "Why didn't it work?"

Keitus turned from Jacob. "All my experimentation with babies proved useless once I got my hands on you. You weren't like any of them. You were stronger. More resilient.

And I'm sure Azuriah informed you that you inherited certain . . . traits . . . which prevented you from turning Lorkon when I expected. In my haste to figure out why, *they* were able to take you away."

He stopped talking, his hands forming fists at his side. Jacob watched as a drop of blood fell to the floor. Keitus resumed walking. "My research suggested I'd be able to unlock your gifts and assume complete control over you once you'd reached the age of maturity. A simple touch was all that was required. But your parents ruined that opportunity by introducing foreign agents to your blood. That attempt to heal you has proven a challenge to overcome." He scowled at Jacob. "I'm forced to resort to other . . . methods. More persuasive, you might call them."

"Why are you telling me all this? Aren't I the enemy?" Jacob hesitated before going on. "I'm just going to tell them everything you've told me. You know that, right?"

Keitus paused, looking away. Then he turned and towered over Jacob. He grabbed Jacob's shoulders and squeezed very tightly, making him gasp as fingernails pierced his skin. An intense expression of greed crossed the Lorkon's face and he pushed Jacob against the stone wall.

43

"Join me. Help me unlock the secrets of the universe. Your life will improve greatly. Anything you want, you'll have. We can rule together."

"Secrets of the universe? Are you serious?" Then the other part of what Keitus had said entered Jacob's mind. He snorted. "Dude, look. I'm not Luke and you aren't Darth Vader. I'm not going to '*join*' you." Jacob smiled. Usually it was Matt who had the quick tongue.

Confusion clouded Keitus's face. "What are you talking about?"

Jacob sighed in exhaustion. "Never mind. Okay, I want to go home. Can we just say we had the conversation, you asked me to come with you, I said no, and call it good?"

Keitus released his hold on Jacob and growled, the color in the air around him changing to bright—very bright—red. He raised his fist to attack, slamming it into the wall near Jacob's head instead. Rock and bits of mortar fell to the floor.

He took a deep breath, speaking through clenched teeth. "I *created* you so we could work *together*. Do I need to repeat myself? I'll give you *everything* you want."

Jacob's mouth popped open. Did Keitus actually think he could convince him? "You can't give me my family. Or friendship. Or love. Or happiness."

Keitus held his breath, then released it slowly. "Is it happiness you want? I can give it to you. I can provide anything."

"I don't want counterfeit happiness. I want the real thing." Jacob stepped out from under Keitus's arm. "And I can't live my life in dishonesty. You're a living lie. You think you're happy, but it's obvious you aren't."

"I—"

"I can see emotions. The truth is coloring the air around you."

Keitus frowned, hesitating for several seconds, then he pushed Jacob to the wall, pinning him there. "You *will* help me. You'll die if you don't."

Jacob tried to look brave, even though he definitely didn't feel that way. "If I die, that means you'll never get what you want."

The Lorkon swung Jacob around, dragging him back down the hall and into the room where the other Lorkon waited. "I've tried to reason with you," he said as he stormed. "You are an impertinent, insolent brat." He motioned to the other Lorkon. "We'll do things the old-fashioned way."

One of the Lorkon laughed gleefully, his excitement evident in the colors around him. He strode to a curtain and pulled out a chair with chains and leather straps attached to it. Another Lorkon dragged a table to the center of the room. It was covered with sharp instruments.

Panic hit Jacob. He wasn't an idiot—he knew right away what they intended to do.

"Wait, wait, wait! Okay, I'll do whatever you want!"

Keitus threw him to the ground. "I know that voice—

you're lying. You're going to try to find a way out of here." He motioned to the other Lorkon. "Strap him in the chair."

"No!" Jacob said, ignoring the pain in his hip where he'd hit the floor. "I promise! I'll help!"

Spittle built up at the corner of Keitus's mouth. "I can only tolerate being the *good guy* for so long, Jacob." His sneer grew broader. "See into the past. Seek out and find the Key of Ayunli."

"Okay, I'll try!" Jacob took a deep breath. "But I only just started learning this ability."

Keitus growled in anger and Jacob rolled to the side, trying to dodge the Lorkon's foot. He didn't go far enough, and the tip of Keitus's boot struck him in the side. Jacob gasped at the sharp pain.

"Find it. Now!"

Jacob held his arms over his ribs. He couldn't help the tears that streamed down his face. He coughed, dragging himself to his knees, holding a hand up in a gesture of surrender.

"Finally," Keitus said. "We're getting somewhere."

Jacob dragged in a breath. "I . . . I need time. Takes time."

Keitus motioned to the table that had the food on it. "Make yourself at home. We'll wait."

Jacob pulled himself up and got into the chair. His body still tense, he massaged his forehead, trying to get the headache to leave. How was he supposed to concentrate well enough to see into the past? And why did they want the Key of Ayunli, anyway? Wouldn't the Key of Kilenya be enough? Then it dawned on Jacob—Keitus wanted *him* for the Key of Kilenya. It only worked when *he* used it.

He took a deep breath. "If you want this key, I'm going to need information. When was the last time it was seen? Who had it? How many years ago?"

Keitus motioned to one of the Lorkon, who pulled a roll of

parchment from his robes.

The Lorkon glanced over the parchment. "It has been four hundred years since it was carried from the castle by a hooded man." He looked up. "That is all we know."

Jacob's heart fell, disappointment flooding through him. "That doesn't give me *anything*." He put his face in his hands. "It's going to take forever to get to a spot four hundred years in the past!"

Keitus leaned forward in his chair. "Then you'd better start, hadn't you?"

"You need to understand something," Jacob said. "Doing this is very dangerous, and I have to build up my endurance. Azuriah told me it could kill me."

"I'm losing my patience with you, Danilo." Keitus glared at him, the bright red and green of his eyes boring into Jacob's. "*Get started!*"

Jacob nodded. He couldn't afford to make Keitus any angrier than he already was. No telling what the Lorkon would do. Jacob put his elbows on the table in front of him, resting his head in his hands, then focused on the wall in front of him, concentrating on the time period he wanted to See.

Everything around him broke into commotion as his reality shifted. He tried to grasp onto something—anything—that would give him a clue to the whereabouts of the Key of Ayunli. He strained into the past—further and further away from the current time. The pain in his chest amplified with each hundred years he scanned until he felt his body would explode.

Finally, he caught a brief glimpse of the hooded man. Then, it was as if the curtains had fallen on Jacob's vision, and he slammed back to the current time.

He opened his eyes and gasped. He must have flopped out of his chair. Keitus held him up by the collar of his shirt.

"Did you find it?"

Jacob shook his head.

In disgust, Keitus dropped him and walked back to the throne, his cloak swirling behind him. "Then keep going."

Jacob gasped for breath, his bones aching from all the times he'd been flung to the ground. He used the chair to pull himself up again, then sat, wishing now more than ever that he was at home. Why hadn't he gone through the door *before* everyone else?

Nearly whimpering, he tried Time-Seeing again. The pain in his chest began as he glared ahead and he focused on it, willing it to spread to his entire body. Slowly, the intensity crawled from his heart and to his lungs, then it finally made that familiar pop as it pulsated over him.

A thousand flashes. Jacob felt his body being pulled in every direction. It took him what seemed forever to grasp on to the image of the hooded man. He finally did, but nothing else worked. His ears roared, he felt a constant sensation of vertigo—as if he were about to fall off a cliff—and his eyes burned.

Whipping around, Jacob flew back to the present time. He found himself on the floor once more and tasted bile in his mouth. Keitus had risen from the throne, his hand reaching toward Jacob, an intense expression on his face.

"Success? Did you see where it is?"

Jacob shook his head. "Only the man. He's holding a small leather package. It all happened too long ago. I have to build up to it. It could take days—weeks, even."

Keitus growled in anger and jumped to the table, flinging it on its side. Food scattered across the floor. "Get it! Now!" He hovered over Jacob. "I'm in no mood to wait!"

"I know, but Keitus—"

"You foolish, naive, useless boy!" Keitus stormed from the room, calling over his shoulder. "Return him to his cell. He'll practice there."

44

With a nod from one of the Lorkon, the Molg nearest Jacob picked him up and carried him through the fortress. One Lorkon trailed behind.

"Put him down," the Lorkon said when they got to the cell.

The Molg flung Jacob onto the cot. Jacob bounced off and cracked his knee on the stone floor. He called out in pain, and the Lorkon grabbed the Molg by the throat.

"I didn't say throw him!"

The Molg grunted in response and he and the Lorkon left, slamming the door behind them. Jacob heard the Lorkon give muffled orders to the Molg, having the beast stand guard near Jacob's door.

He got up and wiped off the floor slime as best he could. He couldn't wait to get home and to a shower. He bit his lip in fear, wondering what would happen if he never got out. No— he couldn't think that way. He had to remain positive.

Jacob lay on the cot gingerly, trying not to cause himself any extra pain. This just wasn't fair. He shut his eyes tightly. Crying wasn't going to happen, no matter how exhausted he was and no matter how much he hurt.

It seemed like everything bad in the world happened to him. In *both* worlds. Getting kidnapped. Not making varsity. Nearly being turned into a Lorkon. And Aloren dating *Kevin*, of all people. Sure, he'd had plenty of time to adjust to it. But that did little to make him feel better, especially now, in his current predicament.

He sat up. Enough self-pity. He needed to concentrate on how to get out of the room.

Starting near the door, Jacob felt his way around the walls again, going up as high as possible, pulling his cot around the room to stand on so he could inspect every possible inch, dealing with the slime on his hands.

Nothing.

He searched the entire floor with no luck. The ceiling was a couple of inches too high. But he couldn't skip it—he had to do everything possible.

An idea popped into his head. He flipped the cot up against the wall, then climbed the underside like a ladder. He smiled—that was perfect.

It took an hour at least to feel every bit of the stone above him. But just like the walls and floor, there wasn't even a fraction of an inch that emitted heat. How was it possible that the Shiengols had constructed this place so incredibly well?

Jacob righted the cot and sat on it, fully discouraged now. Early rapped on the window and he scooted the cot under the glass to be near her. He waved, giving her a little smile. She sat on the window sill and waved back. It was good to have her company, even if talking to each other wasn't possible.

He sighed, turning his mind back to the dilemma at hand —escaping. It was obvious to him now that he couldn't mold his way out of the room. Maybe he'd be able to bribe the Molgs?

But when a Molg brought him dinner, the expression on the beast's face told him he'd have more luck convincing the fortress to open itself up for him than he would getting the creature on his side.

The sun set while Jacob watched, face pressed against the window. Hours had passed since Keitus had him locked up again.

A while after the last rays of light had disappeared, Jacob finally lay down. The pain and exhaustion from the day caught up to him, and he fell asleep.

SUNLIGHT through the window woke him the next morning and Jacob jerked up, looking around in panic. It took a couple of moments before he remembered where he was and what had happened.

He fell back onto the cot, sighing in frustration. He hated being in such complete solitude. Yes, he knew others had experienced worse—being stuck in rooms that were so small they couldn't stand or fully lay out, and bathroom facilities lowered through the ceiling by way of a bucket. 'Course, the bucket idea wasn't new to him. He sent a withering glance to his own bucket in the corner of the room.

Jacob ran his hand through his hair, almost immediately wishing he hadn't. He desperately needed a shower. And breakfast. His stomach growled. Hopefully, it wouldn't be long before someone brought him something to eat. He tipped his head back and closed his eyes, feeling grateful for yet another thing—good food that hadn't been poisoned.

His mind wandered as he gazed at the ceiling. How did the Lorkon get Molgs all the way out here?

He rolled over, then jumped when a Molg opened the door, putting a tray of food on the floor. The Molg sneered at him and slammed the door shut.

Jacob bounced off the cot and grabbed the tray. It only

took a minute to down breakfast, satisfying his empty stomach.

When he'd finished eating, he thought about home, wondering how his family was doing. They had to be completely panicked. He'd never disappeared like this before. 'Course, he was positive they'd figured everything out, especially with Early's messages.

And another thing was bothering him—how much school had he missed? Today was . . . Tuesday. Or maybe Wednesday. That meant he'd missed five days. Last Monday and Tuesday, and the first half of this week.

Jacob spent the next couple of hours in boredom, scratching designs in the slime on the nearest wall. Sometime around ten or maybe eleven—he couldn't tell—he decided he should probably be practicing his Time-Seeing ability. Maybe he'd be able to find the Key of Ayunli, and then not tell Keitus he'd seen it. Jacob seriously doubted he'd be able to accomplish the goal that day. But if the Lorkon kept him there for the rest of his life, he'd definitely be able to do it with practice.

He sat on the cot, facing the door, and concentrated on the Key of Ayunli. He unfocused his eyes and centered on the pain in his chest, willing it to grow and envelop him.

With a pop, it did. And things were different this time— easier. Everything around him changed, and he was in a much different castle from any he'd ever seen before. All the walls were covered with ornate tapestries, the floors with rugs. Not one inch of stone was visible. He only knew it was a castle because of the spaciousness, and the fact that he could see towers through the many windows.

He turned his attention to the hooded man who stood in front of him, holding the key in one hand, gaping at it. He held the leather package with his other.

This was the most detail Jacob had been able to see yet. He

looked around in wonder, taking in the entire room. Beautiful tapestries and swords hung decoratively on the wall. Gold and marble statues graced the hall, and the carpet underfoot appeared to be plush, though Jacob couldn't feel it. There was a hallway behind him lined with stained-glass windows. Sunlight filtered in, making colored patterns on the floor.

With a start, Jacob realized the man had left. Dang it! How had he missed that? He tried Time-Seeing to find the man, but everything went black.

Jacob found himself waking up on the floor of his cell. The light from the window was different—it was late afternoon, almost twilight. Several hours had passed. Had he blacked out? How long had he been Time-Seeing? He tried to get up, but his body freaked out with spasms of pain and he was barely able to roll onto his side. What was wrong? He'd been sore that morning when he woke up, but not *that* sore.

He rolled to a sitting position, groaning. The food tray had been replaced with a full one, and something dawned on Jacob. The Lorkon must have returned. Horror washed over him. Would they attack him while he was unconscious? They must have done something—his entire body ached.

He pulled up his shirt—sure enough, his stomach was black and blue. He felt like retching. Why would the Lorkon do that? Were they the reason he blacked out? Or had he blacked out because he'd been Time-Seeing too long, making the Lorkon frustrated when they couldn't wake him?

An urgency to get out of his situation flooded over him, replacing the horror he'd felt earlier. He had to get home! He had to get away!

But how?

Jacob eased himself off the floor and onto the cot. He slumped in exhaustion, noticing he was covered with slime again. So much for keeping it off—nothing he could do about it anyway.

Early rapped on the window, and he scooted over to where he could see her. They kept each other company. She danced on the window sill, smiling at him, mouthing things he didn't understand.

He couldn't help but wonder why she wasn't able to break through the window. Maybe her magic had a rule that prevented her from breaking things? He didn't know. 'Course, it wouldn't do him any good for her to get the glass open. He was way too high above the ground to jump. But it really would be nice to talk to her. Even though her conversation was trivial, it was still conversation. And they'd done a lot together in the past month—he'd really grown to care for and appreciate her.

The sun was about to set, and he watched the rays fly across the sky. A moment of stupor hit him—he hadn't allowed himself to relax or take a mental vacation for a long time. He invited it in, enjoying its simple calmness.

But then, a few minutes later, Jacob shook his head to clear it. He'd wasted precious time and energy trying to find the key when he should've been focusing on Seeing how the Lorkon had trapped him. There had to be something special about the fortress or this room that hadn't been the case earlier. If he found out what it was, perhaps it would give him the needed information to escape.

45

Jacob Time-Saw to the castle in Maivoryl city, "rewinding" until he reached the point before the Lorkon left to come to August Fortress. An involuntary shudder crossed him when he saw Keitus on his throne with the other Lorkon around him. He remembered how it had felt to be in that room the first time—the awe at seeing the Key of Kilenya, followed by the fear and pain from his encounter with that disgusting individual. That had happened only five months ago, but it felt like ages had passed.

A small burst of flame near Keitus startled Jacob—luckily none of the Lorkon could see him. That flame had been familiar, though, and in surprise, Jacob nearly lost control of his Time-Seeing. He grimaced. He'd seen that flame as he'd been about to go into August Fortress. Apparently, it *was* a fire beetle—they must all have different colors and sizes.

A crackly voice addressed Keitus. "The boy and his group are on their way to release the Shiengols."

Keitus jumped to his feet. "We leave now," he said to the other Lorkon in the room with him.

"You were right, Your Majesty," one of the Lorkon said,

grabbing things from behind a curtain, "about having beetles spy on the boy."

Keitus glared at the Lorkon. "And if you were doing your job, *you* would've thought of the idea."

"Yes, but they can't get into the Makalo village, so it would've been pointless."

Keitus ignored him. "Send for Sindons. And we'll need as many Molgs as possible."

"What about Dusts?"

Keitus's disgusted grunt said enough. Jacob figured he was probably sick of the nearly useless creatures. Maybe training them was too difficult? Jacob felt little hope that was the case.

"You were right about that too, Keitus. You think of everything!"

The Lorkon continued to praise Keitus, and Jacob felt sick at how he received the compliments. Such arrogance! If anyone treated Jacob like that, he'd avoid them.

He fast-forwarded through time, wanting to see what the Lorkon did rather than hear their annoying conversation. They mounted the Sindons—Keitus, of course, sitting on top of one in a rather silly-looking caravan-type thing—embellished with gold and silver and dark blues and purples.

Jacob watched as the group rounded up several Molgs and passed through Maivoryl City and the tunnel in the wall. The Sindon barely fit inside it.

A moment later, when the Lorkon reached the scented air, Jacob slowed down time, watching in interest as the Molgs got stuck. The Lorkon had a hard time pulling the large creatures out. He laughed when he saw Keitus throw a fit from the top of his Sindon, screaming at the other Lorkon to get the Molgs. Then he stopped laughing when Keitus ordered one of the Lorkon to rip Kenji's warning signs out of the ground and throw them into the lake.

Stupid Lorkon.

The three Lorkon in the scented air bickered like little kids, and out of curiosity, Jacob drew near to hear them.

"This is ridiculous," one said.

"If I'd known when I accepted his challenge that I would become a slave . . ."

"Shut your mouth!" the third Lorkon said. "You aren't a slave. If I'm ever in charge, you will be, though."

The first and second Lorkon responded, and it looked like things would escalate. Jacob watched with interest. The Lorkon certainly were childlike sometimes.

Keitus called orders from the top of the carriage, but the other three weren't paying attention. Finally, he stepped down.

"*Enough!*"

The Lorkon stopped and stared at him. At a flick of his hand, they fell to the ground, terror on their faces, groveling before him, begging for forgiveness.

Jacob raised an eyebrow. How had Keitus gotten them to change their attitudes so quickly? Did he have them under a spell?

"My own flesh and blood! How *dare* you act like this? You're worse than Dusts!"

"Father, please—"

"*Shut your mouth!*" Keitus spat. "You *will not* speak until I command it!"

Flesh and blood? Father?

The Lorkon pressed his face into the ground, and Keitus paced. "The next who speaks out of line will become meat for the Molgs!"

Jacob thought that sounded like a dumb threat until he noticed the affect it had on the Lorkon. They were trembling with fear. Why? And it didn't seem like the Molgs had any desire to eat a Lorkon. Speaking of the Molgs, they'd wandered back into the scented air and had stupid grins on their faces. Jacob laughed—they looked even more ridiculous than any human he'd seen there before.

Keitus finally stopped pacing. "I'm undoing this Counter. I'm tired of dealing with it every time we pass through with inferior beings."

Counter?

Keitus lifted his arms waist high and chanted something. He raised his hands higher, still chanting, staring ahead, until his arms were pointed to the sky. The ground shook, every blade of grass, including the dead ones, straightening, pointing up. The brush in the area nearly uprooted itself. A bluish substance, not quite liquid, not quite gas, flowed from the earth all around the group. It rolled along the ground, floating upward, then swirled around Keitus, faster and faster. Like an explosion, the substance burst and then dissipated into air.

After a moment of silence, Keitus lowered his hands and pointed to the Lorkon. "Get up. Now. We have work to do."

The Lorkon and Molgs got back on the Sindons, which had appeared to be unaffected by the scented air. They moved quickly and Jacob zoomed to keep up, finding himself fast-forwarding through time to skip the boring parts.

He was somewhat surprised when the group took a shortcut through Dunsany Mountain, then came out in the city Kenji had called Fornchall. If only Jacob had known that shortcut before. It would have been easier than going around the mountain, and perhaps Seden would still be alive. Then he decided that wouldn't have been good—the Lorkon passed several areas thick with Molgs. If Seden had taken them that way, they would never have made it out.

Jacob fast-forwarded even more, realizing his body would be getting tired soon. Azuriah's warning sounded in his ears—he needed to get to the point quickly, before his body gave out on him.

The group finally stopped near the fortress, on the opposite side from where Jacob and his friends had been.

Another burst of flame near Keitus, and again, a crackly voice reported. "They've found a way into the fortress."

Keitus said something curt in another language—Jacob could tell it was a swear word, due to the tone of the Lorkon's voice and the expression on his face. He motioned for the others to follow him on foot.

They left the Sindons behind and slunk around the huge building to the front, followed by several Molgs. They moved into the trees, and Jacob caught a glimpse of Aldo and Aloren looking up at the fortress wall. Things blacked over for a moment and Jacob worried he was slipping out of consciousness again, but then the scenery returned with usual clarity. The Lorkon were watching Jacob's friends, who were gawking at a hole in the fortress. Jacob realized he must have just gone through that hole.

Two of the Lorkon tried to go forward to attack, but Keitus held them back. A moment later, the Shiengols emerged, and Jacob watched the Lorkon's reaction with surprise. Their emotions went so quickly from eagerness to fear that he nearly jumped in shock. They were afraid of the Shiengols! No wonder they'd trapped the creatures! Could he use that to his advantage?

A few of the Shiengols stared at the Lorkon as they passed, and anger flashed through Jacob. They'd known the Lorkon were there! Why hadn't they done anything about it?

Had Azuriah known?

Jacob gasped when he realized that of course the Shiengol leader knew about the Lorkon. He'd insisted on having Jacob practice his new ability before leaving the fortress. He must have known Jacob would be kidnapped, but how? And why hadn't he done something to stop it? Why hadn't he warned Jacob?

Jacob realized that Keitus and two or three Molgs had gone around a corner, and he opted not to follow them for the time being. He wanted to see what the three Lorkon did. A couple of the Molgs hid behind the door Jacob and his friends had set up. He shook his head, making a mental note to check behind every makeshift door just to be sure nothing was there.

Azuriah came out of the hole in the fortress, followed by . . . then everything got muddled again and Jacob couldn't see details well enough. He tried everything he could—going around the haze, below, above. Nothing worked. He sighed in frustration, realizing there wasn't anything he could do but go See where the Lorkon leader had gone.

But then he felt an odd sensation flooding through him—originating at his heart—and he hesitated. What was wrong? His body—exhaustion crept into his mind. Oh! He was about to black out again! Time for a break.

Lights flashed around him, and he found himself back in his cell. It was nighttime—he'd been Time-Seeing for half an hour at least, if not more. No wonder it'd almost knocked him out.

He rolled to a sitting position on the floor, then jumped when a shape on the other side of the room shifted too.

A Lorkon was with him in the cell.

"Keitus?"

"No. He sent me to check on you. You were Time-Seeing, were you not?"

"Yes."

"What have you to report?"

"Not much. I . . . I still need more time. I mean, I've been trying, but—"

Jacob jerked into the corner when the Lorkon jumped forward, looming over him. Any feelings of smugness Jacob had felt earlier at the ineptitude of the Lorkon fled when he saw the expression on this one's face. Keitus might have been much, much more powerful than the other three, but that didn't mean this guy couldn't inflict a whole lot of damage. "I swear! I'm doing my best! And I have made progress—I saw the entire room the hooded man was in this time! And he went through a hallway. I'm going back to see where he—"

"I don't care about the trivialities. You *will* find what Keitus desires."

The Lorkon rapped on the door, it swung open, and he stepped out.

46

Jacob clutched his chest as soon as he was alone again. Another fright like that—first, nearly going unconscious, then the Lorkon freaking him out—and he'd probably not make it. His heart hurt so badly. What would happen if his body gave out on him while Time-Seeing? Would he be stuck halfway between two places? He hoped not.

In the dim moonlight, he saw a tray of food on the floor and picked it up, then scarfed everything. Why were they feeding him so well? The food was still warm.

His hunger appeased, he lay on the cot, gazing out the window. Early was there—she waved at him and he lifted a hand in response, glad to have her company.

The next morning, he woke before the sun had risen, deciding to start Time-Seeing as soon as possible.

He Saw back into the past and searched through the fortress until he found where Keitus had gone when he left the other Lorkon. He had a couple of Molgs with him, and they were walking down the hall toward Jacob's cell.

Keitus pointed at one of the Molgs. "Go get a door. Our guest will need something to keep him in place."

Jacob wondered where they'd find a door. Hadn't Keitus removed all of them long ago? Maybe they'd brought some with, and Jacob hadn't noticed. The creature ran off, and Keitus and the other Molg entered the cell. Jacob nearly panicked before realizing that in the time line he was seeing, he wouldn't be in the cell yet. He was still outside with his friends.

Keitus stood to the side, allowing the second Molg to bring in a couple of large buckets full of—Jacob looked closer —sludge. Was that what he thought it was? He looked around the cell to verify. Yup. The stone was completely clean.

"Spread it on every inch of rock."

The first Molg returned, hung the door, then the two of them got to work, pulling out gobs of the grease at a time, rubbing it all over the floor, ceiling, and walls. Keitus watched from the doorway for a couple of minutes, an evil smile on his face, then turned to go. "We'll bring the boy soon."

A few moments later, the Molgs finished smearing the stuff everywhere and took the buckets away. Jacob heard grunting in the hallway, then everything went foggy and he couldn't see any longer. He allowed himself to return to the present time, many questions running through his mind.

Why did Keitus put the slime everywhere? Was it to intimidate Jacob? To gross him out? Make him feel dirty and miserable? Or did it have a bigger purpose?

Jacob inspected the wall closest to him. He swiped a finger across it, then looked at the slime up close. "Why did Keitus put you all over my cell?" he whispered.

What if . . . Jacob stared at the door in wonder. Would the stuff counter his ability? Make it useless? But how? And how would Keitus know to concoct something like that?

Jacob used his sleeve to wipe off as much of the gunk on a

spot as he could. Then he put his hand on the stone, trying to warm it. Nothing happened. He shook his head, knitting his eyebrows. The stuff would leave a residue—he wouldn't be able to clean that off without water and lots and lots of rags. And what if everything it touched was permanently immune? It had been all over his hands—had Keitus removed Jacob's ability to mold things?

He felt claustrophobic and took a deep breath, trying to calm himself. He'd find a way out—he had to. If not, he'd be stuck there forever. He kept breathing deeply and glanced out the window, past Early. The sky was clouded over—it'd been snowing.

He had to concentrate. It wouldn't do him any good to panic and stress over things he couldn't control. After several moments of focusing on calming down, Jacob decided he needed to go through his options.

He could wait for the Fat Lady. That is, if she was coming at all, of course. Maybe she'd gotten hold of Gallus's family and they'd send someone. Was there a town closer to the fortress than Macaria? He wasn't sure. He didn't know much about Eklaron, aside from where he'd been already.

He could accept Keitus's offer. He snorted, thinking about that. Yeah, right.

Maybe his family would find another link that would lead them here. His experience with the Eetu fish showed him there were far more links between the two worlds than they'd all originally thought. Perhaps one of them would work. If that were the case, they might be close!

Jacob jumped to his knees, staring out the window. Early flitted up next to him, a hopeful expression on her face. He scanned the forest toward the link to Taga Village and saw nothing, then looked the other way as far as he could —no sign.

He sighed, lowering his head, and pressed his face on the glass.

Wait. "The glass!" he whispered. It didn't have slime all over it! As if in response to this idea, the sun broke through the clouds, lighting his cell.

He was about to touch the surface to warm it when he realized his hands had grease on them. He couldn't afford to infect the glass, too. The fact that the Molgs hadn't touched it, or the frame around it, made him nearly giggle in hysteria—just like Shirley at school. But seriously, how would Keitus react if Jacob were able to escape that way? He'd be furious!

Just then, he heard voices down the hall. Someone was coming! Jacob had always been an awful liar. They'd sense the hope in him—they'd know he was planning something.

He quickly dropped to the floor and closed his eyes, pretending to be Time-Seeing. No—just lying there wouldn't do it. He had to make it believable.

Just as the door opened, he started convulsing.

Would they buy it?

Two Lorkon voices. One laughed. "Stupid human."

Jacob heard the rush of a cloak before the Lorkon's foot connected with his side. His already very bruised side.

A groan of pain slipped out before he could stop it and an involuntary shudder passed through him. One of the Lorkon laughed.

"This boy is idiotic. Why does Keitus want him so badly?"

"Flesh and blood—you know how it is with him."

Jacob heard a smirk in the first Lorkon's voice. "Yeah, well, that didn't help us, did it?"

What were they talking about? Flesh and blood? Then Jacob remembered—Keitus had mentioned blood. His own blood had gone into Jacob, trying to change him into a Lorkon. Was that all they meant?

He realized he'd stopped shaking and hadn't heard

anything from the Lorkon for several seconds. He groaned again and rolled to the other side, hoping—hoping!—the Lorkon would think he was still Time-Seeing.

Silence.

Finally, one of the Lorkon spoke. "We could kill him now."

No response. Jacob held his breath, convulsing occasionally, waiting to hear what the other said.

A grunt. "We could, but . . ." The Lorkon took a deep breath, then let out a watery-sounding cough. "Keitus would never forgive it."

The first Lorkon snorted. "He never forgives anything." Someone nudged Jacob with a foot. "We'd be free from hearing about *Danilo*."

Another pause. "We'll think on it. Leave the food. Let's go."

Something scraped across the floor, then the door shut and Jacob heard footsteps receding down the hall.

He waited for a moment, making sure he was alone, then peeked through his lashes. No one was with him. He got to his knees, a huge sigh of relief expelling itself from his lungs. "Oh, wow, oh, wow," he whispered over and over again. That was way too close!

Jacob pulled the tray of food to himself, not forgetting his decision from earlier to get out through the window. He ate quickly, then looked at the water, wishing he had soap. The water alone would have to do.

But first, he jumped up and looked out the window to the ground below. No one was there. He watched for a moment, waiting to see if anyone would come. When no one did, he got down and poured a trickle of the water on his hands, wiping them off on the underside of his cot—the only place clean enough in the cell.

Thinking better of using all the water, he put the half-empty cup under his cot, behind one of the legs where it wouldn't be immediately visible from the doorway. Just in case.

Then, with clean hands, he jumped up and put his palms against the glass, willing it to heat up.

Nothing happened.

He moaned in despair. The Molgs hadn't put slime on it—he'd been so sure!

He nearly smacked himself in the forehead when he remembered that if something was well built, it *wouldn't* warm up. He felt around the edges of the window and nearly jumped off the bed with excitement when he felt warmth—warmth! He kept going. The frame itself had a few potentially good spots, but the caulking—was that what they called it?—heated up really quickly. He could pull it out, then remove the window!

Jacob got to work, pulling the caulking out, wadding it up, and sticking it to the underside of his cot. He felt like he was six again, with all the stuff he was putting there.

Every time he heard one of his guards moving outside, he dropped to a sitting position, careful not to touch anything. He didn't even have to ask himself what would happen if he got caught removing the sealant. And while he wasn't sure this plan would work, he was positive the Lorkon would either move him or slather the window with sludge.

He had barely a second to fall to a lying position on the cot and pretend to be staring out the window when he heard voices right outside his cell. The door swung open and he turned.

It was Keitus.

47

"Danilo, I'm disappointed."

Jacob sat up, not sure how to read Keitus's emotions. He had multiple colors swirling around him, blending into each other.

"What—what do you mean?"

"You aren't being honest. You haven't tried hard enough. I need to remind you what will happen if you don't find that key."

Jacob's mouth popped open. "But . . . but I *have* tried! It's almost killed me—I fall unconscious all the time and my heart is going to pop with everything I'm putting it through. And I've been working hard! I can see all the way back to where the hooded man leaves the castle. Just give me more time. I'll be able to follow him, I promise!" Most of what he said was true—he really did worry that his body was going to break down. And he really did think he'd be able to follow the man if he tried again.

Keitus looked Jacob in the eye. "Boy, you are a terrible liar. The hooded man *used* the key to go somewhere. Why would he just walk out of the castle when he's got a powerful instrument in his hands?"

Jacob stared at his hands, annoyed with himself and the fact that he hadn't thought of that.

"And it doesn't matter anyway."

Jacob looked up. "It doesn't? Why?"

Keitus strode across the room and looked out the window. Jacob held his breath, praying with every ounce of his body that the Lorkon wouldn't notice what he'd been doing.

"We've decided to kill you."

"What? No!" That wasn't possible. Not after everything Keitus had said!

Keitus turned to face Jacob. "The other Lorkon presented me with a very good argument. They seem to think you'll never join or help me, and if that's the case, I can't have you somehow escaping and making it back to your family.

"I spent years setting things up so you'd be born. You are, shall I say, my pet project. To see you dead would bring me much disappointment." He glared at Jacob. "But if you helped my enemies, it could be my downfall. And I *won't allow that.*"

He grabbed Jacob by the face, pulling him several feet up. Jacob's eyes smarted from the pain in his jaw. "Your death will not be easy for you, nor fast. I will make you cry for mercy, but there will be none to give. And when I'm through with you, I'll move to everyone you love, starting with your little sister."

He dropped Jacob. "Unless, of course, you decide to bind yourself to me." He turned away. "Remember this, boy. Remember it with every part of you. I created you. You belong to me. And if I can't have your powers, *no one* can."

Jacob remained where he'd fallen, motionless. He believed Keitus. The Lorkon really would kill him. And, after Jacob's death, it would only be a matter of time before Keitus found a way to Mendon. A part of his heart shriveled when he thought of what would happen to his baby sister if Keitus ever made it that far. And to Matt. And his parents. And Aloren. Jacob couldn't allow that to happen. He wouldn't. He'd do anything . . . the thought that crossed his mind made him gasp in shock. Was he really considering accepting Keitus's offer?

If it meant saving his family, maybe? Possibly?

He sat up, dropping his eyes to his hands. "I . . ." He hesitated, looking up at the Lorkon, creasing his forehead. "Keitus, I—"

Keitus's cheeks lifted, showing his dirty teeth in what Jacob could only assume was a smile. He must've sensed Jacob's indecision. "I'll return in thirty minutes. Have your decision ready for me. If it's yes, I have many things to teach you. If it's no, you know what to expect."

The door shut behind the Lorkon king, and Jacob slumped on the cot. What was he doing? Was he really considering this? Joining the person who'd made his life incredibly difficult and painful the past several months? How was it possible?

He shook his head. If he did join Keitus, he might actually have more power to help his family.

He got to his feet and paced, making a path in the slime. Was joining Keitus the right thing to do? He searched himself, trying to understand his feelings, and felt shock when he found an element of peace there. Was that because it was right? Was he "meant" to be with Keitus? Would things fall into place for him?

He sat on the cot again. He couldn't think. Things kept slipping from his mental grasp. Okay, a more logical, straightforward reasoning was required. What were the pros and cons?

Pros—he wouldn't die. And he might be able to prevent the deaths of those he loved. He shook his head. He wasn't so naive as to believe Keitus would allow his enemies to live. But maybe, maybe he'd be able to convince Keitus to transport them somewhere far away—somewhere safe, where they'd have no control or influence. Would that be enough?

Other pros. He wracked his brain, concentrating. He could be a spy. He could feed the good guys information. Act as a double agent.

And the cons?

He'd be selling his soul, basically. And he felt strongly that was true. But if it saved the lives of his loved ones, would it be worth it?

Also, he hated the Lorkon. He felt dirty and gross around them. He doubted that would ever go away. He naturally shied away from bad things. Always had. Plus, he knew the Lorkon would probably treat him very poorly. They'd abuse him mentally, emotionally, physically.

Jacob got up to pace again. What could he do? Join the Lorkon, save his loved ones, and lose himself. Or deny Keitus and be killed, knowing his loved ones would follow.

There *was* one more con to joining Keitus.

If he sided with the Lorkon, it would destroy his mother. And he couldn't live with that. He couldn't.

Jacob felt peace then—true peace—and he held on to it as hard as he could. He closed his eyes, picturing his mother's face. He pictured Amberly's sweet smile and Aloren's beautiful eyes. Then he jumped to his feet. He'd wasted five minutes with his moment of weakness. That left him with only twenty-five to escape.

Concentrating, he Time-Saw the fortress, wanting to know where everyone was before he did anything. The Molgs stood guard outside his door still, looking bored. Keitus paced in the throne room. The three Lorkon were at the table there, playing some sort of game with rocks.

Then he looked outside. Molgs were stationed randomly

around the fortress, some pacing, others staring into the forest.

There was the makeshift door where it had been before. Jacob "looked" behind it, making sure no Molgs were there, and then his eyes caught a gleam in the trees behind the door.

The key! The Lorkon hadn't found it! But how did it get way over there? He wondered if Early had moved it. Wasn't it too heavy for her? He zoomed in closer, wanting to be sure that's what it was. It was barely visible—only a sparkle of one of the diamonds and a little metal catching the sunlight—but definitely the key. Relief flooded through him.

He pulled back, seeing the fortress from farther away, counting how many Molgs were outside. Ten, one of which was near the makeshift door, but the rest were placed across the grounds.

He could do this!

Jacob jerked to his cell, making sure he was still alone, then quickly knelt on the cot and resumed warming the caulking. Hurry! Faster! Faster! Early was on the other side, cheering him on. He could see her excitement—it flowed in the air around her.

When he was down to the last bit, he put his hand on the window to steady it, hoping that by yanking hard enough on the caulking, the glass would fall inward, rather than outward.

He tugged on the stuff. The window creaked. He tugged harder, and it shifted visibly. Then he pulled with all his might and the window flipped out of the seal, landing on him. He got knocked to the floor with a thud, and the sheet of glass slid with him. *Ouch.*

But it didn't break.

He breathed a sigh of relief and leaned the glass up against the wall. The floor was too slippery, though, and the pane started sliding. He jumped forward, caught it just in time, and froze, waiting to see if the Molgs outside his door had heard it scraping.

Early flitted to his side, doing somersaults in the air, but Jacob waited.

When nothing happened, he lowered the glass to the floor, where it wouldn't break unless someone stepped on it.

Jacob jumped back up on the cot and looked out the hole he'd just created. His eyes blurred and he pulled himself back in quickly, clutching his chest. The ground was so far below! His head spun and he began hyperventilating. How was he going to do this? He'd always been afraid of heights, and when they were this bad, he had no hope.

"Jacob!" Early said. "You must come now! You've got a way out of the fortress!"

He steadied himself against the wall. He sucked in one deep breath after another, trying to clear his mind. When he felt more ready, more determined, he pulled the last of the water from below his cot and washed his hands. He *would* save himself.

Realizing he wouldn't be able to concentrate well enough to Time-See while he was escaping, he turned to Early. "Go find out where everyone is, then give me updates every couple of seconds. Make sure no one is coming."

She nodded and zoomed back and forth quickly, giving him reports. The Molgs below hadn't noticed anything, and she could see the Lorkon through a window—they were still in the throne room.

Jacob sat on the ledge, legs outside, careful not to look down. "Just like on the wall of the fortress," he muttered. "Just like on the wall of the fortress."

Holding on to the ledge, he turned around, lowering himself. His feet swung wildly in the air as he tried to find somewhere to put them. Nothing.

He paused, breathing deeply, calming his heart.

"Don't look down," Early whispered. "There's a Molg directly below you."

Great. Just great.

His breath came in quick bursts and he closed his eyes as tight as he could. The tower felt like it was falling—his senses were completely messed up.

Finally, when he was sure he could control his panic, he swung his left arm over the ledge, careful not to the touch the slimy interior of the cell, and used the crook of his elbow to hold on, freeing up his right hand.

Jacob heated a deep handhold into the stone, then another one next to it. He made sure there was plenty of stone to grip, fitting it perfectly to himself.

This was easy. He could do it. He pretended the ground was only a foot below. If he fell, it would be like stepping off a curb. Nothing more to it.

48

J acob reached down as far as he could and molded another spot. Then taking a deep breath, he put his right hand in one of the upper holes, letting go of the sill with his elbow. For a moment, his body swung as he tried to put his left hand in the other hole. He nearly slipped.

A warming sensation started on his rear end and he felt lighter, his mind clearing. He would have blushed, but instead felt intense gratitude. Early was helping him. He wondered how she was doing it without sending him shooting into the air.

Finally, Jacob got his fingertips into the other hole. They inched in, and his grip there strengthened. Once he knew he wouldn't slip out, he hung for a moment, letting himself relax as much as possible. He didn't have a lot of experience with rock climbing, but at least basketball and learning sword play had strengthened his upper body considerably.

"Early," he whispered, "can you help me find places to put my feet?"

With Early's guidance, he warmed more holes in the stone and slowly lowered himself, making sure to go to the right from the window, just in case someone looked down. Which he was sure they would. Early gave him frequent updates on Molg and Lorkon activity so he'd know how much time he had.

Several moments later, he neared a corner. After Early checked that no one was watching, he reached around and molded holes, then pulled himself past. He breathed a sigh of relief. He would no longer be visible from the window. So far, so good.

Jacob continued like this—working through shaking muscles, warming up handholds, slowly lowering himself, avoiding windows, and having Early keep watch. It felt like hours had passed, though he knew it had only been maybe ten or fifteen minutes. How much more time did he have? Five minutes? Would Keitus actually wait a full half hour? Jacob doubted it.

He rested for a moment, taking stock of how far he'd gone and how much farther he had left. He was relieved to see that the ground was much closer now. He'd made progress! But the wall ended a couple of feet below. The drop to the next roof was at least ten feet down. That would be difficult to manage.

He made two handholds just above the edge where the wall ended, then lowered himself, closing the distance to the roof below. He shook his head, wondering at the Shiengols' thought process when they'd built this place. Random walls and roofs and ledges everywhere.

With Early encouraging him, he released his grip, landing with a clatter.

Jacob scrambled to find something to hold on to, but couldn't. He started sliding down, gaining speed. Just in time, he caught himself. His legs slid off the edge of the roof, but he held on tight, hanging over the side.

He nearly cried in relief. He'd made it!

Early hovered next to him. "You can't go down this way!" she said. "Too many windows!"

Jacob pulled himself up, got to his hands and feet, and scurried across the large roof, trying to remain out of sight of the Molgs on the ground.

It took him a moment, but he found a side of the fortress where there weren't many windows. Luckily, it wasn't very far from the makeshift door and the key. But how was he going to get down this time? The roof had a ledge that took him too far from the wall. He wouldn't be able to get close enough to mold any holes.

Deciding it was time to figure out where everyone was, he Time-Saw the surrounding area. Molgs were still pacing— none of them had seen him. How was that possible? He Saw the throne room and panicked when he found it empty. He pulled back, searching for Keitus. The Lorkon was just entering the cell.

The anger on Keitus's face was evident, yes, but Jacob could hear the Lorkon's scream, even while Time-Seeing. He jerked back to his surroundings. The Molgs below went berserk, rushing to see what was going on, and Jacob sprawled to his stomach, barely lifting his head a fraction— enough to see that the Molgs were all staring up in the direction of Jacob's former cell.

"Find him!" Keitus bellowed. *"Find him!* He's out there somewhere!"

The Molgs reacted instantly, unsheathing swords and maces. They split up, some going to the right and away from the window, some going into the forest in front of it, and others rushing to the left, closing the distance between themselves and Jacob.

Jacob lowered his head. "What do I do?" he whispered frantically to Early. "How do I get down?"

She shrugged, shaking her head, and wrung her hands frantically.

Then her face lit up. "I'll help you! You drop from here to the ground. I'll be careful—reduce your weight again. It won't hurt as badly if you're lighter."

Jacob nodded, breathing rapidly. The risk of having her shoot him off in some random direction was huge. But this was his only choice. "We'll need to wait for the right moment —there's no way I'm going to make it to the door now without someone seeing me."

Early nodded. "And you can go into the forest and sneak around to the door that way!"

Jacob raised his eyebrows in surprise. "That's a good idea, actually. Thanks, Early!" And if they *did* see him? Without his sword, he had no way to defend himself.

Remembering his sword made him groan. His dad had given it to him. He'd killed a dinosaur with it—he couldn't leave it behind. He didn't care how stupid others would think that was—if at all possible, he wanted to get it.

An idea popped into his mind, and he Time-Saw to see if he could do it. Keitus was pacing in Jacob's cell, his color red so bright it was nearly impossible to see his actual facial expression.

The other Lorkon were searching the halls and rooms nearby.

"He's outside!" Keitus yelled at them. "Go out there and find him!"

The three Lorkon disappeared down some stairs. Jacob quickly Time-Saw to the throne room. Relief hit him. Oh, good. His sword was still there.

The idea continued to formulate, and he quickly figured out how far away the room was from his current position. After a moment of searching, he scanned around and found a stairway leading up near the throne room. He pulled himself back. Now would be his only chance.

"Change of plans," he said. "I'm going after my sword."

"No, Jacob!" Early said. "Bad idea!"

Jacob shook his head. "They think I'm outside. If I go in, I'll avoid them longer, and will be able to get my sword. I'm not leaving without it."

"It's just a sword!"

The room was on the other side of the roof. If he hurried, he might be able to mold his way through the roof and to the staircase while Keitus was still in the cell.

"Keep a lookout—let me know if anyone's coming."

Jacob scurried across the roof, being as careful as he could not to be seen or make a lot of noise.

He was lucky—the Molgs were plenty noisy down on the ground, yelling at each other in their language.

It didn't take long for Jacob to feel his way to a weak spot above the staircase. He Time-Saw one last time—Keitus was just leaving his cell—and molded as quickly as he could. A moment later, he had a hole large enough. Early slowed his decent and he softly fell to the top landing of the steps, then crouched in the shadows of the stairwell. It must have been for servants—it was small and scuffed up, not glamorous like the other staircases he'd seen.

After making sure no one was there, he zipped around a corner and peeked into the throne room. Empty still.

"Keitus is coming!"

Jacob hesitated for a moment, growled, and dashed inside the room anyway, racing for the throne. He fell to the ground, sliding the last couple of feet, and whipped behind the back of the large chair, grabbing his sword and pulling it close to him. Then he tucked his legs in and prayed the back of the chair was big enough to keep him hidden. He heard approaching footsteps.

Keitus entered the room, swearing to himself. Jacob held his breath.

Afraid to close his eyes, he stared at the curtain-covered wall in front of him. The throne shifted when Keitus sat in it, and Jacob was bumped away from the chair a fraction of an inch. He scrambled backward and shut his eyes when he heard the grunting sounds of a Molg echo in the room. Keitus and the creature started a heated discussion.

Jacob saw Early up in the corner of the room and motioned for her to come closer. She did—moving so quickly the other two hopefully wouldn't see her. "Go to the forest on the other side of the fortress from the makeshift door," he whispered to her, trusting Keitus's argument would cover his breathy words. "Do something, anything to make the Molgs think I'm there. Hurry!"

She disappeared and Jacob was alone with Keitus and the Molg. How would he get out? Early had told him that Keitus had only arranged for one exit—the main entrance of the fortress. A lot of attention would be focused there. He bit his lip, concentrating. Would he be able to sneak out that way?

Then he remembered something else—he'd molded a hole in the wall where the Sheingols had been staying. Was it still there? It seemed unlikely—Keitus would have had it filled up as soon as possible.

Could Jacob take the chance? Run that way and see if it still existed? Then he shook his head at himself. He could Time-See. He focused at the wall across from him and held on to the legs of the chair, hoping he wouldn't be gone long enough for his body to convulse or anything.

It didn't take long to find the room, since he started outside. The crates had been moved. Dang it! The hole was covered up. But he zoomed in closer anyway. What he saw made him nearly laugh with happiness. It had been covered with a type of cardboard—enough to make it look like the hole had been patched up, but easy enough for Jacob to get through. He Time-Saw to the other side of the hole. The same thing there. Just so long as the tunnel hadn't been filled with anything, this plan would work.

He returned to his present location and nearly jumped when Keitus screamed.

"He *is not* in the fortress!" Keitus shrieked. "Search the entire forest and the town!"

Footsteps retreating—the Molg left. It was silent for several moments. Was Keitus still there?

49

J acob was about to peek around the corner of the throne when he felt it shift as Keitus changed positions.

The Lorkon muttered something Jacob couldn't understand—maybe he was speaking in a different language— but he stopped when a loud clamor sounded from outside. "What now?" Keitus said.

A Molg's guttural response came from across the room, and Jacob felt the throne move. Footsteps clapped quickly across the floor. Jacob chanced a look beyond the chair and saw Keitus's robes disappearing through the doorway.

Not wanting to lose this chance, Jacob jumped to his feet and dashed across the floor, trying to be quiet. This would be his only opportunity.

He reached the doorway in time to see Keitus stride around a corner at the end of the hall. Unfortunately, that was the only way to get to the room with the hole in the wall. He tiptoed as quickly as he could, following the Lorkon.

Keitus stopped near the entrance to the Shiengols' room to talk to another Lorkon, and Jacob hid behind a corner from them, pressing himself against the wall. He watched the shadows the Lorkon made on the floor.

"Lord, he's in the forest with the volcanic rock. We can't reach—"

"You're sure it's him?"

The shadows moved, indicating the Lorkon were walking toward the front entrance of the fortress.

"Yes—he's . . ."

The voices became a murmur, then died out, and Jacob peeked past the corner. The Lorkon were gone.

Jacob dashed down the hall and through the doorway, gripping his sword tight.

And ran smack into a Molg.

It was the smallest Molg he'd ever seen, but it still freaked Jacob out. And if he hadn't been so afraid, he would have laughed at the expression of shock that crossed the Molg's face.

Instinctively, he swung his sword. The blade connected with the Molg's right arm, cutting it, and surprising the creature even more.

Not waiting to see what the Molg would do, Jacob raced around it into the darkened interior of the Shiengols' room. He sprinted across the floor to the hole, dodging a couple of tables and chairs along the way.

He fell to his knees, skidding the last few feet, then ripped at the cardboard with one hand, holding his sword tightly in the other. He was sure he'd need it.

The Molg roared behind him, and he glanced over his shoulder. It had pulled out its short sword and was charging.

He wouldn't make it through the tunnel in time.

Jacob jumped to his feet, whirled, and barely blocked the Molg's attack. The blow vibrated through Jacob's sword to his arms, and he nearly dropped it, grimacing at the pain in his hands.

The Molg glared and attacked again. Jacob defended himself, but not before the Molg's sword caught his left sleeve, slicing his arm. Jacob barely felt the pain, but was sure it would register later. He stabbed at the Molg, but the beast easily stepped to the side, avoiding Jacob's blade.

The two continued to fight—Jacob attacking in anger and frustration, and the Molg easily getting out of the way.

After only a few parries, Jacob recognized that the beast was enjoying itself. It was toying with him, which meant it knew Jacob wouldn't win—the creature had probably been using a sword its entire life.

What could he do? He needed to get through that hole, and fast. No telling how long the Lorkon would take.

Making a quick decision, Jacob backed away, then ran to the right, skirting the perimeter of the room. He glanced over his shoulder. The Molg glared at him, the colors for annoyance swirling in his air, then raced after Jacob. Good.

They zigzagged between pillars, Jacob every now and then turning to throw in a quick jab. He led the Molg away from the hole to the other side of the darkened room.

Jacob ducked under a table and turned to attack when the creature tried to do the same. He got in another blow, injuring the Molg again, and its colors flashed bright red.

Early returned just then, excitedly babbling about the Lorkon searching the forest for Jacob and how she'd dropped heavy branches.

"Kinda busy right now," Jacob said.

"Oh! Can I help?"

"I need more time before the Lorkon come."

With a flash, Early disappeared, and Jacob, figuring she'd left to make more distractions, ran to a huge table in the center of the room. Why did the Shiengols need a table that big? It was as high as Jacob's shoulders. Sure, the Shiengols were tall, but not *that* tall.

Jacob swung on top of it, then whirled, attacking the Molg's hands when it grabbed the table to hoist itself up. After a couple of seconds, Jacob's hands trembled with relief when he found it was easy to maintain his position there. He gripped his sword tighter.

Jacob wracked his brain, trying to come up with a plan. The Molg looked like it had figured out it wouldn't be able to get on top too. It stepped back, surveying the room with its big, intelligent eyes. It dashed under the table.

Jacob gasped in shock when the table shifted under his feet. He crouched, steadying himself. The Molg attempted to tip the table over, but Jacob counterbalanced from on top, barely staying upright.

Then an idea popped into his brain. It would work—it had to! He only needed Early's help to get things going.

He nearly fell off when the Molg pitched the table hard to his right, but he was able to jump to the left, pushing the surface back down.

Early returned just then, and Jacob told her what to do. She nodded in agreement.

Jacob was finally distracted enough for the Molg to knock the table over, and he spilled to the ground. He jumped to his feet and ran toward the hole, stopping several yards away, then turned in time to block an attack.

The Molg raised its sword again, but Early blasted the creature and it banged off the wall opposite Jacob, landing roughly. Jacob dropped his sword, falling to his knees.

He searched the floor for warmth as quickly as he could. The Molg returned, and Early zapped it again. Jacob continued searching.

Finally, he found a spot where the stone emitted warmth.

Early pushed the Molg away a third time, and Jacob warmed the floor. Rather than pulling the stone up, however, he worked as deeply as he could, creating a section that was at least two feet square. He smoothed the top over, grabbed his sword, and jumped to his feet right as the Molg neared.

Jacob carefully parried with the creature, leading it toward the warmed section.

Right as the stone started to harden, the Molg stepped into it. Jacob distracted the creature by swinging his sword a few times, pretending to be attacking. He backed up. The Molg tried to follow, but couldn't. Its foot stayed in place!

"Early! It worked!"

Early giggled, then disappeared with a flash, reappearing seconds later. "It's clear outside! Go!"

Jacob re-sheathed his sword and wormed his way through the hole. He fell to the ground outside with a thump, his breath getting knocked out of him. Early poked and prodded, trying to get him up, but it wasn't until he dragged in a huge breath that he was able to stand again.

He spotted the makeshift door and ran. He'd nearly reached it when a Molg stepped out from behind. No! He should've checked to make sure no one was there!

The Molg grabbed him around the neck, throwing him to the ground, pinning him. Lights danced across his eyes.

"Fjd arwes aried!" the Molg yelled.

Jacob brought his leg up, kneeing the creature between the legs. Nothing happened. The Molg maintained his grip, preventing Jacob from drawing another breath.

Early flitted through the air nearby, panicked and screaming at the Molg. Jacob wanted to tell her to blast the creature away, but couldn't get the words out. He couldn't hear anything but the pounding in his ears. Everything went bright white as he struggled for air.

Remembering his sword, he stopped trying to push the Molg away, instead focusing on getting the sword out. But then he forgot what he was doing. Blackness caved in on him.

The Molg released him, and Jacob sucked in air, coughing.

His throat seared with pain. He sat up, gasping, clutching his neck.

The Molg had fallen to the ground near him. Early rose, an expression of intensity on her face that Jacob had never seen before.

The Molg stirred right as four more Molgs came running around the corner only a hundred yards away.

"You shall not touch my Jacob!" Early screamed at the Molg. She zapped it again, and the creature flew through the air.

Jacob jumped for the ground behind the door, searching in the grass. Where was it? Where was it? "Early! Help me find the key!"

She zipped past him and pointed. "Over there! I dragged it there—I hid it!"

The key! He saw the glint in the trampled grass and loosened it, pulling it out. Jacob closed it in his fist right as the Molg returned and kicked him, knocking him to the ground. The beast jumped for him, but this time, Jacob rolled away, to the front of the door, before he got pinned down. He pulled out his sword and swung wildly at the beast, lessons forgot, the need for survival the only thing on his mind.

Early blasted the Molg away again, but it didn't go as far as before. She looked exhausted, and the other Molgs were coming closer.

Jacob didn't waste time. He shoved the key into the lock and yelled, "Kenji's house!"

Right as he turned the knob, the door flung open and Azuriah dashed through, a spear in one hand, a sword in the other, robes flashing in the sunlight. Jacob got knocked to the side.

Azuriah screamed something in the Shiengols' language. Jacob's mouth popped open. The Molg—at least a foot taller than Azuriah—parried the blow with his crudely fashioned sword. The other Molgs arrived.

Then came the most extreme, awesome sword fight Jacob had ever seen. Azuriah twirled around the Molgs, advancing, attacking. The beasts were very fast, keeping up. They blocked almost all of Azuriah's attacks, but some of them got through.

One by one, the creatures fell to the ground. The Lorkon came around the corner, saw Jacob and Azuriah, and hurtled themselves across the distance. They were incredibly fast.

Azuriah threw his sword and spear into Kenji's house—someone jumped out of the way just in time—and then he did something with his fingers. A whoosh sounded through the air, like incredibly low bass, rattling Jacob's ribs. A wave rippled through the grass away from Azuriah, and the Molgs and Lorkon were smashed back. They fell to the ground, dazed.

Gallus grabbed Jacob's arm, yanking him through the door.

The last thing Jacob saw of the Lorkon was bright red—their favorite emotion—before Azuriah jumped through, slamming the door behind him.

50

J acob leaned back from the table and patted his stomach, completely satisfied for the first time in days. And not only because he'd just eaten a delicious meal, but also because he was back home, with all the people he loved most. He sighed. Everyone—the entire group—was waiting in the next room.

"Ready, son?" Dad asked from the kitchen doorway.

Jacob nodded.

"All right. Let's get the meeting started."

After Jacob escaped the fortress, Mom and Ebony insisted that Akeno shrink Jacob and put him in a Minya container. It took him a little over a day to heal. He'd only been awake for an hour, and everyone had been hanging around, impatiently waiting to hear what had happened.

Apparently, Early was unable to deliver messages once Jacob got the window worked out of its frame. He'd kept her too busy. Jacob felt bad—his family must've gone completely crazy with worry. He could only imagine how stressful it had been for them—unable to do anything, not knowing what was going on.

And speaking of Early—he hadn't seen her since coming back. How was she? Where had she gone? Probably off to take a break from being ordered around. He smiled to himself. The poor Minya.

He got up from the table and entered the living room, aware of all eyes on him. He felt a flush race across his cheeks and took his seat next to Dad and Mom.

"Start from where you were separated from the group," Dad said.

Jacob explained being knocked unconscious and Keitus trying to force him to find the Key of Ayunli. He briefly described escaping. Aloren interrupted to say he was crazy for going back to get his sword, but Dad laughed. He'd have done the same thing. Jacob then filled them in on everything he'd learned, deciding not to tell them he'd almost joined Keitus.

Mom gasped when she heard about Keitus trying to turn Jacob into a Lorkon. "We would never have known!"

The Fat Lady, who had been quiet up until this point, nodded. "The process is very painful and takes a long time." She looked at Kenji and Brojan. "It's a good thing both of you had the idea to put Rezend in him. Sounds like that really fouled Keitus's plans."

Brojan nodded. "Yes, it's a huge relief to know this, actually."

Jacob glanced at his dad. "Is it all right if I ask a bunch of questions?"

"Of course. And we'll answer the ones we can."

"Azuriah said I inherited things that didn't come from Rezend or the Lorkon. What did he mean?"

Dad laughed. "You ask the question we can't answer without permission from Azuriah." He settled into his chair. "What did he tell you?"

"That the abilities were more pure, more intelligent or something."

Dad nodded. "And he's right. We can't expand beyond that, however. You'll have to wait until Azuriah deems it appropriate for you to know."

Jacob rolled his eyes. "Which means I might not ever find out. He's super, super temperamental."

"Yes, he can be difficult—but you'll get used to that. I'm sure he plans to teach you everything eventually. Next question?"

"What happens now with the Shiengols?"

Aldo motioned out the window with his hand. "They've already left to recruit more of their kind from the other parts of Eklaron. They plan to come back and help us fix things here."

"Not Azuriah, though," Mom said to Jacob. "He's going to be training you when he returns."

Jacob wrinkled his nose. He wasn't sure he'd enjoy those training sessions. "Oh, speaking of recruiting, have we heard from the Wurbies yet?"

Gallus shook his head. "No, not yet. We'll touch bases with Fubble over the next few days."

"And what happens now? With the Lorkon?" Jacob hesitated. "Do you think they'll keep trying to get at me?"

Mom took a long breath. "We've been worried about this."

"The short answer is yes," Ebony said. "We feel Keitus was bluffing about destroying you."

Jacob snorted. "He sure made it believable."

"Well, of course he would. He needed you to think he was telling the truth."

"The point is," the Fat Lady said, "until Keitus gets his hands on the Key of Ayunli or Key of Kilenya—both of which require your help—he's pretty much stuck."

"Unless he finds a way to get the Key of Ayunli without Jacob," Aloren said quietly.

Jacob shivered at that thought. "Is that a possibility?"

Aldo nodded. "Of course. I was unsuccessful at finding the key, but that doesn't mean Keitus will be. For all we know, he has access to a lot more information than we do."

Jacob rubbed his face. "Okay, what happens now?"

"We prepare to defend ourselves—the Lorkon are on the offense, and they're not going to wait for us. They'll do everything they can to move forward with their plans."

Dad made a steeple with his fingers, tapping them on each other. "We need to figure out what *our* plan will be."

Aldo nodded. "Azuriah's instructions were explicit. Jacob must finish learning his abilities. He'll have to act as spy for us, and if he isn't in complete control, he'll put all of us in unnecessary danger." He smiled apologetically at Jacob, then continued. "Also, we need to find out what's going on in Fornchall. We can save that topic for a later time." He turned to Dad. "Have we discussed everything on the agenda?"

"Yes, we're about finished here."

"Good. 'Cause it's about time I got home."

Dad chuckled. "What's left of your home, you mean?"

"Oh, no. I've moved into the Makalos' farming area to oversee the humans there. Many of them will be ready soon for the upcoming war."

Aloren wrinkled her nose. "And we're sure there has to be one?"

Gallus knitted his eyebrows, looking at Aloren. "Not unless you can see another way to get rid of the Lorkon."

She shook her head. "No, not really."

"The Lorkon won't go away peacefully. I'm afraid things will be ugly."

Dad took a deep breath. "Well, this meeting is adjourned. Jacob, go ahead and take everyone home."

Jacob stood up, motioning for the rest to follow. He took Gallus and the Fat Lady back first, then Aldo and the

Makalos. He was about to return home when Kenji stopped him.

"Ebony and I need to talk to you about something."

"Oh? Okay."

Jacob looked at Kenji, but couldn't tell by the Makalo's emotion colors what he was thinking. He keyed them from the tree to their house. It was dark inside and Kenji touched the wall, lighting up the stream of silver in the stone. The Makalos motioned for Jacob to have a seat at the table. They joined him, colors finally starting to swirl around them. They were nervous. Why?

Kenji leaned forward, clasping his hands. "We've spent a great deal of time over the past little while discussing something with Early."

Jacob raised an eyebrow. "Yeah?"

"We were hesitant to bring it up with you at first, knowing how your father feels about Minyas, but Early was very insistent."

Ebony laughed. "And persuasive."

"How does my father feel about Minyas?"

"He doesn't like them," Ebony said, "and they don't like him. Anyway, she doesn't want to belong to the Makalos anymore. She wants you to be her owner now."

Jacob's mouth popped open. "Really?"

Kenji nodded. "And once a Minya has chosen an owner, you can't change their mind."

Ebony hurriedly put her hand on Jacob's arm, and her words rushed out. "Do you want to keep her? You don't have to if you don't want to. We told her not to expect anything. And she won't be too much of a bother—we made her promise not to annoy you—"

"Of *course* I want to keep her! It would be so awesome! How cool!"

Ebony's eyes widened. "Really?"

"Yeah! I mean, she's been like my best friend for the past several days and all. I wouldn't have survived if it hadn't been for her."

"So, that settles it, then," Kenji said. A grin spread across his face. "She's yours to keep."

Just then, something zipped through the air so fast, Jacob wasn't sure what it was until it hit him in the side of the head. Early, of course.

"Oh, Jacob!" she said. "Thank you, thank you! I have a new owner! I get to stay with you forever!"

Jacob beamed at her exuberance. He could see her extreme colors of happiness out of the corner of his eye as the Minya hugged his face.

She stopped. "I'm gonna go tell September. He didn't think you'd want me!" With a flash, she disappeared.

Jacob laughed. "Wow."

He couldn't believe his luck—he had his very own Minya!

Kenji and Ebony grinned.

Jacob stopped smiling, realizing something. He couldn't take care of another pet—Tito and the chickens were hard enough as it was. "What does this mean, though?" he asked. "How do I take care of her?"

Kenji shrugged. "It's not hard. She'll feed and entertain herself. It just means she most likely won't answer so quickly when we call for her, but that she'll check up on you all the time—it might even get annoying with how frequently." He stood. "Like Aloren's Hazel, Early may choose to have a permanent Minya container placed in your room for her to sleep in. She'll go everywhere with you, unless she wants to do something else."

Jacob nodded, his smile broadening again.

Early flitted back to him and nestled in his hair. Kenji

chuckled, and Ebony gave Jacob a hug goodbye. Jacob let himself out, deciding to walk to the tree and key home from there.

51

When he got back, Mom and Dad were waiting for him in the living room. The expressions on their faces said they had something serious to talk about, and Jacob quickly put thoughts of Early out of his mind.

"Honey," Mom said, motioning for Jacob to have a seat next to her, "your dad and I have been discussing a few things. Well, one in particular."

Jacob didn't like her tone of voice. Not only that, but the colors swirling around her indicated discomfort. His heart beat sped up. "Yeah? About?"

"You—your future. You've got a lot of work ahead of you. Azuriah made it clear that he expects to train with you for several hours a day."

Jacob thought he could see where this was going. "I'll be really stressed, I know. I've been thinking about it, and I know I can't overdo things. I figured out really quickly while in the fortress that pressure and Time-Seeing don't go together."

"Not only that," Dad said. He looked uncomfortable. "But . . ."

Jacob swallowed. "Okay, just spit it out. You're making me really nervous."

Dad took a deep breath. "We've been thinking about pulling you out of school and hiring a tutor."

Jacob's jaw dropped. "But . . . that means . . . basketball . . ."

"You'd have to quit JV," Dad said, nodding. "Which is important to you. This, however, is more important."

"I don't understand—I did everything fine before, when we were getting ready to rescue Aloren."

"Honey, we know," Mom said. "But it's much different—this time, almost everything depends on how you handle things. We don't want to over-stress you, and your dad and I feel that if you had one-on-one time with a teacher a few times a week, it would be better than having you gone several hours a day."

Jacob felt his eyes smart—he wasn't about to cry. Not in front of his parents. "But I've worked so hard!"

Mom put her arms around him. "You have. You really have. Think about it this way—if things go smoothly, you'll be able to register again your senior year. You'll make it on varsity easily."

"I can't just drop out! I've never *not* been on a team! And everyone will think it's because I didn't make varsity."

"Think it over," Dad said. "We'll give you some time to adjust to the idea."

Jacob stood. "I—"

He couldn't continue the conversation. He had to be alone. He quickly walked out of the room and ran up the stairs to his bedroom, shut his door, then fell on the bed. Without basketball, he wasn't sure where he'd be. He needed it! It helped him concentrate and feel good and . . . and . . . it wasn't fair! Why didn't anyone else have to sacrifice like this? Why weren't they telling Aloren she couldn't go to school? Or Matt?

Jacob jerked to his side, answering his own question. Because they didn't have "special abilities." Well, curse his gifts! He didn't ask for them and he didn't want them!

He scowled at the wall, feeling the bitterness creep across him. A part of him recognized that maybe, if he threw a big enough fit, he'd be able to continue playing basketball at the school. He let those emotions rush over him—getting his way. Pushing other people around.

Then he took a deep breath—that wasn't how he was, and he didn't want to hurt his family.

He rolled to his back again. But then . . . the only thing he *could* do was to go along with his parents.

Jacob covered his face with his pillow.

———

AN HOUR LATER, someone knocked on his door. Matt didn't wait for the go-ahead to come in. He grabbed Jacob's desk chair, spun it around, and straddled it.

Neither said anything for several moments.

Finally, Matt cleared his throat. "Mom just told me what's going on."

Jacob nodded, putting the pillow aside.

"I'm sorry—I know how much it sucks."

Jacob nodded again. He didn't need to respond.

"I've been thinking, though." Matt paused. "You're working toward getting on varsity, right?"

"Yeah."

"And you don't have to stop playing ball just because you can't be on the team anymore, right?"

Jacob took a deep breath, then sat up. He hadn't thought of that. "I guess so."

"Well, look at it this way. We'll all help you keep up on your skills. You won't fall behind—you were already way ahead anyway. And not only that, but I really do believe what Aldo said about the Lorkon intending to come and destroy everything. We can't just stay here, ignoring them. It will happen eventually." He paused again. "So . . . by dropping out for a while to work on your abilities and figure things out in Eklaron, you're actually working toward making varsity. 'Cause if we don't stop the Lorkon, there won't be a varsity team in a couple of years anyway."

Jacob thought on that for several moments, then nodded. "Maybe you're right." When put that way, it made sense. There wasn't any way the Lorkon would let Jacob continue playing basketball if they took over his life.

"Cheer up, Jake. This isn't the worst thing ever. Other people have had to make bigger sacrifices."

Jacob looked his brother in the eye for a moment. "I know. But it's still really dumb."

Matt agreed and leaned forward, resting his chin on his hand. He played with the rungs in the back of the chair, possibly giving Jacob time to think.

Jacob ran his hand through his hair. What Matt said really hit him—sacrificing. If it meant saving his family and loved ones and even basketball, he could sacrifice his biggest goals for a season. It was a noble thing to do—putting the needs of other people ahead of his own. He'd already had a lot of practice doing that, and had even considered joining Keitus to save his family.

He took a few deep breaths. "I've got so much to do. I don't know how I'll get everything done."

Matt sagged in the chair. "Yeah, I'm glad I'm not in your spot."

Jacob reached over and playfully slugged his brother on the shoulder. "It would've been better if you were—you could've figured everything out by now."

Matt shook his head. "Nah. You've done a really good job."

Jacob looked at his hands. "Thanks."

"Wanna play a game of one-on-one?"

Jacob looked up and snorted. "Why? So you can lose?"

Matt rolled his eyes. "Whatever. I practiced while you were gone. I'm even better than before."

Jacob laughed. "I doubt that."

"Oh! A challenge! Game's on!"

The brothers jumped up to leave the room, Matt's colors switching from concerned to cheerful. He paused before they headed down the stairs. "I've only got one request."

"What's that?"

"Hurry up and save the world so I can still be captain of the football team."

ABOUT THE AUTHOR

USA Today bestselling author Andrea Pearson is an avid reader and outdoor enthusiast who plays several instruments, not including the banjo, and loves putting together musical arrangements. Her favorite sports are basketball and football, though several knee surgeries and incurably awful coordination prevent her from playing them.

Andrea graduated from Brigham Young University with a

bachelor of science degree in Communications Disorders. She is the author of many full-length novels (the Kilenya Series and Mosaic Chronicles) and several novellas. Writing is the chocolate of her life - it is, in fact, the only thing she ever craves. Being with her family and close friends is where she's happiest, and she loves thunderstorms, the ocean, hiking, public speaking, painting, and traveling.

Learn more about her from her website: www.andreapearsonbooks.com

Made in United States
Troutdale, OR
11/20/2023

14765298R00196